Mission to Malaspiga

MISSION TO MALASPIGA

by

Evelyn Anthony

Coward, McCann &
Geoghegan, Inc.
New York

To Leonard and Sylvia,
with love and thanks

1

It was the fifth morning, and still there was no letter. No message. She had waked early. Having slept deeply for the first time since she had arrived, she didn't immediately recognize her surroundings.

The windows showed her an unfamiliar view of red Tuscan tiled roofs and a hot blue sky. She was in Florence, in a hotel bedroom. She showered and dressed; the maid brought her breakfast; the coffee was superb; she didn't eat anything. Nine o'clock. It was time to go downstairs and approach the reception desk and ask the same question.

The clerk looked up at her and smiled. He also shook his head.

"Good morning, Signorina Dexter. Nothing has come, I'm sorry." The pigeonhole with her room number was empty. The clerk assumed that she was waiting to hear from a lover. She could tell by the sympathetic look he gave her. And like all Italians he was nice to women. He had shown special interest in her since he saw the second name on her passport when she registered. The manager himself had approached her in the restaurant, asked her if she was comfortable and to let him know if there was anything she wanted. It had set her apart from the other foreign visitors in the hotel. It gave her an uneasy feeling to know that in spite of her American nationality, the Florentines regarded her as part of themselves.

"I'm going out," Katharine Dexter told the clerk. "I'll be in late this afternoon. If anyone calls for me, ask them to leave a telephone number."

"Certainly," he promised. She looked unusually pretty that morning. He had his countrymen's love of blondes, and her hair was a beautiful golden color. The eyes, surprisingly, were brown. It was an odd combination, and he thought it a pity. He preferred a blonde to have blue eyes. She looked anxious and ill at ease. He wasn't deceived by the guidebooks and the tours which occupied her time. She wasn't an ordinary tourist, however hard she tried to act the part. She was waiting for a letter, a telephone call. Whoever the man was, he was behaving very badly.

"Don't worry, Signorina," he said. "If anyone calls, I will take the message."

It was early May, and Florence languished under an unexpected heat wave. She had arrived a week ago, after an exhausting flight from New York via Rome, and landed at Pisa airport. She had been too tired to appreciate the taxi driver's detour past the Campo Santo, so that she could see the splendor of the great twelfth-century Duomo and the actuality of the leaning Bell Tower. She had looked out of the window, dazed with travel fatigue and a deep sickness of the spirit, the aftermath of grief and anger, not caring about or appreciating the glimpse of a wonder of the ancient world. During the long drive along the autostrada to Florence, she had dozed, awaking with a sense of panic to find herself in the city itself, the taxi drawing up outside the sixteenth-century palazzo, on the Piazza Santa Maria Novella, which had been gutted and converted into a modern hotel. Seven days ago. It seemed as long as her whole life. She walked down to the Via dei Fossi and hesitated, the crowds of Florentines and tourists pushing past her, people with a purpose, herself an island of indecision in the human sea. No letter. No telephone message. Five days since she had made the approach and there was no response. And they were not away. She had telephoned the villa the day she arrived and hung up when she was told the family was at home. They might never reply.

She could have telephoned. It would have been the shortest way, but she had told herself it would be better if she wrote. It was a good excuse for cowardice. A letter was like a pole with which to touch a dreaded object. She remembered the old adage from her childhood about those supping with the Devil needing a long spoon. . . . Perhaps tomorrow there would be an answer. She stepped into the moving stream and turned toward the far end of the Via dei Fossi, where the broad Arno River bisected the city. It was a different route from the others she had taken. She paused by the antique shops, drawn by the simplicity and elegance with which they displayed their treasures. She was more attuned to the atmosphere. She felt less strange, less disoriented. There were times when she lost herself in the city, when in spite of the reason for her presence there, she fell a victim to its beauty and the magnetism of the Florentines. They were an energetic people; there was no evidence of the lethargy of the Southern Italian, enervated by poverty, a harsh terrain and brutal heat. They were shrewd, ambitious, with a marvelous respect for money and a passionate enjoyment in doing business. They had invented banking; it was perhaps the least of their many gifts to the civilized world. She paused, seeing her own reflection in the window of a shop displaying swathes of silk and printed linens. She looked like an American, slim and neat in a cool linen dress. She was thirty-one, unmarried, and unattached. She began to walk toward the river and turned down the Lungarno Corsini toward that morning's destination. The Pitti Palace. She had read her guidebook before going out. It would give her something to do if there was yet another day of futile waiting. She had already seen the great Duomo, the Baptistry with its incredible bronze doors. There was so much that was beautiful and unique, such an opportunity for pleasure if the circumstances had been different. The day before she had walked along the road beside the river—the Lungarno Amerigo Vespucci—on the right the Stars and Stripes fluttered suddenly at her, like someone waving a handkerchief in a strange crowd. The American Consulate—a superb façade, gilded wrought-iron gates, and behind them the familiarity of home. American faces and voices. That morning she walked on in the opposite direction to the Ponte Vecchio, the medieval survival into modern times, crossing the ribbon of the river to her right, its houses stacked on top of the bridge as if a child had built them out of brightly colored bricks.

There was a narrow, cobbled road across the bridge, only open to those on foot, hemmed in on either side by row on row of jeweler's shops and silversmiths. It was the ancient center of the Florentine art of making beautiful ornaments for the women and the houses of the rich. There was a pervading glitter that sparkled from one end of the bridge to the other, made up of precious stones and gold, from the high-priced gems of the quality jewelers to the cheap adulterated goldwork of the shops that preyed on greedy tourists. Katharine passed through them without being tempted. She hadn't bought anything since she arrived. It would have seemed frivolous under the circumstances. She reached the other bank of the Arno and turned to the right, taking the road toward the Piazza Pitti. She had spent two days exploring the enormous treasure house of the Uffizi Gallery, bemused at first and then gradually absorbing what she saw. Forty-two galleries, containing some of the greatest pictures in the world; rooms filled with sculptures, ceramics, jewels and oddities, the garnering of talent and wealth by the Medici rulers of the city, which their descendant, with a rare sense of history and knowing herself to be the last, had bequeathed forever to the citizens of Florence in the eighteenth century.

The Palace was erected on top of a steep slope. She walked up the cobbled surface of the Piazza, one of a stream of tourists, and because it was so beautiful and the interest around her was infectious, her spirits rose and she began to enjoy herself. The Pitti was a magnificent Renaissance building; grand and self-contained in a city where size and splendor were commonplace.

She bought a ticket and began to climb the enormously wide staircase. From the first-floor gallery, even before she paid attention to the pictures, she paused by one of the windows. The Pitti had been built by Eleanor of Toledo, wife of one of the Medici princes. She had also created the famous Boboli gardens that spread out below.

People swarmed everywhere, enjoying the sunshine. There was a preponderance of students, lounging against the steps of the amphitheater which had been built in imitation of the Roman circus but with less sinister purpose. Plays and operas had been performed outside in the lee of the Palace. The steps where the twentieth-century children squatted, eating ice cream, reading, gossiping in groups, had been the seats of the Florentine nobility. As Katharine watched, a cheer went up; some twenty students had sighted another group. She thought suddenly that there was a gaiety about Italian youth which was absent among the Americans and English. Comparisons were odious, and she tried not to make them, but there was a love of life and a natural spontaneity which didn't have its origin in drugs or mystical religions. They were young—the world was a place where the sun shone and the wine was cheap. A cluster of middle-aged Germans, shepherded by a guide, came to a halt close by her. The guide explained the history of the painting immediately in front of them. "Judith with the head of Holofernes," by Allori. Katharine had taken German at college. She understood everything the guide was saying, noticing the distortions of his Italian accent. It was not an easy language, unlike Italian, which she learned to speak as easily as if it were her own. She had majored in Renaissance literature, a curious subject in her father's opinion. He didn't see how it could assist her in the department store business, which was where her family had made their money, or to make a nice, conventional marriage. He had been worried that his daughter might turn out to be an intellectual. He had been unlucky in his children. He and her mother were ordinary affectionate parents, responsible citizens, prepared to cope with the average disorders that might overtake their kind of family.

They hadn't a hope of understanding what had happened to their son.

Katharine moved forward, following the Germans, half listening, pausing at something which touched her imagination or aroused her curiosity, until they had passed on into the next gallery. She found herself standing alone in front of a large portrait. Normally pictures of children did not appeal to her. They usually suffered from the artist's desire to please, and the results were often mawkish and unreal. This was a boy, painted life-size. A pale face, full lips without a smile, enormous eyes. He wore the costume of the early sixteenth century, crimson embroidered with gold, a velvet cap with ostrich plumes and a massive jeweled pin. There was a narrow sword by his side, and one hand rested on the hilt. A hound crouched at his feet. The predominant color was red. A crimson curtain provided the figure with its background.

It was the most arrogant face she had ever seen. It was almost obscene that a boy so young and so physically beautiful should convey such a degree of cold-heartedness and pride. There was a plaque below.

Alfredo, Prince of Malaspiga, aged nine, 1512, and the artist's name, A. Vitali. Presented to the Pitti Palace by Ernesto, Duke of Malaspiga, 1921.

Katharine stood in front of it; and a man brushed against her, apologizing. Malaspiga. Confronted by it, she felt shaken. In a way they were just a name, something she had never thought about as being real. Even now, alone in their city, Florence, Katharine hadn't invested them with tangibility. It was a threat, that name. Malaspiga. But it was the second name on her own passport. The reason why, as she left the cemetery after her brother's funeral in New England, men like Ben Harper and Frank Carpenter had come into her life.

It had been the most beautiful spring day she could remember. April in New England was a lovely month, crisp and cloudless, but on that morning it seemed the sun was brighter, the colors of leaf and daffodil more pure. In films it always rained at funerals; the mourners shuffled to the graveside under glistening umbrellas, and the rain fell like tears. All that was left of Peter James di Malaspiga Dexter was contained in a metal urn eighteen inches high, and the minister had just committed it to a two-foot hole in the ground.

It reminded Katharine of a grave for a pet dog. Once, during a period of convalescence, her brother had spoken of Catholic burial with abhorrence.

She had granted his wish to be cremated; had chosen New England as it, at least, was a place Peter had remembered with some happiness. There were only two people present at the service, the family lawyer, who had gone through the formality of his will, and herself. There had been nothing to leave anyone. She heard the closing words of the service and found no comfort in them. The minister came over and shook hands, murmuring about his sympathy. Katharine didn't listen, but she thanked him anyway. A single wreath of spring flowers was laid by the side of the newly cut turf. Her writing was on the card.

He had gone out of the world as he had lived in it for the last seven years. Uncared for and unmourned by anyone except her. He had been twenty-seven when he died. She had a handkerchief in her hand; she had no tears left, and she put it away and began to walk toward the cemetery gates.

Two men had been watching the funeral. They were waiting by the entrance and as she came up, one of them moved away from the railing.

"Miss Dexter?" The man took off his hat; he was going slightly bald, and he had hard brown eyes. She had never seen him before, and yet he was familiar.

"Yes," she said.

"My name is Harper. Ben Harper. And this is Frank Carpenter. We'd like to offer you our sympathy."

"What do you want?" she said. They seemed to have closed in on her. The man called Harper produced an identification card, and then she understood.

"I'm sorry," she said. "I made a statement to the police. There's nothing more I can tell you." He didn't stand aside. His voice was soft, gentler than she expected.

"We'd like to talk to you," he said. "We'd like to buy you a cup of coffee or a drink. Just a few minutes of your time."

She looked at them in turn. The second man was taller, younger, but he had the same hard face and wary eyes. Men who lived in their world couldn't be expected to have pity left. Suddenly she was too tired to resist. It had all happened so often before. Questions, answers that didn't help.

"All right," she said. "There's a drive-in café down the road. I'll meet you there." She got into her car and drove away. They chose a table near the window. She found herself with the light on her face; theirs were in shadow. It was a pleasant little café, decorated in cedar wood, with brass fittings and checked tablecloths. Frank Carpenter ordered coffee for them.

"We've done a lot of checking on this case," Ben Harper said.

"I don't know why," Katharine said slowly. "It's exactly like all the other cases. It's finished the way they all do."

"It has a very special feature," Frank Carpenter said. She saw the older man put a restraining hand on his sleeve.

"You cared for your brother for seven years," Harper said. "Not many people can take it that long. He must have meant a lot to you."

She didn't want to look at them. To men like these, Peter was just another statistic. "I didn't believe it had to end like this," she said. "I thought with someone to care about him, with medical help—"

"You must feel pretty bitter," Frank Carpenter said. He stirred his coffee. Ben Harper was watching her.

"It's the sense of waste, isn't it," he said quietly. "The failure. I've been with the narcotics bureau for twenty years. I've seen thousands of lives just thrown away."

"He tried," Katharine said. "Believe me, he tried. But it was hopeless. Clinics, psychiatrists, everything. He hadn't a dollar or a friend in the world when he died."

"Except you," Ben Harper said. "I saw your face when I showed my ID, Miss Dexter. Just another cop wanting to know where he got it. Well we know, all right. We even know the pusher who supplied him. But we're not interested in him, or in the thousands of smalltime operators like him. The petty crooks, the addicts, selling to keep themselves supplied— they're not what we're after.

"We want the top men, Miss Dexter. We want the millionaires, who run yachts on getting heroin to people like your brother. It wasn't just dope that killed him; it was organized crime. The biggest moneymaking racket in the world. Do you know what the street price of one kilo of heroin is in New York City? A half a million dollars! I want the men who put that in their pockets. That's why we've come down here to see you today. I believe you can help us get them." And that was how it had begun.

She turned away from the portrait of the Malaspiga prince; even the lofty rooms of the Pitti seemed claustrophobic, the murmuring crowds threatened to drag her forward with them when she wanted to get out. She turned back, pushing her way through knots of people by the doorways, going against the stream. At the top of the staircase she began to hurry down. There were gardens outside, sunshine and normality. She wouldn't admit it, but she wanted to escape from the implications of that magnificently evil portrait. Outside in the brilliant sunlight, she paused, uncertain and a little out of breath. She had run away from what—from the memory of her brother's funeral? From the reminder that she had committed herself to do something which grief and anger had made feasible at the time. Katharine didn't know. She made her way to the amphitheater and found a vacant space on the steps. Carpenter had been against the mission from the start. Ben Harper had assigned him as her instructor. A crash course, that was what he said. A month of intensive training before she went to Florence. It had seemed easy at the time. It had offered a purpose when nothing faced her but a vacuum now that her brother was dead. She had turned to Ben Harper at the final interview, a week after their meeting at the funeral.

"If what you say is true—if these people are at the head of it—then no one has a better right to go out there than I do. I owe it to Peter."

And Harper had looked at her and said, "Maybe you're more Italian than you think."

She had packed up her apartment in Greenwich Village. It was not a district she would have chosen if her circumstances had been normal. Before her brother's condition became chronic, she lived on the upper floor of a brownstone on East Sixty-seventh between Madison and Park that belonged to her aunt. She had a job in a prestige publishing house, her brother had left to get his MBA at the Harvard Business School, and the family planned to spend summer weekends together in Southampton. Life had never seemed more satisfying; she loved her job, a college romance had gently blown itself out, she felt free and excited by the future. Within three months she had discovered that her brother, the person she loved best and admired most, was a heroin addict. It wasn't apparent at first. Later she learned to recognize the signs, but to begin with he seemed simply to be going through a phase. Finding his feet, her father called it. His son had never given any cause for worry. He was a fine athlete, an adequate scholar without any of the academic pretensions that had disturbed them about Katharine—handsome, friendly, popular with everyone. Only Katharine, who was so close to him, sensed that something fundamental had changed. He had always been responsible; his interests were active, his habits gregarious. He became slack, uncaring; he spent hours sleeping or sitting vacantly, listening to his stereo. He began to drop his friends and then he left Harvard without his degree. The pattern of dependence and then degeneracy was developing before their eyes, but even Katharine couldn't see the cause.

And then one night he came to the house on Sixty-seventh. It was two in the morning and he woke her up. He sat on her bed and told her. It began during his final year at Princeton. Somebody had some "horse"—at first she hadn't understood the meaning of the jargon used by addicts. Smack. Stuff. Heroin. He'd smoked pot in common with his contemporaries. There wasn't much kick to it, and that night it had seemed like fun to try something a little stronger. First it was sniffing cocaine—but that paled, too, and the need for stronger rushes drove him on to heroin. She had held him in her arms while he wept and shook and told her how he had tried to stop and couldn't. Couldn't . . . That was what his parents didn't understand. That one word.

He went away for cures; he tried psychiatry, group therapy, a long cruise with Katharine, who'd given up her job to keep him company, but nothing helped. He had to have the heroin. His mother had a heart attack and died, and from then on his home was closed against him. Katharine had never forgiven her father; he had abandoned his son.

For seven years she had lived with him, fought for him and gone from hope to despair, seeing the person she knew transformed into a stranger. A liar, a thief, capable of stealing from her when her back was turned, a reject who only felt comfortable with other addicts. If she hadn't supported him, she knew he would have joined the army of the addicted who in turn pushed drugs. It had been a long journey to that cemetery in New England—to the two-foot square plot with its urn full of ash.

She left the amphitheater and began to walk up the very steep steps to the top of the Boboli gardens. She looked at her watch; it was almost twelve o'clock. Everything closed at one until four in the afternoon. She didn't want to eat anything, but she was hot and tired.

She had gone to the Drug Enforcement Administration center in Manhattan. Frank Carpenter had met her there. It was the second time she'd seen him since the funeral. He had been curt and irritable. He hadn't spared her that first morning. "If you think that penetrating an organization like the Malaspiga's is going to be easy, then you'd better walk right out of here and take up social work instead. It's going to be tough, Miss Dexter. And having one of them as a grandmother may be a great introduction, but after that you're on your own."

Malaspiga. There was a china cabinet in her parents' drawing room. Her mother's collection of Italian ceramics was kept in it. There were Capo di Monte boxes and jars with an armorial crest on them, two miniatures in gilt frames, one set with pearls and a lock of dark hair coiled into the back, a gold locket, a coronet in diamonds on one lid. Her mother had given her a ring when she graduated. It had a lapis lazuli stone, carved intaglio with the same coat of arms as the ceramics, and it had belonged to her grandmother. A wreath of laurel surmounted by the coronet. Coming through the center of the wreath was an ear of corn; it ended in a sharp spike. There was something sinister in the crest instead of romantic. She had disliked the little ring and never worn it. She remembered being irritated by her mother's reference to their noble Italian connections. Her mother was a small, energetic woman, devoted to her husband, and an active member of their community. Katharine had loved her but regretted that she was such a snob. Her grandmother was a vague figure, recalled from early childhood. Dark and slight, sitting in a chair with a tartan rug over her knees. Everybody seemed to be afraid of her. The story was that she had run away from home to marry their grandfather, who was the son of a poor tradesman. They had emigrated to the States, where he had established himself in business and ended by founding one of the biggest chain department stores on the East Coast. Her mother had never cared to emphasize that aspect of her family, and when she married Richard Dexter, whose father was a lawyer, she ignored it altogether. Only the mementos of her grandmother, the reputed Italian aristocrat who had abandoned all for love, were kept on display around the house. Katharine had thought it ridiculous but harmless. She felt the same way about the name being included when they were baptized. Katharine di Malaspiga Dexter. That was what had brought Ben Harper to the cemetery. That was why she followed Carpenter down to his office to begin her training. Her brother was a known addict. The notification of his death had disclosed that curious second name. And it had a very special significance for the narcotics bureau.

She turned left at the top of the stairs leading from the well of the amphitheater. Cypress trees formed a velvet green background to the massive classical statues which the Medici princess had bought to enhance the symmetry of her gardens. Katharine turned left, following the trickle of people who still walked in the heat. There was a little bell tower, rose pink and crowned with its cupola and bell, and beyond it a natural panoramic view from the hill, with chairs and tables to accommodate those who were weary or just wished to enjoy the sight of the city from above. She went to the edge and looked over. It was a city of infinite variety. Somebody had described a beautiful woman in those words—Shakespeare, extolling the charm of Cleopatra. Infinite variety. The pink plaster, the gray domes, the slender towers. The birthplace of the Renaissance, the second greatest civilizing movement in man's history since ancient Greece. The trading center of the medieval world. The city where the Duke of Malaspiga and his family lived during the spring. It had sounded easy. She had the means of introducing herself without suspicion. All she had to do was make a contact, get to know them, and use the training Carpenter had given her. Given unwillingly and without disguising his belief that she was going on a one-way mission. She sat in the Florentine sunshine, listening to the distant mellow tolling of the great Cathedral bell for Matins, and wondered what Frank Carpenter was doing in New York.

It was the first time Carpenter had disagreed with his chief. He had been with the bureau for twelve years and directly responsible to Ben Harper for the last four. He had never found cause to criticize his policies or his judgment, until he enrolled Katharine Dexter. To Carpenter, the idea of using women on high-risk missions was bad enough—to bring in an amateur was making certain of disaster. He had gone to the funeral without much misgiving. He was certain that whoever this girl was, she'd have the sense to refuse. He hadn't even reminded Harper about Firelli, because he hadn't believed the idea would come to anything. When Harper told him Katharine Dexter had agreed to do it, he made a reasoned protest which ended up with his banging Harper's door and stamping back to his own office.

"It's our only chance," Harper had insisted. "We know those bastards are connected with it, and people like that don't come in except at the top. We've tried getting to them and we've failed. They're too smart to let anyone penetrate that organization. This girl is a chance in a million!"

"That's what we thought about Firelli," Carpenter pointed out. "He looked cast iron. One of the most experienced agents we had—right background, knowledge of antiques, everything. And he disappeared. A crack shot, a judo expert, a really bright guy. Vanished. And not a thing anyone can pin on them. I'm sorry, Ben, you want me to train this girl and get her ready to go out and take on a setup like that? It's not just crazy, it's a death sentence, and you know it."

"We haven't any choice," Harper responded. "We've got to crack this. The stuff's pouring in and all we get is a few pushers. We got that lead through an act of God. I'm not going to let it pass."

It was in an Interpol report. The driver of a truck that had arrived at Genoa with a shipment of antiques for New York was stopped by the customs for questioning. He was recognized by one of the officers as a known drug smuggler who had previously operated in Naples. Nothing was found in his load or on his person, and he had to be released and his shipment cleared. The goods he was carrying came from Malaspiga. The Italian narcotics authorities had carried out discreet investigations in the town of that name and found nothing to connect it with the smuggling trade. The truck driver was unknown there. The town itself was a sleepy Tuscan community, resentful of questions from outsiders, and feudally attached to its hereditary Duke. The antiques were part of a collection sent by him to the United States, and there was nothing illegal to be found anywhere. Without evidence except the coincidence of the truck driver's previous connection with narcotics in another part of Italy, the authorities declined to approach the Duke or investigate further. And there the matter rested. It was a narcotics agent in the Florence office of Interpol who noticed a police report that the driver of the truck had been found garroted in a derelict warehouse in Genoa within a week of his detention by the customs.

The Italian agent was known to Harper; a man of strong convictions and fierce integrity. On a visit to the States he had stayed at Harper's house. He was known as Raphael. He hadn't been able to convince his superiors, so he cabled his finding to Harper. There was a connection between Malaspiga and the smuggling of drugs. Nothing could be proved, but in his experience the Mafia-type murder of the man who had attracted attention was evidence enough. He hoped Harper might make use of it, since the shipment, innocent though it turned out to be, was destined for New York. That was Harper's act of God, that clue. And he had sent Firelli in to penetrate the family and investigate the town. A month after his arrival, well covered as an antique dealer, he had disappeared. Leaving one garbled telephone call for Raphael. Italian communications were bad, the telephone lines outside the major cities were deplorable. Little of what he was saying had got through. A word here and there. *Dangerous . . . I've found . . . Angelo.* That had been repeated twice, before the line went dead. *Angelo.* He had apparently checked out of his hotel in Florence, again by telephone, his luggage was picked up, and he was never heard from again.

So now, as Harper pointed out, there was no doubt that Malaspiga was involved. And sending in an agent with a genuine connection was the best chance they'd ever have of going to the heart of the organization. The Italian authorities wouldn't move without absolute proof, Raphael assured him of that. There was a strong political bias about his attitude to titled families and official deference to them. Interpol would assist, and he would act as liaison.

"I want you to give this girl everything you've got," Harper told Frank Carpenter. "I've seen you turn the rawest material into something first rate. You can do it, and I'm not accepting any excuses. Okay, she's a woman, and you don't like women in this kind of work. And she's a complete outsider, no police training, no service affiliation, nothing. But she's got the means of getting to them, if anyone has. I want you to show her the works, cram as much in as you can, and don't let your prejudices get in the way. And that's an order."

Carpenter had met her again the next morning prepared to dislike her as much as he disliked her mission. It hadn't been easy for him. She proved to be intelligent, thorough. As if she sensed his hostility, she set out to do better than he expected, and soon enough he had to admit that her ability was exceptional. She had near perfect recall and a natural eye for detail. She mastered the mechanics of simple electronic bugging, and showed a rare facility for identification.

There was no evidence of a neurotic personality or of any-thing more than a natural feminine diffidence in what was such a very masculine preserve. Nobody got to see her or know her. She stayed in the section of the DEA building that was reserved for special training. At the end of three weeks she was making such good progress that he had to report to Harper that she would soon be ready. One element of training she refused, and in spite of himself, Carpenter respected her for it.

She wouldn't learn to fire or carry a gun. "I'd never use it," Katharine said. "No matter what happened, I couldn't shoot anybody. So why carry it?" He hadn't argued. He had even felt relieved. Harper was triumphant, called her in to congratulate her and gave her a departure date the following weekend. The night before she left for Italy, Frank Carpenter had taken her to dinner. They went to a small restaurant on West Fifty-sixth. He hadn't taken a woman out for a meal since his divorce.

"Do you come here very often?" Katharine leaned back; she hadn't realized that she was tired. There was a niggling ache in the middle of her spine from bending over Carpenter's files. He looked more relaxed than she had ever seen him.

"I come here for a drink sometimes," he said. "With a friend of mine; he's a bureau man too. We have a beer to-gether on our way home."

"Is home far away?"

"Out along Pelham Bay Parkway, beyond the golf course. I have a small apartment in New Rochelle and sometimes grab a weekend game." He offered her a cigarette and lit it for her.

"You're not married?" She had noticed that he never said "we" in any context.

"Not anymore." The tone of voice didn't invite further questions. Silence developed between them. She took out her mirror, used a lipstick, looked around at the people standing by the bar. He didn't seem to mind not talking.

She had moved into a small hotel on East Fiftieth just off Third. She had stored her furniture from the Village apartment; the memories of Peter were too strong. She never wanted to see any of it again. He had come out of a well known clinic in upstate New York after a stay of six months. And for the first time it seemed as if there was hope of a cure. A week later she left him alone in the apartment. When she came back he had disappeared. A few hours later she found him in Bellevue Hospital, dead of an overdose. She wondered suddenly whether the man sitting opposite her had any real idea of the receiving end of drug addiction. Of the misery, the fear, the sense of isolation which was part of being with an addict.

His marriage had been a failure; it was obvious from the way he answered that the experience had hurt. He was very professional, very reserved. She admired him, but after a month she knew nothing about him at all.

"You didn't marry again?"

Their drinks had arrived. Lager for him and Scotch for her. He sipped the beer.

"I don't have time for a wife," he said. "In my experience that's something you've got to give a woman to keep her happy. Plenty of time. I work a sixteen hour day; I have to fly off any place at a moment's notice. This is a job for bachelors."

"Was that what went wrong?"

"In a way, yes. My wife was lonely; she got suspicious. She couldn't believe it was work keeping me away from home. So she invented other women. We had a rough two years before we got divorced. She's remarried now, and she's very happy. So." He shrugged. "That's my life story. How about yours?"

"I should think you know it all. I know how your department checks up!" He smiled at her; he didn't usually smile, and it made him look relaxed and attractive. His eyes were friendly.

"I know your age, where you were born, educated; no criminal record, one boyfriend that dropped out after you left college. Another that didn't last long—he couldn't take the setup with Peter. Seven years taking care of your brother. And you've never been married. That's surprising. You're an attractive girl."

"Addicts need time, too," Katharine said. "Anyway, I'm old-fashioned. I never met anyone I really cared about. I need to be in love before I marry. Right now, all I want to do is get to Italy." Carpenter didn't answer.

She looked less tired than when they came in. He had driven her hard but just as much in her own interest. Every time he looked at her he saw his friend Firelli—one of the experts in the department, with all the skills at his command. Firelli had gone to Malaspiga and vanished. He had a good sense of humor, and he was popular. He used to come to the same place with Frank, have a few drinks and eat dinner with another bureau man, Jim Nathan. The three of them had been good friends. They used to sit around and kid the waitress . . . He leaned across the table toward Katharine.

"I shouldn't say any of this to you," he said. "But I've told Ben what I think of the idea. I think it stinks. I've done my job . . ." He looked up at her briefly. "I've taught you how to plant bugs in a room, how to memorize facts and faces, the elementary things an agent has to know. But I don't call it training. It takes years, Kate, not weeks. I feel really bad about this. I told you about an agent named Firelli. He was a great guy. We used to come here together. He got one message through which made no sense, and then he disappeared. I want you to think about that. He's dead. And that's what you're walking into. I told you the first morning you came to the bureau, being a relative isn't going to help you. When you get out there you're on your own."

"I know all that," Katharine said quietly. "I'm not doing it under any misconception. You realize what the odds are? There must be twenty million Americans with Italian ancestry. But my grandmother was a Malaspiga. I believe that's fate."

"It wasn't fate that killed Firelli." Carpenter's expression was grim. They didn't mention the subject again. There seemed nothing more to say.

He brought her back to her hotel, and on the steps outside he kissed her urgently. In four weeks of being constantly together, he had never put his hand on her.

"Be careful," he said. "For Christ's sake don't take any risks. Promise me."

"I promise," Katharine said. He turned and went back to his car. He drove off without looking back. The next morning she left Kennedy Airport on the first leg of her journey to Florence. She had never felt more alone in her life.

2

She saw the letter even before the reception clerk signaled to her. There was a white triangle in the slot below her room number, and it was the only one. She walked over to the desk, and the clerk reached up and gave it to her. He smiled, thinking she would be pleased.

"It came by hand after you'd gone out this morning," he said. He was watching her with an expectant look on his face.

"Thank you," Katharine said. On the back of the envelope, embossed in crimson, was the crest of the Dukes of Malaspiga. She went up to her room and opened the letter.

It was very brief—four lines running boldly across the page, unevenly spaced.

Dear Signorina Dexter, Thank you for your kind letter and welcome to Florence. We should be pleased if you can take tea with us on Wednesday at five o'clock. Isabella di Malaspiga.

The signature was large, the letters ended with an artificial flourish that suggested years of practice. It was the way someone signed his name when he believed that name itself to be important. Isabella di Malaspiga. She had written to the Duke, her cousin; he must have passed her letter to his mother. How very correct they were, this family of aristocrats, self-consciously admitting a distant kinswoman to take tea.

Tea. She thought only the English indulged in that habit. She folded the letter in its envelope and locked it away in her case. She was not nervous. She lit a cigarette defiantly to prove to herself that her hand was steady, and threw the match away because it trembled in her fingers. There was something about that sinister crest that frightened her, a tonal quality in the name that held menace. Malaspiga. Perhaps she had been scared by some story about them when she was a child—she couldn't remember. It was as if she had deliberately shut all thought of them out of her mind. She sat on the edge of the bed, relit the cigarette and smoked, thinking quietly. Her letter had introduced her as the granddaughter of Maria Gemma di Malaspiga, niece of the twelfth duke, who had married and gone to America. It had taken her a long time to write it. Several attempts had been made and the results thrown away before she felt it was exactly right. When telling a lie, Frank Carpenter used to say, always hide it in the middle of truth. She had said she was making a pilgrimage to her ancestral city, recovering from the loss of her brother who had recently died, and would very much like to make the acquaintance of her cousins, and if possible see some of the family treasures. She hoped they would forgive the intrusion, but meeting them would mean a great deal to her. She had added a hypocritical flourish, much against her will, to the effect that she had dreamed of coming to Florence and seeing her grandmother's old home ever since she was a child. Thinking of Carpenter gave her courage. Feminine nervousness couldn't be helped; she owed a basic self-confidence to him. He had been hardhearted but wise. Hard on himself too—the way he had kissed her told her that. She threw the cigarette away. The invitation needed an answer.

Another letter. She rebelled against that. There was a telephone at the Villa Malaspiga. These were human beings,
capable of normal communication. It was ridiculous to feel
in awe. She picked up the phone and asked the switchboard
to get the number for her. The unfamiliar whine continued
until she almost gave up. Then a voice answered, and speaking in Italian, Katharine asked for the Duchess di Malaspiga,
and gave her own name. Katharine di Malaspiga Dexter.

There was a long wait, so long she wondered if they had
been disconnected. Then a high-pitched voice sounded through
the receiver.

"Isabella di Malaspiga is speaking. Is that Signorina Dexter who wrote to us?"

"Yes," Katharine said. "It is. I've just received your letter.
I'd be delighted to come for tea on Wednesday. It's very kind
of you."

"Not at all." The voice sounded like a young girl, friendly
and excited. There was no suggestion of grandeur or patron-
age. "We are so looking forward to meeting you, my dear
child. My son is especially pleased. He is so happy to have
found a new cousin. Until Wednesday then. Good-bye."

She had been very welcoming, very warm. It was ridiculous to feel afraid of them one moment and then charmed
by a few friendly words over the telephone.

The taxi crossed the Ponte Alla Carraroia; the bridges of
Florence were dramatically beautiful, wide and gracefully
arched over the broad sweep of the Arno. Churches raised
proud domes on the skyline, and the distinctive Italian bell
towers fingered the blue. Even the name for them was musical.
Campanile. For all its beauty and its ancient culture, there
was a toughness, an arrogance about Florence which was
reflected in the Florentines themselves, yet it was so difficult
to find fault when every street revealed an architectural treasure, with the gleaming river running through the center and
the colossal splendor of the great Cathedral, its Bell Tower
and Baptistry dominating the city's heart. It was the city of
the Medicis, the de la Riveras, the Malaspigas, the workshop

of Michelangelo, of Donatello, of Ghiberti. Time was not important, even to the busy Florentines. It was made for man, and not man for time. Eating, not dieting, was the occupation of the women, all of whom seemed to have enormous appetites and superb figures. The vanities were different; sex was implicit without in any way intruding. There were no vulgar signboards, none of the suggestive advertising that was so much a part of American life. It was assumed the men were virile, the women seductive. By contrast with the tourists of all nationalities who crowded the city, the Florentines stood out, dark and sinuous as cats, gracefully sharpening their claws for the exploitation of the foreigner.

Katharine spoke their language fluently and with a grace that they appreciated, not because she had studied hard, but because it came naturally to her. And a passionate love of the arts had awakened in her. Beauty, visual and tactile, was displayed all around her, in the architecture, the paintings, the rich fabrics, even the food. The waiter at her hotel, who took tremendous trouble advising what to choose on the menu, informed her proudly that French cooking owed its excellence to the importation of her Florentine cooks by Catherine de' Medici.

She could never be a part of these people, her background and attitudes were too different, but now and again something unfamiliar stirred in her, roused by a sight or a sound which was wholly Italian. The moment she saw the Villa Malaspiga, it happened again. The Viale Galileo wound upward behind the center of Florence on the other side of the Arno. Pine trees stood sentinel over the enormous houses, shielded behind ornamental gates. The road rose higher, climbing steeply; when they turned into the entrance of the villa, Florence lay stretched out below them, glittering and displaying itself in the sunshine, the roof of the Cathedral glowing red. The crest was everywhere. On the wrought-iron gates, which were twenty feet high, above the pillared doorway, carved in stone. On the mosaic floor of the entrance hall. The coronet, the wreath pierced by the corn shaft. A manservant waited beside her. He wore a white coat, and the crest was embossed on the brass buttons. She noticed in amazement, that he also wore white cotton gloves. She gave her name and followed him through the entrance hall, which was dominated by a pair of magnificent marble statues. There were massive double doors, elaborately carved. When they opened she found herself looking into a long, cool room, and immediately a musty smell intruded. Her heart was racing. A man came toward her, a tall, slim man, pale and smooth like ivory. The best-looking man she had ever seen in her life.

"Signorina Dexter? I am Alessandro di Malaspiga." She gave him her hand, and he brought it up to his mouth, without actually touching it. His eyes were black, large, heavy lidded. After a second's pause, they smiled at her in keeping with his lips.

"Please come in; my mother is waiting for you." The length of the room was exaggerated in her mind. Afterward, when she was used to it, it didn't seem too large. That day it was like a vast corridor, the walls covered with tapestries, a huge table standing in the center, and around a fireplace painted, carved and gilded with the Malaspiga coat of arms, she came upon a group of people. There were two servants standing behind a table, which was covered with a white cloth and glittering with silver. In a long chair, her feet raised on a foot rest, a woman looked up at Katharine and held out a pale hand, flashing with rings.

It was the same bell-like voice, beautifully modulated. "How delightful this is. I am Alessandro's mother. We talked on the telephone. Do come and sit beside me; let me look at you." It was a beautiful face, impossibly white-skinned, with great black eyes that glowed, a mouth painted bright scarlet. Delicate waves of gray-black hair curved from under a wide brimmed hat, with a wisp of veil falling from the crown. On the left lapel of her black silk dress she wore a pale pink rose. After the first shock of seeing her, Katharine realized that she must be nearly eighty years old. Two other figures rose from a settee; one moved with the grace so natural to Italian women. Katharine shook hands with a painfully slim girl with a handsome face and coal black eyes. She wore no makeup except black liner which emphasized the density of her eyes and detracted from fine features and a beautiful mouth.

"My daughter-in-law, Francesca," the old Duchess said. "And this is our friend, Mr. Driver."

She pronounced the English name with emphasis. Her presentation of the young Duchess di Malaspiga had been hasty by comparison. He came forward and shook Katharine's hand. He was a young man, somewhere in his early thirties, with fair hair and gray eyes, fine teeth—she thought irrelevantly that you could disguise every feature except the magnificent dentistry of the North Americans.

"Hullo," he said. "John Driver—nice to meet you, Miss Dexter." The accent was Canadian.

"Sit down," the old Duchess suggested again, "close to me, my dear. I don't hear all that clearly." She gave Katharine a beautiful smile.

Then the servants began to serve tea. It was an extraordinary ritual. Tea was poured from a huge silver pot into cups so small they contained only a mouthful. Sugar and milk were presented on a silver salver. Plates of rich pastries and an enormous confection of icing and walnut were solemnly cut and slices passed round. Nobody ate anything, except the Canadian, and the Duke, who took one pastry and left half of it. She was too nervous to eat herself. She finished the tiny cup of tea and sat balancing it, wondering suddenly if Ben Harper or Frank had any idea what they were asking her to do when they suggested she get to know her family. Family. It was ridiculous to use the word in connection with these unreal, stylized people. The beautiful, mummified old woman in her picture hat and fresh rose, the impossibly handsome Duke di Malaspiga, his wife with her sad expression—only the man named Driver was real. He asked for more tea, talked to the Duchess, and watched her with friendly eyes.

Her cousin the Duke leaned toward her.

"You have a family resemblance," he said. "Did you know that? A distinct resemblance to one of my aunts. She was a blonde too, like you. I must show you her portrait. She died three years ago, but she was very beautiful."

They were all beautiful. Katharine didn't doubt that. He had wonderful eyes, dark and expressive, a mouth that was too well molded for a man, and yet there was nothing feminine about him. He was completely male. He reminded her of an animal, something proud and swift that moved among trees. He said suddenly, in a quiet voice, "Don't be nervous of us, Signorina Dexter. Let me take that silly little cup away from you. I hate tea, but my mother insists upon it."

"I'm not nervous," she protested. "At least, I don't mean to be. You've all been so kind."

"Then you are shy," he said gently. "I didn't know American ladies could be shy. It's not a common attribute."

"Maybe not," she countered quickly. "But we're not all brash widows from the Midwest, either."

"You are from New York?" He accepted the retort, and she had a feeling that he respected her for making it.

"Yes. We live in New York now."

"I've been looking up my family records," the Duke said. "I have some papers relating to your grandmother. And her marriage. I thought you'd be interested to see them."

"I would," Katharine said. "I'd love to see them. I hope you didn't mind me introducing myself. But I'm alone now, and it seemed such a perfect opportunity to look up my grandmother's family and see all the places she used to talk about."

"We're very happy you wrote to us, aren't we, Mamia?" He turned to the old Duchess. He raised his voice and repeated the question. Katharine wondered why the old lady didn't wear a hearing aid. She nodded and waved one dainty hand —it was a coquettish gesture, perfected many years ago.

"Very happy. Tell me about yourself, my dear. Who did your mother marry—I'm sure I met some Dexters after the war. Probably your relations." She waited, still with the encouraging smile on her painted lips.

"My father's family came from Philadelphia," Katharine said calmly. "We used to live in Philadelphia when I was a child, but then my father decided to live in New York. He's still there. My brother and I lived together. When he died I decided to take this trip." She had perfected the story, and repeating it helped.

"You won't regret coming over," John Driver interposed. "I came on a short visit and I'm still here." He laughed. It was a pleasant sound. She couldn't imagine any of the others making it. "I fell in love with Florence," he continued. "People talk about Rome and Venice, but I found the heart of the Renaissance right here. Even the heart of Italy. And then I met Alessandro and that changed everything." He looked across at Katharine's cousin; he had an attractive, extro-verted face, not strictly good-looking because the conforma-tion was irregular, but likable and humorous. He seemed aware of her unease. Being so at home himself, he was try-ing to convey to her that she too would learn to relax with them all.

"How long have you been here?" Katharine asked him.

"Four years and two months. Your cousins won't let me go home!"

"We'd miss you, John." It was the first contribution Fran-cesca di Malaspiga had made. "Sandro and I will keep you forever, if we can." She handed her empty cup to one of the servants. The old Duchess gave a signal and the service was cleared away.

"You have a very warm-hearted family, Miss Dexter," John Driver said. "They've been wonderful to me."

"If you would like to come to the library with me," the Duke said, "I could show you the portrait of my aunt. The likeness is extraordinary."

It seemed a long way to walk down the room. One of the white-coated servants had gone ahead, and he opened the door for them. She passed through first, followed by her cousin. She wondered if he ever opened anything for himself, or whether even in the bedroom he shared with that unhappy-looking wife, a servant was on duty.

In the hallway he paused. "We can go to the library first," he said. "And then I could take you for a little tour. We have a lot of family portraits here, and a number of bronzes. Are you in a hurry?"

Katharine looked into the smiling face. The charm was very powerful; he was using it deliberately like someone displaying a talent. He wanted her to stay and see around the villa. For all his exquisite manners, he wouldn't have suggested it otherwise. "I'm not in a hurry," she said. "But I don't want to be a nuisance."

"That wouldn't be possible," the Duke said gently. "It isn't every day one finds a beautiful cousin from America. Come, this way." He took her by the arm. His touch was light, reminding her suddenly of the strong, hard fingers of Frank Carpenter when he had held her in his arms that last night. Alessandro didn't grip, he guided. There was no resemblance between them, except that both gave the impression of great physical strength. He brought her to the library.

"This is my favorite room," he said. "My mother prefers the long salon—she adores the tapestries, but I find them musty. I like the smell of wood and leather." So that was what she had noticed about the long room. The smell of tapestries woven hundreds of years before, perhaps hanging undisturbed for years.

"This is lovely," Katharine said, and it was true. It was a beautifully proportioned room, paneled in oak, with three walls of books behind exquisite grillwork. There was another twelve-foot fireplace, the Malaspiga coat of arms in carved wood above it. The floor was marble, the furniture very old and dark. An enormous iron chandelier hung above their heads.

"Here," the Duke said, "is your aunt. Now, isn't she like you?" It was a pastel portrait, as big as a large photograph, standing in an elaborate gilt frame on one of the side tables.

It showed a young woman in the fashion of twenty years ago, blond and dark-eyed, and remarkably like herself.

"You're right," Katharine said. "There is a look—even I can see it, and it's very difficult to see a likeness to yourself. What was her name?"

"Elsabetta di Carnevale; she was a famous beauty. She married a Venetian, a prince with a fortune. That's a rare commodity for our aristocracy these days. We've begun to marry rich American ladies."

"That's surely an old European habit," Katharine answered. "The English and French have been doing it for years."

He laughed. "You mustn't mind if I tease you, my dear cousin. It's only my way, and I always tease people I like. And I like you. I adore America and Americans, so don't misunderstand me."

"Have you been to the States?"

"Yes, some years ago. I went there on honeymoon with Francesca. She hated it. I found it very exciting."

"And when was that? How long have you been married?"

"Seven years," he said. "Look, here is a little gem. Bernini carved that bust of our ancestor, the sixth Duke. He has a wicked face, don't you think? He's supposed to look like me."

"He doesn't," she said.

"You're very forthright," he remarked. There was a change of expression in the dark eyes. He wasn't used to being contradicted.

"Most Americans are," Katharine said. "You must have noticed that. Tell me, where did you go in the States?"

Now the memory which Carpenter had trained was tuned like a machine, waiting to record every detail. Information was what they wanted: when he had gone to the States, how long and where he had stayed. Any contacts he might have made.

"We went to New York first, then on to California to stay with friends of my father—Hollywood, of course. I was fascinated."

She could imagine he would be; equally, the people whose business was fantasy must have been fascinated by him.

"Did anyone offer you a film contract?"

"How funny you should ask—yes, they did. I was very flattered. Francesca was horrified. Some of her attitudes are very bourgeois—odd, because she is wellborn."

It was not even subtle, and this surprised her. He should have been a subtle man, smooth and deft at hinting. There was no mistaking the contempt with which he spoke of his wife.

He took out a gold cigarette case—she saw the coronet in rubies and diamonds at the corner—and lit a cigarette. "I'm sorry, do you smoke? Nobody does in the house except me. I forget about visitors."

"Thank you." They were long, filtered, with a monogram printed on them. Specially made for him.

"I have the papers concerning your grandmother here," he said. "But I'm not going to show them to you today. Then you will have to come again."

"I was hoping you'd invite me." Katharine wasn't good at this kind of game. He was a master, and he made it easy for her. He seemed to be enjoying the light fencing match, through which his attraction toward her flashed like a beacon.

Women would find him an irresistible force. "I'll take you upstairs now," he said. "And then we'll rejoin my family in the salon."

"Who did you stay with in California—someone connected with the film world?"

"Yes, a couple called John Julius and his wife. He was a famous star before the war. He'd met my father in Italy and they became friends. He took us everywhere and showed us everything. Turn up these stairs here and be careful of that rug at the top—it slips." Again the grip on her elbow, pretending to support her. She eased herself free of him as they walked down a wide landing.

"Portraits," he said. "All Malaspigas, but of the eighteenth and nineteenth centuries. The earlier pictures are at the castle. Over there is your great-great-grandfather."

It was an unattractive portrait, showing a man standing three-quarter length in the dress of the early eighteen hundreds. He had a dark, arrogant face with a black beard. She stared at the picture without emotion. "Federigo di Malaspiga, second son of the tenth Duke," her cousin said. "His son was your grandmother's father. There is no picture of him, but your great-grandmother is over there."

"She looks very proud," Katharine said. "I don't envy my grandmother when she wanted to marry a poor man."

"A *common* man," Alessandro corrected. "Poverty was not a disgrace in those days, whatever stigma is attached to it now. Your grandmother wanted to marry a social inferior. That was impossible."

She didn't answer. To call him snobbish and old-fashioned was a pointless truism. Living in a house like the villa, surrounded by the ritual of a world which only existed for the few, made such an attribute inevitable. Her purpose was to penetrate, to ingratiate herself. She walked beside him slowly, pausing to look at pictures he thought might interest her. She lost count of the great-aunts and uncles, the cousins, the relatives by marriage who adorned the gallery walls.

He looked at his watch. Cartier, with an elegant crocodile strap. There might be some poor Italian aristocrats, but the Duke di Malaspiga wasn't one of them. "It's past six—we must go downstairs and have a drink with my mother. Fortunately, John is very good with her. He keeps her entertained, otherwise she gets very bored."

"He seems so fond of you all," Katharine said.

"It's entirely mutual. Besides which, he has a great talent. I hope the ancestors haven't bored you?"

"Of course not—it was terribly interesting for me. Thank you."

"Please," he said, leading her back toward the salon, "call me Alessandro. If I may call you Katharine. Miss Dexter is ridiculously formal between cousins."

The Duchess' salon was full of subdued lights. The smell of the tapestries was mingled with a different, sweeter smell. As well as electric light, candles were burning on the big center table, and she realized that the wax was scented. The tea table was shining with crystal glasses and decanters. One servant, instead of two, was offering drinks. The Duchess di Malaspiga had gone; only the old lady and the Canadian remained. They were sitting close together and laughing. Both looked up as they approached. There were two little spots of red on the old Duchess' cheeks and her eyes sparkled. She looked so young in the deceptive light that Katharine was startled. Her glance at her son was mischievous.

"There you both are," she said. "What a long time you kept Miss Dexter, Sandro. She must be sick of her ancestors by now! Come and have a cocktail, my dear child. My son is so selfish, keeping you away from me . . ." The laugh was a bright trill, with a sweet note of malice in it. Katharine sat near her on the other side of John Driver. She laid a hand as dried and thin as old paper on top of hers. On the little finger she wore a crested ring which was the twin of the one Katharine had in her hotel room and had forgotten to wear.

"Have something to drink," she invited. "John will make you a wonderful old-fashioned. He taught Bernardo to do it, but he can't get it right. Or would you prefer champagne . . ."

"Just whiskey please," Katharine said. She could feel Alessandro watching her; the amused glances of his mother were making her uneasy.

"And another of those delicious cocktails for me," the old lady demanded. She took the glass and sipped it greedily. "When you get old," she said to Katharine, "life has few compensations. One lives for something as simple as an old-fashioned! When I was young I only drank wine—spirits were not suitable for women. Now wine disagrees with me. Old age is a sad thing, my dear. Enjoy your youth—you don't know how precious it is."

"Come now," John Driver said gently. "You look like a girl tonight, doesn't she, Sandro?"

"You have the secret of eternal youth, Mother," he said. "Our cousin is going to think we don't look after you, if you talk like that. No more cocktails tonight; you're becoming sad."

It was said with gentleness, but the old lady put her glass down. It seemed she understood her son.

"I must change my dress for dinner," she announced. The beautiful, painted face turned to Katharine, and the smile showed the same superficial friendliness.

"You must visit us again, my dear," she said.

It was a dismissal, and Katharine got up immediately. The Duke and John Driver came to the entrance hall with her.

"I'll take Miss Dexter back to her hotel," John Driver said. "My car's outside."

Alessandro bowed over her hand. This time his lips brushed the back of it.

"Would you like to come tomorrow and look at the papers?"

"Yes," she said quickly, "if that's convenient—I'd love to."

"Good," the Duke said. "John will take you home now. I will collect you at one o'clock tomorrow, and we will have lunch. Good night."

As they crossed the Ponte Alla Carraroia, Driver looked at her and grinned.

"Don't be overpowered," he said. "I felt just the same when I first met Sandro. He sort of takes you over. He doesn't mean anything, it comes naturally to him."

"So it seems," Katharine said. "It's just that I'm used to being asked."

"Would you have said no, if he had asked you?"

"I guess not," she admitted. But not for the reason Driver thought—not because she was overcome by his looks and his charm. Now that she was out of the villa and sitting next to an ordinary human being, she felt that Alessandro di Malaspiga was the most frightening man she had ever met. She felt as if she had come out of a tomb. The smell of the scented candles and the fading tapestries was still with her, cloying and unhealthy. Nothing except her purpose in coming to Florence would have made her see any of them again.

"Women never say no to him," Driver said. "That's the trouble. He lifts a little finger, and they stumble over themselves running."

"Well, I hate to tell you, here's one who won't. Anyway I think you're putting the wrong interpretation on it. I'm a stranger and his cousin. He's just asked me out to lunch."

"Oh, sure." He gave the same friendly grin. "But being so pretty helps. He's great company—you'll enjoy your lunch."

"I'm sure I will. I didn't mean to be ungrateful; it was very nice of him to ask me." They shook hands outside the hotel.

"Maybe you'll lunch with me one day," he said. "I'd like that."

"So would I," Katharine answered. She found that she meant it. There was something real and warm about John Driver. A great talent, Alessandro had said. She wondered what it was.

"What's the matter with Frank? He won't even come out for a beer." James Nathan had worked with the old Federal Bureau of Narcotics before it became assimilated into the BWDD, then the Justice Department's Drug Enforcement Administration. He was a veteran of fifteen years, small and tough, with a reputation for getting rough with suspects. His methods and his attitudes were disliked by men as progressive as Ben Harper. After a few drinks he was inclined to express his opinion of the softer handling of addicts as typical of the left-wing sellout that was undermining the American people.

"Hit 'em," he would say, slamming a fist on the bar. "And hit 'em hard. It's all they understand." But a lot of people liked Jim Nathan; everyone respected his professionalism. He spoke to a younger colleague of Frank Carpenter's.

"He always comes and has a beer on a Friday at that little

joint around the corner. Last two times I asked him he was busy. What's up with him?"

The younger man shrugged. "He's running a training program. You know Frank, he never lets up. Try him now; he was around this morning seeing the old man."

"I have tried him," Nathan said. "He gave me thumbs down. Christ, what's he doing training rookies—he's way past all that stuff."

"Special rookie," the other man said. "Pretty important mission. I don't know much about it, but the word's out that we're on to something with Firelli's assignment."

"Italy?" Nathan asked. He smoked a chewed-up pipe, which he took out, stuffed untidily with tobacco and lit.

"Could be," was the answer. Nathan balanced on one buttock on the other man's desk.

"First I've heard of it," Nathan said. "So what's the special mission? Another undercover agent?"

"I guess so." The other man's telephone began to ring. He picked it up and gave his name. Nathan slid down to the floor, rubbing his bottom. A special mission, an undercover agent needing Frank's crash course instruction. Nathan raised an eyebrow and sucked on his pipe. He looked at his watch —seven thirty-five. He waved to the man who was telephoning, then he went out of the office, down in the elevator and through the main hall, where he checked out. He was off duty till nine the next morning. Free. He wandered toward the bar where he and Frank Carpenter met for a beer, and had a drink by himself. He looked at his watch again. Firelli's assignment. He was posted missing, presumed dead. A statistic on the ledgers of the most lucrative business in the world. The old-time gangsters hadn't begun to realize the potential of drugs. They ran liquor, gambling, women, and made themselves millionaires. Then they discovered the labor unions and netted themselves new revenue. But a kilo of heroin was worth half a million dollars. An ounce brought fifteen thousand. He drew on his pipe and the ashes glowed. Millions and millions of dollars. Pounds, Deutsche marks, francs, yen.

Every currency in the world for the dust that brought dreams. A lot of his old associates had thought exactly the same thoughts as he was thinking, and the process had only led one way. The old bureau had been amalgamated because it contained a hard core of corrupted officers, men who stole the impounded heroin and cocaine and re-sold it on the market. Men who took bribes, suppressed evidence, gave protection. He had known many of them. The Mafia had reached them all. He had never taken anything from them. They were the Wops—the scum. It was after eight o'clock. He checked his watch again and went to the telephone booth in the corner of the bar. He dialed a Brooklyn number.

"Honey? Yeah, it's me. Okay—sure. I'm having a beer. I'll be home soon. You fix us something to eat. Be a good girl now." He hung up, found some loose change and started another call. This time there was no answer. He waited, listening to the ringing. He said "shit" under his breath and hung up. Eight thirty. He'd have to try again, when he got home. He bought some more tobacco and left the bar.

Being a frugal man he traveled by subway. He read the paper, his reflexes tuned for trouble. Even in the early evening, the trains were places where robbery and murder happened regularly. Nathan wasn't bothered. He could take care of himself. He would have welcomed some young mugger trying to take him on; he was in that kind of mood. He got out at Grand Army Plaza and walked the three blocks to his home on Eastern Parkway, stuffed the pipe in his pocket, because his wife didn't like the smell of the tobacco. They had been married three years. There had been another marriage, but it had ended years ago, and he never thought about it. He opened the apartment door, and went in. There was a smell of roasting chicken. He sniffed it and smiled.

"Marie? I'm home." She came to meet him. She was thin and small, with dark hair tied back in a pony tail. She looked like a teenager with an old face. He kissed her, slipping his arm around her waist. "How's my girl," he asked.

"I'm fine," she said. "Just fine. Hungry?"

"Starving," Nathan said. He kissed her again. Three years; three years of being married to the only human being he had loved in his life. He didn't use the word "love" except in connection with Marie. His family relationships hadn't been easy. They were a poor, immigrant Jewish family of Russian origin, struggling to make a living. He hadn't liked his parents, and his home had been very different from the sentimental myth about close-knit Jewish clans presided over by the mother. His father was poor, anxious and bad-tempered. He hit his children and bullied his wife. His three sons didn't like him, his only daughter liked him too much and ended up living with a woman buyer for one of the Park Avenue stores. Nathan didn't acknowledge her. He would have preferred a sister who was a whore to a self-confessed dyke. One brother, Bud, was working in a Brooklyn supermarket, where he was manager; he was married with three children, and occasionally he and Nathan and the wives got together. The other brother had been killed in a highway accident ten years earlier. His parents were dead, and Marie had no family. They were on their own, and Nathan liked it. His private life was very private. He took a beer out of the icebox and drank it in the kitchen watching his wife get the dinner ready. At thirty she had the figure of a teenage girl; he was proud of it. He liked being seen out with her on a Sunday, when he went bowling— she looked so young. She was the most vulnerable woman he had ever met, and in the course of his career as a policeman and then a specialist in Narcotics, Nathan had met some pathetic specimens of humanity. Few had roused him to pity. Criminals filled him with hate, and it was a hate born of self-knowledge. If he hadn't been a policeman, Nathan would have been a criminal. He sensed this without understanding it, and pursued the thieves and pimps, the blackmailers and murderers with brutal fanaticism because they were a mirror in which he saw himself. He had met his wife in a police raid. She was working as a waitress in a coffee shop which was a known meeting place for addicts in the hippie-dominated East Village.

It was decided to clean the place out, and Nathan led the squad. He remembered the wispy, hollow-eyed girl, trembling and mute with fear, standing backed up against a wall while the arrests were made. Something touched a sympathy in him he didn't know existed. He felt sorry for the kid. Sorry enough to go and tell her there was nothing to be scared about. If she was clean. He'd known immediately that she wasn't. Only heroin gave that jaundice color to the skin, the limpid brightness to the eyes. She was hopped up and the moment she was booked into the precinct station she was on the way to jail. Nathan hadn't arrested her.

And the next night he was back at the coffee shop, looking for her. He wasn't surprised to find she had disappeared. Pursued by fear, by debt, by the police, people like Marie were always running. And equally she wasn't difficult to find. She had another job, cleaning up in a seedy hotel patronized largely by hookers and their clients, whose manager complained angrily to Nathan that the hippie chicks supporting themselves as amateurs were ruining his business. Nathan didn't know himself what he wanted with her. He just knew that she worried him—it was like a toothache. He felt none of the disgust and contempt most addicts inspired in him. He gave her a meal she didn't eat, and tried to get her to talk about herself. It wasn't successful. He was a cop, and she just sat and stared at him, her eyes bigger than before and almost as frightened. It took a long time for Nathan to get through to her; in the next few weeks he made certain the hotel manager and his wife paid her a decent salary and didn't let her get into trouble. An attempt to escape responsibility, and he'd see their place was cleaned up. This was a departure from the free use of the whores or the cash handouts usually extorted from people in their line of business, but they kept their bargain so carefully that they hardly allowed Marie outside. She'd been seeing Nathan regularly for two months when she confessed she was on heroin.

"You can't go on seeing me," she had said, quite without warning when they were walking through Prospect Park on his Sunday off. "I'm hooked on the stuff. I'm no good to you. So thanks for everything and good-bye." She had turned and rushed in the opposite direction. It took Nathan a few seconds to catch up with her. She was crying, and that was when he decided he would have to marry her. Someone had to help her kick the habit—someone had to take care of her. He looked at her tenderly as they ate their evening meal. She was the exception, the single statistic that meant success. She had taken a cure, under Nathan's direction, and she married him clean. And she'd stayed clean. She was house-proud, frugal, a good cook, and he loved her so much that the emotion was a pain. She had offered to become a Jew, which he rejected, having given up religion as a boy, but the suggestion touched him profoundly. She owed him everything and she never stopped trying to say thank you. The beautifully cooked kosher meal was another way. She had been three years without slipping, or showing any sign she wanted to slip. She was safe. He helped her clear the table and dried the dishes. They talked a lot while they worked. She made him laugh, telling him small details of her day. It was almost ten o'clock when he went to the telephone.

"Get me a cup of coffee, honey." He sent her back to the kitchen and dialed the same number. This time it was answered after half a dozen rings.

"This is Nathan." He lowered his voice.

"Yes."

Nathan glanced at the door; his wife couldn't hear anything in the kitchen. He didn't take time out to be polite.

"There's another pigeon being trained. Yeah—as soon as I know I will. But the heat's on. Let your end know."

He hung up, just before the door opened and Marie came in with two cups. "Were you calling somebody?"

"Just the office." He smiled. In a dozen years they had never got to him, and they had tried, many times. Money, threats, cutting him in. But it was inevitable the moment he married Marie. They had the lever and they applied it. He hadn't even tried to fight; he almost admitted to himself that he had known it would happen and accepted it. Now he was bound to them, fighting on their side. If he didn't do as they had told him, he would come home one night and find she'd had visitors. And the visitors had put the needle in her again.

He put his arm around his wife and sipped his coffee. "You want to watch the Thursday night movie, Jimmy?"

Nathan looked at the television set. "Okay," he said. "We can catch the first half. Then maybe I'll take you to bed." She reached up and kissed him. He smiled and squeezed her. To hell with the bureau. Nothing was going to happen to his wife.

Katharine was downstairs waiting in the hotel lobby by five minutes to one. She had taken a lot of trouble to get ready, choosing a lightweight dress in pale yellow, putting on the little signet ring she hated. She carried a large shoulder bag. Inside it was the set of tiny bugs and the recording device Carpenter had given her in New York. It had been arranged that she could spend the afternoon alone, looking up her family records. And the records were in the library. The Duke had said it was his favorite room. There couldn't be a better place to set a recording device, and she would have time to do so as soon as he left her there. Alessandro called for her at one o'clock, driving a wicked-looking Ferrari, the small Ducal crest painted on its doors. He was casually dressed, wearing a canary yellow sweater and a silk scarf. He kissed her hand and told her how charming she looked. They lunched at the Loggia Restaurant on the Piazzale Michelangelo, set high up in the Florentine hills, and dominated by a copy of the great master's statue of David, which stood in the center of the Piazzale itself, looking down on the city.

If there was a single word that described Alessandro di Malaspiga, it was magnetism. Katharine had never met anyone who possessed it to such a degree. There was a drawing power about him which transcended the obvious star

quality of being a Duke with charm and money. He was a
man who would have made an impression under any circumstances. When they came into the restaurant, everybody stared
at them; several people smiled and waved. He hadn't introduced her, he had taken her arm in his proprietary way and
guided her straight to their table, preceded by the manager
himself. "I have already ordered lunch," he said. "Something
very special. And some nice wine." He looked across at her
and smiled. "This is a celebration," he said.

She thought quite dispassionately that a woman would
have to be very brave or very foolish to become involved
with him. You might admire the fearful beauty of the tiger,
but you didn't take it in your arms.

"What are you thinking about?"

"You," Katharine answered truthfully. "You're not at all
what I expected."

"And what was that—some effete degenerate out of a Fellini
film? I'm sorry if you're disappointed."

"How could I be," she said. "You don't need me to flatter
you. And I didn't expect you to be so friendly. I'm only a
distant relative—very distant. A quick trip around the villa
would have been enough for most people."

"Believe me," Alessandro said, "that's exactly what most
people would have got. But you don't need flattery any more
than I do. A beautiful flower has blossomed on our family
tree!" He laughed out loud. "You have the most delightfully
expressive face—don't look so disgusted, it was only a joke.
Do you know, Italian women don't make faces—they're so
frightened of getting wrinkles! It always irritates me to sit
opposite a mask. I love people who show what they feel."

"I can't help it," she said. "Is that how your mother looks
so incredibly young? I've never seen anything like her."

"Eighty-two years old," he said. "Only her body betrays
her. She is still beautiful. I remember seeing her as a little
boy, dressed to go to a reception. It was before the war, and
she was wearing the Malaspiga diamonds. She was so lovely
it was like a vision. Then the war came, the diamonds were

sold, we lost nearly everything. My father had collaborated with the Fascists, you see, and we were outcasts for a time. And becoming poorer. Not even marrying Francesca helped, because she didn't have enough money to restore what had been lost." He lit one of the monogrammed cigarettes. Sunshine beat down on the green hills, silvering the roofs of Florence. The windows of the restaurant were shaded by vines coming into leaf, and from the position high up, a cool breeze countered the heat below them.

"Is that why you married her—for her money?" Katharine asked the question, made bold by his frankness. He glanced at her for a moment before he answered.

Suddenly he smiled. "You certainly are forthright," he said. "I like it. Yes, of course, money was a consideration. She was very suitable as a wife. Except for one very important detail, which unfortunately we didn't know about at the time. She can't have children. So for that alone, the marriage has been a disaster. It's not her fault, of course, and she broods over it. I've told her not to feel guilty. It's an act of God."

"It must be terrible for her. Knowing how much you want them. I'm sorry."

"You have a kind heart," he said. "I think you really are sorry for someone you have only met once. I don't think she spoke a word to you beyond hello, did she? She's a very quiet woman. In old age she is the type who will turn to religion to compensate for her disappointments. At the moment she is too bitter even to go to Mass. I insist that she does so when we're at the castle. It's expected."

"If you're so poor," Katharine said, "I don't understand how you can keep the villa and a castle—maybe I'm being forthright again, but your life-style looks like money to me."

"I didn't say I was poor now," he replied. "I said we were becoming so after the war. Fortunately, with my wife's money I began a business. I've made a great success of it."

"What sort of business?"

"Antiques. Furniture, china, sculpture, objects of art. I have a thriving export business and a number of shops in the capital cities. Paris, New York, West Berlin, Stockholm. That's the most recent—we opened there a year ago. It isn't easy to get the Swedes to appreciate the art of the South. They incline to the somber. Their furniture is rather like their women. Beautiful lines but strictly functional. I'm going to take you home and leave you with your family papers. I have an appointment at three."

She saw no one when they arrived at the villa. The same servant opened the door; he looked sleepy. There was a silence which made the closing of the front door sound like a gunshot.

"Siesta," Alessandro said. "They are all sleeping. I think it's a stupid habit. I haven't time to waste. There is the library; everything has been left out for you on the table. I should be back by five. Mother has asked you to take tea with her again. Enjoy yourself."

The library was cool; the shutters had been half drawn to keep out the sun. She stood looking around for a moment and then went to the center table. A small heap of letters tied with brown ribbon, an album of photographs, a large envelope with a broken seal on the back of it, full of documents. She pulled a chair to the table and sat down, unfastening the letters first. Her watch showed ten minutes to three. She wondered where the servant had gone—probably to his room to sleep. She pretended to read the letters, listening for any sounds of activity outside. She heard nothing. She went to the window and looked out. The library was at the back of the villa and it faced the elaborate gardens, so large and formal they would have done credit to a country mansion. Italian gardens had a style of their own; water was a prominent feature in all of them. Fountains, pools, rock gardens with a waterfall, and always the beautiful marble statuary, gleaming in dark green corners, clothed in ivy, or displayed in the center of a brilliant flower bed or a sweep of lawn. She pulled the shutter half-closed. The gardens were deserted too. She made a careful examination of the room. The central point was the fireplace, where the most comfortable chairs were arranged. There was a fine marble table on an elaborately carved ebony base, supporting a huge, ugly baroque clock. She took the tiny bug out of her bag. It was fitted with a magnetic surface. The recording device which taped what the bug picked up, was the size of a cigarette pack. To be effective, the bug should be at a minimum of five feet from the ground, otherwise the voice levels didn't carry clearly, without a complicated electrical system which had to be incorporated in the structure.

Frank Carpenter had given her a simple, portable device, suitable for limited use in a room. She ran her fingers under the marble table; they were black with dust. Nobody at the villa cleaned underneath the furniture. She fitted the little recording machine under the tabletop, hidden at the back. Two suction pads held it in place. The bug was more difficult to conceal. She looked upward. A splendid landscape painting hung on one wall, but there was always the danger of the frame being dusted and the little bug dislodged. The wall on the other side of the fireplace was a bookcase, covered by the delicate gilded grill. She inspected the tenth row of books, standing on her toes. They were a complete set of ornithological works, and when she touched them with a finger, they were as dusty as the table base. Nobody was likely to move them or even clean them at that height. She slipped the bug inside the grill and clamped it to the wall. Provided that there was no excessive background noise, anyone talking in the library would be clearly recorded on the tiny voice-activated tape machine hidden under the table. When she had finished, she lit a cigarette; it tasted stale and she threw it away. Smoking in Italy wasn't the pleasure it had been at home. Perhaps it was the change of atmosphere. The first step had been taken; she was surprised at how easy it had been. But then her cousin trusted her. He had left her alone in his house with freedom to go where she liked, to look at anything, however private. There was a desk near the fireplace and a telephone. She went to the desk and was surprised again when the flap opened. None of the drawers were locked. There was no reason for her to hesitate, or for the feeling of uneasiness that overcame her as she began to search the desk. This was what she had come to do. It was illogical to feel guilty about reading private papers, opening other people's drawers.

Inside, everything was fanatically neat—papers, clips, ink, an assortment of pens from ballpoint to gold-nibbed Parkers, a leather address book. She hurried through that, looking for something without knowing what. It read like the *Almanach de Gotha*. Princes, counts, dukes, English aristocracy, half a dozen Blue Book American names she recognized, and then in a separate section, a list of addresses which she guessed must refer to his business. Paris, Rome, London, which he hadn't mentioned, Stockholm, Brussels, Beirut, and New York. 493 Park Avenue, New York. E. Taylor, and the Manhattan telephone number, 212–PL 8-2790.

He could have been making as much money as he said out of exporting antiques all over the world. He could be the high-powered businessman who had rescued his family and rebuilt their fortune. Or he *could* be growing rich on a different kind of trade from bronzes and Renaissance art. She closed the desk; there was nothing in the drawers but more photograph albums, boxes of embossed writing paper, a carton of the Duke's special cigarettes, and an empty velvet box which had once contained Perugino chocolates and was now full of broken glass pieces, drops and loops from a chandelier. She went back to the table and picked up the letters. It was now four o'clock. She would be asked about the letters, the family documents. She began to read through them, skipping large sections, memorizing small items. The admonishments of her great-grandmother to the lovesick Maria Gemma, refusing to receive her lover and threatening to disown and disinherit her. They were an unlovable family, consumed by pride, impatient of feeling. Merciless, even to their own children unless their will was obeyed. The implacable mother was only an echo of the furious father, affronted at his daughter's temerity in loving a man inferior in social caste. It made Katharine wince for her grandmother when she read them. She at least had truly loved; it wasn't an emotion common to the Malaspigas. "The marriage has been a disaster." So coolly and without sentiment, Alessandro had dismissed the ruin of a human life, the cruelty of her barren state. Poor Francesca di Malaspiga. She must have been in love with him, dazzled by the marriage. Now, in his casual description, she was a silent woman, embittered against God. Katharine thought suddenly that there could only be one thing worse than hating her cousin, and that would be to love him.

By five o'clock she had read hurriedly through everything, and was looking through the photograph album, when the servant knocked on the door and announced that the Duchess was expecting her in the salon.

Both women, the old and the young, were waiting for her. The Duchess gave her a slight smile, and relinquished the seat next to her mother-in-law. "Please sit here so Mamia can talk to you."

"How pretty you look today," the old lady said. She wore a hat of pale straw, a silk dress of the same neutral color, and another pink rose, fastened with a diamond pin. She trailed a brown chiffon scarf in one hand. Her daughter-in-law looked stark and austere in black, relieved by huge matched pearls around her neck and in her ears.

"Sandro isn't here," the old Duchess said. "He left a message saying he wouldn't be home till this evening. He asked us to take care of you. He works so hard, poor Sandro. He's done so much for us all. Bernardo, pass the signorina some tea! And my John isn't here, either—he always looks after me when Sandro isn't here."

"Where has he gone?" Katharine didn't want to know, but a silence was developing. The Duchess was drinking her tea; her daughter-in-law said nothing.

"I don't know," the old lady said. "He just goes off, and never tells me anything. Where has he gone?" She turned suddenly to Francesca.

"He's gone to the Belvedere, to see the exhibition. He told you so this morning." She stirred her tea, without looking at her mother-in-law.

"He's so foolish, wasting his time on that modern rubbish," the Duchess complained. She appeared mollified by the information. "There's been no great art since the Renaissance; he knows that. You must see some of his work."

"Alessandro said he was talented," Katharine said. "But he didn't say how. Is he a painter?"

It was Francesca who answered. "He's a sculptor," she said. "Sandro discovered him. I think he will be one of the world's great sculptors."

"Oh, come." The old Duchess gave a little laugh. "You do exaggerate. He's good, but only centuries will determine his greatness . . ."

"Excuse me." Francesca di Malaspiga got up. She came over to Katharine. "I have something to do for my husband; I quite forgot. I hope you will come again." She held out her hand and for a moment took Katharine's in a limp clasp. The black eyes were empty, cold as pit water. She went out of the room.

The old Duchess di Malaspiga sighed. "Oh, dear," she said gently. "I upset her by suggesting John wasn't guaranteed greatness. Now she will be angry for the whole evening. There will be an atmosphere." Katharine didn't know what to say. The exchange seemed so unreal and exaggerated that she stayed silent. She felt the old woman's great dark eyes watching her.

"I'm very fond of John," the Duchess said. "He's kind, and he amuses me. He doesn't make me feel a nuisance and that's important when one is old. But I cannot pretend to admire him as much as my son and Francesca do. I can understand her in a way; she is extreme in her attitudes. Personally I find that people who over-emphasize everything are bores. But I find Sandro's belief in him more difficult. He really thinks he will produce great work. Perhaps he's right." She sighed again. "I shouldn't have contradicted her," she said. "I should have been patient."

"It won't matter," Katharine said. "She'll have forgotten it. I shouldn't worry about it." Again there was silence.

"I've had a fascinating time," she said. "Reading my great-grandmother's letters. It's been so kind of Alessandro to make everything available to me."

"I know it's given him pleasure," the Duchess said. "His family means so much to him. All the Malaspigas are very proud. Being forced to leave the castle helped to kill his father. It was very difficult for us after the war."

Katharine looked down at her clasped hands. They were gripped very tight. "It's amazing how he's restored everything," she said slowly. "He was telling me about it at lunch. And it's all been done so quickly."

"He's an extraordinary man," the Duchess said. "Nothing deters him. He promised his father he would make up for all that we had lost. A number of my friends were ruined after the war." She shrugged. "Politics are always dangerous, but men love to play at them. I've never understood what fascinates them. Our friends supported the Fascists, just as my husband did. But most of them have remained ruined. We owe everything to my son." She smiled at Katharine. "I hope I haven't bored you talking about family matters. It must seem very strange, coming from the United States."

"A little," Katharine admitted. She looked at the beautiful old woman, wreathed in chiffon, emphasizing her remarks with graceful gestures and that constant smile, and wondered how much she had deliberately suppressed a keen intelligence in order to accommodate the conventions of her generation. Isabella di Malaspiga was not a fool; she was a woman of taste and judgment who had assumed the role allotted her by circumstances and the accident of her exquisite beauty. Her destiny had been relinquished into the hands of her husband, and her son. An extraordinary man, she called him. A man whom nothing deterred, who had given a deathbed promise and carried it out. It should have sounded like melodrama, but it didn't. There was a cool, factual quality about the magnificent old lady and her acceptance of what he had achieved. Men ordered the world in which the Duchess lived. If one was fortunate, they governed wisely. Otherwise one suffered as a result of their mistakes. Whatever happened there was nothing to be done about it.

Katharine recalled herself to the present and to the purpose which had brought her there. She was shocked at how easily she had slipped away, and how pervasive even the old Duchess was as a personality.

"I didn't have time to read everything," she said. "I was so absorbed I didn't realize that it was getting late. I wonder— do you think Alessandro would mind if I came back and finished all the letters?"

"But of course not," the Duchess said. "Come whenever you like." It was easy then to get up and take the hand that was as light as a leaf.

"Thank you for tea," Katharine said. "I'll come again in a day or two."

"I shall look forward to it," Isabella di Malaspiga said. "We can have another talk." The bright smile was still on the Duchess when Katharine left the room, but her eyes were looking somewhere else. Katharine realized suddenly that this was her secret, the recipe for her survival. Nothing and no one came too close to Isabella di Malaspiga. The beautiful smile, the gracious manner were an impenetrable barrier against the outside world. As she began the long walk down the Viale Galileo to the bridge, Katharine envied her that barred and bolted attitude to life. She herself had never felt more vulnerable or more uncertain. Her home and the life she had lived, even the nightmare of her brother's addiction and death, all seemed to have blurred around the edges. It was as if she were losing her contact with the real world and slipping into that inhabited by her cousins. Alessandro di Malaspiga had disturbed her. She hated his arrogance, his cynicism—she had to fight consciously against his charm. It was a mistake to analyze him, to probe into the reasons why he was what he had become, to pass opinions on his mother. It was getting too close, becoming involved. That didn't make it easier to go through his desk, to record his conversations.

She had to remember that none of them were what they seemed. She had placed the bug and the recorder; the fact that her hands shook and she felt frightened afterwards were healthy reactions. Her unwillingness to go back and do it again were not. She had made the opening, saying she needed more time to look at her family papers. But as she crossed over the river and found a taxi to take her to the hotel, Katharine knew that the last thing in the world she wanted was to go to the villa or see any member of the family again. Back in the hotel she took a hot bath, trying to relax. She admitted her confidence was shaken; thinking of the moments when she was reading the address book and searching the drawers, she felt numb with fright. If the door had opened, if the Duke had returned unexpectedly . . . Angrily, she reminded herself that in spite of these reactions, she had learned two very important things. Malaspiga's honeymoon visit to Hollywood and the name of the film star, John Julius.

Carpenter had emphasized the need to pass on information as soon as possible. She ordered herself a Campari soda and dialed the Florence telephone number which was the Interpol contact with the narcotics bureau.

The same number Firelli had dialed before he disappeared. A woman answered and Katharine gave the code word. It was a man who came on the line.

"This is Cousin Rose," she said. "I've made contact and I want to report."

"Any progress?"

"Yes, I think so."

"Then we had better meet. I will be outside the east door of the Baptistry in half an hour. I will carry a large sketch pad under my arm, and I shall wear a panama hat with a green band. Use your call sign—mine will be Raphael."

In the Piazzale del Duoma there were little groups of tourists on the steps of the Baptistry staring at the Ghiberti bronze doors, which were one of the wonders of the city, fingering the little raised figures, and listening to the explanations of a guide. She saw him standing a little apart, the sketch pad under his left arm, wearing the hat with the green ribbon, and she walked up to him.

"I'm Cousin Rose," she said. He took off his hat, showing a semi-bald scalp with a fringe of curly black hair. He shook hands with her and smiled.

"Raphael," he said. "I'm glad to meet you. Let's go and have a drink. There's a nice little café over there, on the other side of the piazzale."

The place was full of tourists, drinking coffee, and eating ice cream; a few Italians sat sipping glasses of Stock, with the usual tumbler of iced water on the side. They found a corner table, and he tucked himself in, apologizing for the crush. He seemed a nice, ordinary man in his mid-forties. He could have been behind the counter in the café. He leaned toward her.

"Welcome to Florence," he said. "How do you like our city?"

"Very much," Katharine said.

"Have you been sightseeing yet?"

"Yes." She wondered how long he was going to waste time. "I went to the Uffizi and the Pitti when I first arrived."

"Good," he said. "I didn't order you a drink—what would you like?"

"Nothing," Katharine said impatiently.

"That wouldn't look natural," he said. "If anyone is watching us they've got to think we've come here to enjoy ourselves. Relax, Cousin Rose. Smile at me. I'll hear your report in good time."

"I'm sorry," Katharine said. "You're quite right. I'll have a coffee—cappuccino, please."

"I've been a policeman for twenty-two years," he said. He had two front teeth with gold base caps and they glittered when he smiled. "I've learned to take my time. It isn't easy."

She tried to smile, to relax as he intended, but his presence across the table had added a frightening dimension to her situation. The worst part of her mission had proved to be the easiest. Meeting her relations, getting on friendly terms with Malaspiga, all had been accomplished without difficulty.

None of the complications she had imagined before going to the villa had impeded her progress. They had been friendly, hospitable; and the Duke had been warm and charming to his new cousin. Perhaps a little too warm. . .

The coffee came and she sipped it; the tiny cups of espresso were too strong. To her surprise, she found that drinking even such a small quantity made her nervous.

"You're worried, aren't you?" Raphael said quietly. When she shook her head he smiled. "This is a very nasty business. Any intelligent person would be afraid. Tell me about it."

"I've been here ten days," she said. "Maybe I've lost touch with reality. I don't know how much you've been told about me, but I'm just an ordinary person who has been picked out to do this, given some quick basic training and sent out. I felt confident when I agreed to do it. I had a special motive."

"Yes," Raphael said. "Your brother."

"He was an addict, he died. I saw him go through hell and there wasn't anything I could do to save him. They picked me up right after his funeral and made me the proposition. I said yes." She lit a cigarette. "Nobody forced me, in fact my instructor spent most of his time trying to scare me off. But I was determined to stop these people. I wanted to hit back."

"And now you're not sure?"

"I'm not sure I can do it," she said slowly. "I've met the Malaspiga family. I've done the first thing I was sent to do, and that's make friends. They're not at all what I expected."

"Nicer?" he prompted. She hesitated. The word was ill-chosen, it didn't apply to the old Duchess, still less to her cousin, the Duke. It was too small a word for people fashioned on such a grand scale.

"Different," she said. "I can't explain it. It seems impossible they could be mixed up in this." She gave a shrug, exasperated at herself. "Maybe I just don't like spying; I went through his desk today," she said. "I feel unclean. I wish there were another way. I don't feel I've got the nerve or the experience to carry something like this through to the end. I suppose the trouble is, three weeks' instruction wasn't enough."

"It was very little, for this type of work," he said. He didn't

seem disturbed or critical. His eyes were calm and understanding.

"You're a nice girl, from a nice background. You were
brought up not to go through other people's drawers or read
their letters. Obviously, you are honest, because of the way
you've talked about yourself. I understand all this. You're the
sort of woman who would never search her husband's pockets when he was asleep." His gold teeth flashed in a smile.
"You expected these Malaspigas to be monsters, Mafia vil-
lains easily identifiable, didn't you? Instead, you meet a
cultured, charming family of Italian aristocrats, and believe
me, charm is the passport issued to that class at birth. You
feel cheated. They're not so easy to hate. They've been
friendly to you, and you don't like spying on them. Also
you're in Florence, and the States and what happened to your
brother seem a little far away. A bad dream? Am I exag-
gerating?"

"No," Katharine said quietly. "I don't think you are."

He leaned back in his chair, tipping it a little.

"Ben Harper thought this might happen," he said. "He's a
very good psychologist. Tell me something—do you want to
give up and go home?"

"No," Katharine answered. "I'd never forgive myself if I
did that."

"Just self-doubt, a little weakening of resolve, is that all?"

"They're my relations," she said slowly. "My grandmother
was a Malaspiga. That's why I was chosen."

"Oh? And you've been taken to the bosom of your family—
no wonder you feel uncomfortable. I know how strong the
blood tie is with all Italians. Even of humble origin." For the
first time she sensed hostility. He hadn't minded her confession of nervousness, her irrational sense of guilt for what she
was doing. But he resented her being connected to the Malaspigas.

He leaned toward her across the table.

"You asked me if I knew about you. I didn't know you
were one of *them.* Harper didn't tell me that. But he expected

you to have second thoughts, and so he prepared me for it. Before you feel guilty about betraying family trust, or allow yourself to be seduced by their charm, there is one thing that you should know, which Harper didn't tell you. The real reason why your brother died, just when it seemed he had a chance of being cured."

"What do you mean—" she said. "What do you mean, the real reason. . ."

"He spent six weeks in that clinic in upstate New York, didn't he? Then three months at the convalescent home. They told you he was rehabilitated, that the miracle had happened. He was off heroin and there was hope, for the first time."

"Yes," she whispered. Tears had come into her eyes. The memory was vivid. Peter coming back with her in the car, looking alert, able to talk about the future; he'd put on weight, he looked in possession of himself for the first time in years. She would never forget that afternoon. Hope, the Italian had said. The staff of the home had come out to see them off, shaking hands and waving as they drove away. She put a hand up to her eyes as if to shut the memory out.

"He was going to live," Raphael persisted. "You thought you'd won, didn't you. For the first few days you stayed with him day and night, watching him, not quite believing it was true—and then you went out to the theater. He stayed at home."

"I've never forgiven myself," she said. He was a hard man, inured to pain by long experience. He didn't flinch at the misery he saw on her face.

"When you came home," he said, "he'd disappeared. I can imagine how you felt. The anxiety, the despair. Admitting to yourself that it had all been an illusion. You never saw him alive again, did you?"

"No." She said it very low. "No. When I got to Bellevue he was dead."

"He was murdered," Raphael said. "When they found him, he was lying in a back street, unconscious from an overdose. His body was badly bruised. Your brother didn't go out to look for drugs—the pusher came and looked for him. As soon as he was left alone, they came and forced a fix on him. He must have struggled, from the way he was marked. He didn't want it. But they made him. He was underweight and weak. He hadn't a chance. They gave him a lethal dose and took him out of your apartment to die in the street. You mustn't cry—people are watching you."

"I don't care," she whispered. "Oh, God—why didn't Harper tell me?"

"Because you didn't need to know it then; you had a strong motive. He kept the ace in my sleeve. You know why they killed him, don't you?"

She shook her head. She found a handkerchief and pressed it to her eyes. Raphael was leaning over the table, holding her hand. To the onlooker, it seemed as if he were comforting her.

"The police run regular checks on the roster of clinics like the place where your brother went. They ran one around the time he left. The pushers weren't taking any chances on his breaking under questioning. So they killed him to make sure. It's the mark of the Malaspiga operatives. They never lose sight of their customers." He let go of her hand, lit a cigarette and passed it to her.

"How do you feel about your cousins now? Still guilty about deceiving them? If you have any doubts left now, about yourself or anything else"—his voice was pitched low, but full of emphasis—"then you'd better go back to the States tomorrow."

Katharine opened her bag, and put the handkerchief away. She drew on the cigarette he had given her, and then as suddenly stubbed it out. She looked at him.

"You've played your ace," she said. "You know the answer. I blamed myself and I blamed my brother. I thought he'd just given in again. Now at least I know he tried. What you've just told me makes my cousin Malaspiga his murderer."

"As surely as if he shot him," Raphael said. "Policies like that are made at the top. Would you like to tell me what you've found out?"

"I went to tea with them," she said. "The old Duchess, my cousin, his wife and a Canadian, a sculptor who lives with them. The Duke is his patron."

"Yes, we know about him. He came over from Toronto about four years ago. His background is routine, farming family, no money, artistic talent. It would amuse those sort of people to have him around. They love to imitate their ancestors."

"My cousin took me out to lunch today," she said. She felt sick and shaken but in command of herself. He had given her a brutal shock, and at the same time she felt curiously relieved. Peter had tried. The tragedy at the end was not because of his weakness or venality. There was a cold sensation inside her and it was spreading as she talked.

"He told me a lot about himself," she said. "He loves talking about the family, and he feels I'm interested. I discovered a lot."

Raphael interrupted her. "You're looking very pale," he said. "Are you feeling all right? Shall I get you a drink—"

"No, nothing. I'm fine. Just let me go on talking; I don't want to forget anything important."

"What did you find out?"

"The Duke said they were poor after the war. He said he'd financed an antique business with his wife's money and was making a great success of it. It certainly seemed as if they'd plenty of money. The villa was full of lovely things, there were servants all over the place, and he had all those little extras that go with the rich. Handmade cigarettes, Cartier watch and cigarette case—that kind of thing. I'd say there was a great deal of money there."

"If our suspicions are correct," Raphael said gently, "he must be a multimillionaire. Which is what they were before the war. Like all the top Fascists, they were only interested in protecting their money against Communism. Do you mind if I smoke? That cigarette I gave you seemed to upset you."

Katharine shook her head, and he lit a cheap cigarette and sucked at it.

"So, there is evidence of a considerable fortune. That's very interesting. The antiques couldn't account for all of it, but at any rate they're a good cover. What else?"

"He has an antique shop in New York," Katharine said. "It's called Florence Antiques, 493 Park Avenue and the name of the man who runs it is Taylor. E. Taylor. I saw it in his address book this afternoon. I was alone in the library looking at some family papers, and I found it when I searched his desk."

"Yes," Raphael said. "His outlet in the States is known."

"There were other antique shops in the book—all over Europe and one in Beirut. A mass of personal entries but mostly princes and counts. I set a bug and a recorder in the library, and I'll be going back again in a day or so and I can get it."

"You've been very enterprising for someone who's so new," he said. "Congratulations."

"But perhaps the most important thing I discovered was that both the Duke and his wife went to America about seven years ago. They stayed in Beverly Hills with a film star named John Julius. Can you remember all this?"

"No," he said. "But I don't have to; I have something in my pocket which is taking down everything you say. That way, there won't be any mistakes."

"Will you pass this on to New York as soon as you can? They can investigate this film star. Some of those Hollywood people are pretty degenerate. There could be a drug connection there."

"Of course."

"But what about the antiques?" Katharine asked.

"I ran a check on one of Malaspiga's exports to Paris, but we found nothing," Raphael said.

"Did they know?"

"No. It was done in the customs. I had an expert go over the pieces looking for false drawers, bottoms, hollow handles. We found nothing. It seemed a dead end. My opinion is that they don't send drugs with every shipment. The last was three months ago."

"Then you think the next one—"

"It could be. How friendly *are* you with your cousin?"

"He seems to like me," Katharine said. She shivered, in spite of the heat in the café. She still felt cold, as if she had been chilled. Hate should be fiery, it should burn. . . If she shut her eyes she would see Peter lying dead in the hospital room, and the nurse taking her by the arm, brisk and callous through overexposure to such cases. "Too late, I'm afraid, he's gone."

"That's understandable," Raphael said. "You're very pretty. He has a reputation for women. Can you take advantage of that?"

"No!" She said it sharply. "After what you've told me, how could you suggest. . ."

He raised his hand. "I didn't suggest anything," he said. "Just that you encourage his friendship, get as close to him and the family as you can. You can't afford scruples. If he's attracted to you—and obviously he is—then this could encourage him to talk. Italian men always talk to women, unless they happen to be married to them. I have a girl friend in Lucca and I tell her everything." He smiled at Katharine. His expression was mild and friendly again. He had a schizoid attitude she found disconcerting. His revelation of how her brother died had been merciless. As if he knew her thoughts, he said quietly, "Forgive me for being brutal with you. But you needed the shock. I didn't enjoy giving it. We are both working for the same ends. Try to forgive me."

"Of course," she said. "You did the right thing. I'm very grateful. Nothing would shake me now. I'll keep my head, don't worry."

"I'm sure you will," he said. "Now your real job is to find out when the next consignment of antiques is leaving for the States. We can't show our hand by holding up every shipment. We've got to get the dirty one—the one with the drugs. Only you are in a position to find out which one it will be. Go to the villa as often as possible. Make a note of anyone who visits there, especially foreign contacts."

"I think I can do that," Katharine said. "But it may take time."

"Not too long," he said. "That shipment will be on its way. If not to America, then to one of the other places. I want to know when and where it's going."

"I'll do my best," she said. "There's something I'd like to ask you—"

"Yes?"

"How far did Firelli get?"

He took a thousand-lire note out of a shabby wallet and folded it in the bill.

"We'll never know," he said. "His last telephone call didn't make sense. The line was so bad that only a word here and there came through. He wasn't alone, that was obvious. And whatever he was trying to tell us had to be disguised. *Angelo* —that was the only clue. It didn't connect with anything. There's nobody with that name among the Malaspiga family or their staff. But it meant something to Firelli. He knew he'd never make another call and he was trying to get it through to us. He was a very brave man. I liked him."

"And he was never heard of again—it seems incredible. Why didn't the police investigate?"

"They did," Raphael said. "He was using a firm of antique exporters as a cover. The Duke said he left after a business interview, his hotel received a telephone call asking them to pack his luggage, which was picked up by taxi, and after that there wasn't a trace. The caller said he was Firelli and flying back to the States."

"It's horrible," she said slowly. "It's worse than knowing for certain he's dead."

"Oh, there's no doubt about that," Raphael said. "They murdered him because he was on to something. Firelli's dead, but we will never find him. Take my advice. Don't be afraid to be afraid. Fear breeds caution, and you need to be very cautious dealing with your family. Don't imagine that a blood tie would protect you. Be very careful."

"I will," she said. He got up and they squeezed out between the tables.

"I think you should leave first," he said. "I will pay the bill. I look forward to your next report and I will pass on this information to New York. You've done very well."

They shook hands briefly, and Katharine went outside. It was dusk, a warm, humid evening. Crowds of people were crossing the piazza, breaking up into groups, to linger and look. The Florentines were setting out for the bars and cafés before going home. Everywhere the shops were open, lights blazing. The scene had a medieval quality, with the great Cathedral and the Baptistry brooding over the scurrying people. High above her, a bell began to toll; a flock of pigeons rose whirring in alarm and then as quickly settled. Bells began to ring in different parts of the city. The sound was indescribably sad and beautiful. A pair of sharply dressed Italian men paused as they came by her, one of them half turned back, a smile of invitation on his face. Katharine turned quickly before he had time to accost her, and walked toward the Via Vecchia. In the main street she waited a few minutes on the pavement until she found an empty taxi to take her back to the hotel.

Be very careful, the little policeman had said. *A blood tie won't protect you.* Her handsome cousin, with his princely bearing and his charm, would kill her as pitilessly as he had Firelli. As those who worked for him had killed her brother.

She went upstairs to her bedroom; she didn't want to eat anything. She felt sick and weary. There was a huge parcel wrapped in cellophane and tied with a pink ribbon in her room with a card pinned to the front. She saw the familiar crest in red on the envelope. She opened it first.

"Thank you for lunching with me. I'm sorry I was delayed and didn't see you. Until tomorrow. Alessandro."

Under the cellophane there was a gilded wicker basket full of flowers. Pale pink flowers, heavily scented. The same out-of-season roses his mother wore.

3

Frank Carpenter flew out to the Coast on a Thursday; his telephone call to John Julius resulted in a lunchtime appointment, made by a secretary. For someone who hadn't appeared in a major film for ten years, the actor seemed to live in style. It was a day of travel poster sunshine; the smog had lifted and everything sparkled in the heat. Carpenter took a taxi out to the Julius mansion in Beverly Hills. He knew California well and had never liked its artificiality. When he was in the country he liked it to be raw. He had several times taken a hunting trip to Vermont, living in a cabin with two other men. His wife had suspected him of being with a woman. Nothing could have been further from Carpenter's idea of relaxation than taking his sex life into the hills to shoot deer. Hollywood held no magic for him; it reminded him of a fantasy city, built to delude the eye, like the streets and houses on a film set. A plastic place inhabited by plastic beings, pretending to be human. The air in the Hills was cooler; in spite of the busloads of sightseers crawling past the mansions of the stars, there was elegance and space, handsome trees and beautifully laid-out avenues. He turned left off Sunset and up a long drive lined with Queen Palms. At the end of it they came to the typical lavish mock-Spanish villa, white stuccoed and red tile-roofed, set in a perimeter of flowering shrubs. A Hawaiian butler appeared at the door. He was built like a prizefighter. It reminded Carpenter of the opening shot of an indifferent thriller movie.

"Mr. Julius is expecting you." In contrast to his appearance the butler had a friendly voice and a pleasant smile. Carpenter went with him inside.

It was cool and green, the rooms open plan, a vast reception area leading off the hall. One wall was constructed of multicolored glass, which gave a weird kaleidoscopic effect, alarming and yet beautiful. Sofas the size of ocean liners, single pieces of modern sculpture in aluminum and stone, a room full of soft furniture and hard surfaces, dominated by an erotic mural over the open fireplace.

"Sit down, please, sir. Mr. Julius will be right with you. Can I get you a drink?" Carpenter looked into the smooth dark face.

"A beer," he said. "Thank you."

He recognized the face as soon as the actor came into the room. Handsome, with gray hair, blue eyes, a well-preserved body in expensive casual clothes, a young man's walk. He shook hands firmly, gave a professional smile and sat opposite.

"What can I do for you," he said. The appointment had been made under the guise of an interview with a well-known film magazine. Carpenter took out his DEA badge and passed it across. John Julius looked at it, and for a moment the Great Movie Star smile slipped sideways.

"What the hell is this? I thought you came for an interview!"

"In a way I have." Carpenter was used to honest citizens getting annoyed and even more used to the dishonest showing indignation. "I want to ask you some questions, Mr. Julius."

"Couldn't you have said so in the first place, instead of making up a lot of crap about *Fan Fare!*"

"You mightn't have seen me," Carpenter said. "People don't like talking to policemen. Especially my kind of policeman. I just hope you can help me."

John Julius got up. He pushed his fists into his trouser pockets and glared down at Carpenter. "I don't like being taken for a fool," he said. "I've a perfect right to throw you out of here."

"But you won't," Carpenter answered, "unless you've got something to hide."

"Hona!" The call brought the Hawaiian running. Carpenter guessed he couldn't have been far away. For a moment Julius hesitated. There was a line of red coming up from his smart silk shirt collar, reaching to beneath his ears. He was genuinely angry. And genuinely afraid too. Fear showed in the eyes—bright blue, ladykillers, with fear blinking in them.

"Hona, bring me a Buck's Fizz! And tell Jumie this gentleman won't be staying for lunch after all." He turned away from Carpenter and sat down.

"All right," he said. "You've come into my home under false pretenses. This doesn't help, as far as I'm concerned. But I have a duty as a citizen. If you've got questions, ask them."

"I'm sorry," Frank Carpenter said. "I should have said right out what I wanted. But a lot of people do scare off. Some of this will be pretty personal, so I'll wait till you get your drink. Can I ask you something?"

Julius nodded. The red around his neck was fading.

"What the hell's a Buck's Fizz?"

"Champagne and fresh orange juice." He didn't suggest that Carpenter try one. He sipped it. "Let's get on with it," he said. "What do you want to know?"

Carpenter lit a cigarette. "About six or seven years ago you entertained the Duke and Duchess of Malaspiga here, didn't you?"

"Sandro and Francesca—yes. They came on their honey-moon. Why?"

"Would you mind telling me how you met them?"

"I knew Sandro's father. He was much older of course, but I was filming in Italy, and we were introduced. He asked if I could show his son and daughter-in-law around Holly-wood. They stayed with us for ten days. I remember my wife gave a big party for them. It made every gossip column in the country."

"I'll bet," Carpenter said. "And do you still see them?"

"No," John Julius said. "I don't. We lost touch after my wife died."

"But you remember them pretty well, don't you—seven years is a long time and you must have had a lot of people staying since then. But you remembered them right away."

"It was a memorable visit," the actor said.

"Could you tell me anything about them? Anything at all, any recollection."

"Not till you've told me why you want to know," he said. "I don't talk about my friends."

"They're hardly friends," Carpenter suggested, "as you haven't seen them in seven years. Or is it only since your wife died. She died two years ago, didn't she?"

"Yes," Julius said. "I think she corresponded with them. She liked titles."

"But you weren't impressed," Carpenter said.

"He was impressive," Julius said. Carpenter leaned forward and lit a cigarette for him; the service seemed to ease the tension between them. He leaned a little back in his chair and crossed his leg over the other. "Nobody could help being impressed by Malaspiga."

"Why not? What was so special about him?"

Julius waved the cigarette. "He was a beautiful man. And don't misunderstand me, Mr. Carpenter. I mean beautiful in the aesthetic sense. He'd have made a fortune on the screen. He had presence, magnetism. In fact he was the only Duke I've ever met who looked the part. There were half a dozen producers fighting to sign him when they were over here. As for the women—well."

"How did he take it all?"

"As his due," John Julius said. "He was amused by flattery. He had a very good sense of humor and he made fun of a lot of people. I didn't mind that; I could see how we'd look like a lot of exotics to him. My wife resented it, but she was a native Californian."

"You're English, aren't you?"

"Originally, yes, but I took out U.S. citizenship twenty years ago. I consider myself an American." It was the sort of answer he'd have given had it been an interview.

"Although your wife resented his attitude, she still kept up with them—but you didn't."

"That's right. I told you, my wife was a snob. I didn't invite them to visit again."

There was a contradiction in the answer, but Carpenter decided not to follow it up at that stage. He himself was relaxed, he asked his questions in a quiet voice. John Julius was no longer as angry, or as frightened as he had been. Carpenter encouraged him.

"These must seem very unrelated questions, Mr. Julius," he said. "And by the way, I appreciate the way you're giving me the answers. It's good of you to cooperate after what I pulled on you."

"I suppose that's part of your job," the actor shrugged. He called for the butler, who was a little longer coming this time, and ordered a second Buck's Fizz. There was a second's pause and then he offered one to Carpenter.

"It's very refreshing—the orange takes the acid out of the champagne. It's great if you have a hangover."

"No thanks." Carpenter shook his head. "But I'd like another beer. Tell me, among all the women who chased after Malaspiga, was there one in particular he fell for? Some of the most beautiful girls in the world hang around here. He must have had a ball."

"As a matter of fact he didn't." Julius leaned a little forward. He wrinkled his forehead; he looked exactly like an English actor playing an English actor.

"He seemed to be very much in love with his wife. It was quite a phenomenon. There was one very famous movie actress, no names, you understand, but she was the sex goddess at Paramount, and she made a play for him one night. You've never seen anything like it. He brushed her off like a true gentleman."

"So you wouldn't say he made any close friends while he was staying with you?"

"No. Truer to say he made a few enemies, including the goddess, who'd never laid it on the line and been told to take it home before." He put his head back and laughed with pleasure at the memory. "Jesus, was she mad!"

Carpenter allowed himself to grin. "I can imagine. When you don't want it they'll give it away."

Julius looked at him. "You mean all women or just movie stars?"

"All women," Carpenter said. "You haven't said anything about the Duchess. What was she like?" It was an irrelevant question, and he didn't know why he'd asked it, except to stall before the next one, which was important.

The actor's face closed like a fist. "Nothing much to look at. I don't remember her all that clearly."

"She must have had something to keep a man like that on a short leash. If it wasn't beauty, what was it?"

"I've no idea," Julius said coldly. "She was rather dull—pretty in a way if you like very dark women. Not at all sophisticated."

The lurking fear was back behind the eyes. He picked up his drink and put it down again. He wasn't worried about answering questions concerned with Malaspiga, but the young Duchess had the opposite effect. He looked at his watch.

Carpenter knew that he was going to cut the interview short. He asked his original question.

"Did the Duke and Duchess go anywhere more than once

when they stayed with you—weren't there any social contacts that might have stuck? This is a very important question, Mr. Julius. Try to remember."

He couldn't and he wasn't going to try; even before he answered Carpenter knew it would be a negative.

"They didn't make any real friends," he said. "Ten days isn't very long. Now, Mr. Carpenter, I'm afraid you'll have to excuse me."

"Sure." Carpenter held out his hand. Julius took it, but his reluctance showed. "Don't you want to know why I'm asking about them?" Carpenter asked quietly. "Or do you know?"

Suddenly Julius looked his age. The lined forehead was real, the blue eyes held fear and revulsion. "I expect I know," he said. "You've come to dig up some dirt connected with Elise. Well, you won't get anything from me. Hona! Show the gentleman out."

Outside in the brilliant sunshine, Carpenter walked slowly between the line of palm trees to the avenue. Before going to interview John Julius, he had made a quick investigation of the star and his background. He was a respected member of the film community. There were no scandals in his life— his marriage to a rich socialite, Elise Bohun, had lasted fifteen years until her death. He had no children, and was one of the few postwar Hollywood stars to keep his money, as well as having married it. And presumably benefited from the will. He didn't maintain that house on television royalties from old films. He had disliked the Duke of Malaspiga, at the same time as he admired him. His description fitted the kind of arrogant upper-class bastard Carpenter thoroughly despised. A beautiful man, magnetic, sophisticated, contemptuous of people he considered his inferiors. He had made fun of the movie colony. How they must have hated him for that—they were already so insecure. He had disliked the Duke, but he hadn't been able to hide his hatred of the Duchess.

There was pain, as well as defiance in the suddenly aged face, when he said those last words. "You've come to dig up some dirt connected with Elise. . . ." Until that moment, Carpenter hadn't known there was any dirt to dig for. On arrival in New York, he went straight to his office.

The previous day, he had asked Jim Nathan to investigate Edward D. Taylor's background and early connections. At eight o'clock that night, Nathan phoned in.

"I tried to get you earlier, Frank. They said you were out of town."

"I went out to the Coast. You coming in, or going home now?"

"I'm on my way," Nathan said. "But I could make a progress report over a beer. How about meeting me at Noni's in twenty minutes?"

Half an hour later, Carpenter went to the bar where he and Jim usually met, and saw Nathan in a corner booth. He went over and Nathan shook hands.

"Well." He raised his glass to Frank Carpenter. "So how was the sunshine state—black with smog as usual?"

"No. Sun was shining. Pretty stewardess on the flight back, too. All in all, a good day. What'd you get me on Taylor?"

Nathan shrugged, drawing his mouth down.

"Nothing much. He runs a very classy antique business now. I went in for a look. They have a beautiful stock, no junk or repro stuff. What's the angle on the place?"

"I don't know yet," Carpenter said. "But it's a link with our new drug pipeline. Where was he before he opened the shop on Park?" Carpenter asked the question casually. Nathan paused to light his pipe; he looked down at the bowl, stuffing the tobacco in with his fingers, before he put the match to it.

"He had a place up in Beverly Hills," he said. "But that was sold years ago. I checked very carefully."

"Did he own that, too?"

"Yeah," Nathan said. He sucked hard, drawing on the pipe. "I went into all the details. He bought the place, ran it for a year or two and then sold out. There's no connection with drugs there, Frank. I guess he's just another antique dealer. Sorry."

"I'm not so sure," Carpenter said. "Go on digging. Get the layout—who he sells to, private clients, other dealers—everything you can find out."

"Okay." Nathan shrugged. "If you say so, but I think it's a waste of time. What makes you think Taylor's involved in the new pipeline?"

"There's a connection," Carpenter said. "And I'm relying on you, Jim. Keep digging. We'll find something. I know it."

"Tell me," Nathan said, "how big is this pipeline—where's it coming from?"

"Not out of Marseilles this time. Italy," Frank Carpenter answered. He rubbed out his cigarette in the metal ashtray and used the stub to draw patterns in the ash. "Italy. We're sure of that." Nathan called the waitress over.

"Have another beer?" he asked.

Frank shook his head. "Not for me."

"So what's the matter with you, Frank?" Nathan rolled his eyes; he liked to play the ethnic ham. He spread his hands and put on a heavy Yiddish accent. "You don't drink, you don't screw around, so what's the matter with you? You sick or something? So go on, live dangerously, have another beer!"

Carpenter laughed. "Okay. But I've got work to do." He liked Nathan. When his marriage broke up, the older man had proved a good friend, with a rare understanding of his feelings.

"It's Mafia controlled, then?"

"It must be at least affiliated, or they'd have wiped the operation out. They don't encourage independent organizations. This is a bastard to pin down, but my guess is it started from small beginnings and it's slowly building up. Now there's a big network in New York and a suspicion that it's spread to the Coast. What we need is some hard facts, something to act on."

"And you haven't got that yet?" Nathan asked him.

"No," Carpenter said. "All we have is circumstantial evidence. We've got to get solid proof."

"How?" Nathan said. He sipped his beer. His skin was cold, his hands moist with sweat. *Marie. . . .* The name was repeated in the accelerated heartbeat. *Marie. Carpenter was getting close. Firelli had got close, too. Carpenter wouldn't give up on Eddy Taylor. Go on digging, we'll find something. He had to find out what was happening, give Taylor warning. It wasn't enough just to block them in investigating Taylor's connections. He had to get information. Otherwise something would happen to Marie.* His left arm ached, as if he'd pulled a muscle.

"What's your plan of attack?"

"Penetration," Frank said. "From inside."

"Jesus," Nathan muttered. "That's giving somebody a one-way ticket. Was that what happened to Firelli? I was up to my balls on the Marley case when I heard he'd disappeared. This is all news to me."

"That was Firelli," Carpenter said. "But it's the only way to nail the bastards in a hurry. Give them a couple of years more and they'll have grown too big to cut down. There's no time to waste. I'm glad you're helping me out on this, Jim. I've got a feeling it'll give me gray hairs. Now I'll buy you a beer."

"No." Nathan shook his head. "I'll go home smashed and Marie'll murder me. The way that girl bullies me it's a crime!"

"The way she spoils you, you mean. You know something —you're the only happily married people I know."

"You're getting sour," Jim Nathan said. His ugly face was soft, the dark eyes mild. "You should get married again. It's a great life—with the right girl. I was lucky, Jesus, how lucky —but you mustn't let one bum deal spoil the whole game. Look for a nice girl and try again!"

"Nice girls don't marry cops," Frank said. "They marry nice guys with regular jobs, reasonable working hours and a hefty paycheck. I'm happy single, thanks. It's easier that way."

"Okay. I'll be glad to work with you, Frank. What's the

connection with California? Anything to do with the agent we're sending in?"

"No," Carpenter said. He had a professional dislike of direct questions, even those asked by colleagues. And by nature he was a taciturn man. "It's just a lead. But I'm hopeful. Give my love to Marie."

"I'll do that," Jim Nathan said. "You must come for dinner. I'll talk to her."

They parted, Nathan on the way to his car. Carpenter stayed on in the bar. He ordered himself a chicken sandwich. By a coincidence they were sitting in the booth where he and Katharine had eaten their first meal. When her message was relayed through from Interpol, Harper had called him in. He hadn't shown any feelings; he was sure his relief was concealed even from eyes as sharp as Ben's. She was making good progress and her contact said she seemed cheerful and confident. *A one-way ticket,* Nathan had said. He couldn't afford to think about her or allow himself to get personally involved. He lived a celibate life except for occasional casual one-night stands. That was one of the reasons why he hadn't made love to Katharine Dexter the night before she left for Italy. He didn't want to involve her or get involved himself.

If he had established a physical bond with her, it might have been very difficult to be impersonal. Difficult to fish around in California and drink beer with Jim Nathan while she faced the menace that had destroyed Firelli. He forced her out of his mind; the effort cost him more than he realized. He didn't want to go back to his apartment, because it meant being alone, and he knew the problems would chase themselves on a roller coaster through his mind. Loneliness overcame him—it was the first time in years he had felt so isolated from his fellows and so much in need of human company. He thought of Nathan, with his wife, sitting together watching TV, enclosed against the emptiness outside, and felt unhappy and envious. This was also for the first time. He called for coffee and the bill, angry with himself for a weakness he didn't understand. He wouldn't go home. He would go to a late movie. It was a cheerless prospect and he resented it. Even when he chose the movie, paid and took his seat, he was depressed. He woke after an hour, found he'd missed half the main feature, and decided to go home to bed.

"John *caro?* Is that you?"

Isabella di Malaspiga was sitting in the garden. She wore a wide-brimmed straw hat, and sheltered under a canvas umbrella. In the shade, she looked like a beautiful young woman. She had never permitted the sun to scorch her complexion; the modern woman's passion for roasting her skin was incomprehensible to her.

She waved at the figure of John Driver as he crossed the lawn. He turned and came toward her. She smiled, and the exquisite mask broke into a thousand wrinkles.

"Caro," she said. "Come and talk to me; I'm lonely." Driver bent over and kissed her cheek. She smelled of the pink rose she wore pinned to her blouse. She had used the same scent for forty years; it was made specially for her by a firm of perfumiers in Florence. Its base was attar of roses. She had adopted the flower as her emblem, and her countless lovers had been selected by the gift of the one she was wearing. The old Duchess had always had a sense of theater, and such gestures delighted her. Again, she had nothing in common with the modern women of her class, who bestowed themselves upon men as casually as if they were giving them a buttonhole. The Duchess had chosen her men from two motives. Attraction and wealth. Her most cherished piece of jewelry was a large diamond and ruby rose, the central bloom mounted on a spring so that it trembled delicately. It was the memento of a brief liaison with a nephew of the King.

John Driver took a chair beside her. They overlooked the lovely formal garden Katharine had seen from the library window. It was very hot, even for mid-spring, and a distant fountain shimmered in the sunshine.

"Where did you go to yesterday? I missed you."

"I went to look at some bronzes Alessandro liked. I think they look right to me."

"You have wonderful taste," the old lady said. "But you should be working on your own pieces, instead of looking at other people's creations. It's wasting your talent. I shall tell Sandro."

"I like to help," John said. "And I've plenty of time. You're not to say anything to him about it. Promise me?"

"Very well. But you must do something for me."

"Anything," he said gently. "Just ask."

"I'm worried about this cousin, Katharine Dexter."

"Why? She seems a nice girl—don't you like her?"

"John, you are such a baby—liking hasn't got anything to do with it. Anyway, I've never liked my own sex." She gave a little bright laugh, naturally coquettish.

He leaned over and held her hand. "Why are you worried about her—tell me?"

"Sandro is interested in her," she said. Now she was serious. The enormous black eyes were unhappy as she looked at him. "I know the signs, John. He's been restless; I hear him and Francesca quarreling again. Haven't you seen how miserable she's been looking lately? Now this girl comes here. She has taken his fancy—I knew it immediately the first afternoon. I spoke to my florist this morning, and she said he'd sent a huge bouquet of my roses to this girl. They were worried in case they couldn't supply me until the end of the week. And when Sandro starts sending flowers—you know it means another one! More scenes with Francesca, more atmospheres. I'm getting too old for it. It upsets me."

"I don't think she'll be impressed," Driver said. "I wouldn't worry about it too much. She isn't staying long."

"You don't know my son," the old Duchess said. "Not when it comes to women. No woman has ever resisted him —not since he was fifteen. This girl isn't going to be the exception."

"What do you want me to do?"

"Take her out," the Duchess said. "Talk to her. Warn her that as far as he's concerned it's just a game. American women don't understand this sort of thing. They don't realize that Italian men never leave their wives, and having a love affair with a stranger means nothing to them. Frighten her off. Please, *caro*, will you do it?"

"I'll try," John Driver said.

"For Francesca's sake," she added. "She takes these things so seriously. If only she'd had children she wouldn't have minded. It's all such a pity. People complicate their lives so. I pity this generation. I always did exactly what I wanted and enjoyed it. You young people have lost the capacity."

"Perhaps," he said. "Perhaps you didn't have our sense of guilt."

"I was never guilty about anything unless it was ugly or stupid," she said. "Those are the only real sins. I learned that from Sandro's father. I had complete respect for his judgment."

"And you have the same for Sandro," Driver said. "They're natural leaders, the Malaspigas. If he'd lived in Cellini's time, he'd have sculpted him in armor on a horse, instead of Cosimo de' Medici."

"And that is the tragedy," she said. "He is the last. And I'm responsible. I suggested Francesca for him. He has never once reproached me."

"He loves you," John said gently. "He knows you only acted from the best motives. She's everything a man would want in a wife, except for that one rotten piece of luck. She's sweet and gentle." For a moment his expression tightened. Under her heavy painted lids, the old Duchess saw it, as she had seen it many times before. She gave no sign.

"My son doesn't love me," she interrupted. "He doesn't love anyone. None of the Malaspigas can love. I discovered that soon after I was married. It didn't destroy me because I arranged my life accordingly. My husband had mistresses, but there was never any scandal. I had admirers; I was equally discreet. But Sandro flaunts women in her face. It's ugly and I've told him so. I don't want it to happen with this American girl. I'm too old for family dramas. Please, see if you can persuade her to go home quickly. I don't want her coming here."

"I'll do my best, and don't you worry. I'll take her out and talk to her." The Duchess watched him walk away across the lawns to the house. He had a good figure, broad shoulders, narrow hips. Strong and faithful, simple and kind. Her son had found him and taken him up, playing the patron to the artist in the best Florentine tradition. He had become part of the family. The place he occupied was ambiguous, in that although they treated him as an equal, she knew he didn't regard himself in the same way. She didn't really care if her daughter-in-law suffered—she had no patience with jealous wives. Francesca's quarrels with her husband didn't distress her; it aroused her impatience to watch the younger woman mishandling the situation. The Canadian was in love with Francesca. The old Duchess could have shaken her daughter-in-law for pretending not to know it. She didn't care what Alessandro did with women; she wouldn't have cared what her daughter-in-law did with the sculptor, provided that it was done with discretion. But she cared very much about the disruption of her life; the war had broken her world and forced reality upon her. She had been comparatively poor, socially ostracized, deprived of the privileges she had always taken as a right. Alessandro had restored the balance. Now she was rich, pampered and secure. And that depended upon Alessandro. An Italian mistress, the wife of a friend, a film actress perhaps—none of these would have disturbed her as the American girl with family connections had done. She was different. She came from outside. And her son's reaction to her was different, too. His mother knew it, with her sharp survivor's instinct. Her anxiety was increased when Alessandro did not appear for lunch, and the manservant gave her the message that he was spending the afternoon showing Signorina Dexter the sights of the city.

"How did you like my roses?" He was looking down at her, smiling.

"They're beautiful," Katharine said. "It was very kind of you."

The Duke laughed. They were walking across the lobby of her hotel, and heads were swiveling to watch them. "Don't be so formal with me," he said. "It wasn't kind at all. I wanted to send them to you. I love roses."

"So does your mother," she said. "It must run in the family."

"My mother has always worn one; except during the war. My first memory of her as a little boy is the smell of roses and the flower she wore every day. My car is over there. First we will go to the San Mineato Church, and I shall take you down into the crypt to see your ancestors; there's a marvelous Cellini tomb, and then we will have lunch." He took her arm as they went into the street. The same low-built Ferrari slid through the traffic up the Viale Galileo to the Viale Michelangelo.

"What happens to your business," she asked, "when you take days off like this? You must have it very well organized."

"I do," he said. "I delegate. Isn't that the secret of all successful tycoons—I make the decisions and other people do the work. I can see by your face you don't approve. My dear cousin, that is quite untypical of your family. We never show our feelings! Now you are smiling. That's better."

"Why don't you keep your eyes on the traffic?" Katharine suggested. She made a conscious effort not to be affected by the charm. Such a cold man, and yet so warm; so familiar and easy and yet so unapproachable. There were so many contradictions about him that she felt herself swept away in confusion. Know the enemy. Watch them, tune in to their habits, expressions, moods. That way they won't be able to take you by surprise. Whenever she was with Malaspiga, she clung to what Frank Carpenter had taught her. He lulled, as deadly as the drugs that stole away the will. He had taken her arm again, guiding her through the dark cool Church of San Mineato al Monte, pausing to point out the magnificent frescoes by Spinello Aretino which decorated the ceiling in the Sacristy, explaining the history of the superb marble pulpit, made for the Urbino Dukes and given by them to the Church. She had known men of culture before, but nobody like him. He amused as well as instructed, he made the incidents of centuries alive and relevant and the touch on her arm was as light as it was positive. *Come with me, follow me, I know the way* . . .

"We'll go to the crypt," he said. "I arranged to bring you this morning. It's only shown at certain hours on Tuesdays and Fridays. That's where all our family are buried. Except for two Dukes, who died on the Crusades."

A sacristan in a musty green soutane guided them through a side door, and down a flight of steep steps incongruously lit by bare electric bulbs in the wall. It seemed a long way down and the atmosphere grew colder. She shivered, and immediately he noticed. "Take my coat," he said. "How stupid of me, I should have made you bring something to put on."

"No," Katharine said quickly; she almost panicked as he tried to put it around her shoulders. She didn't want him to touch her, she didn't want to wear what he had worn. It was a light, silk jacket. It hung on her. "Please," she said. "I don't need it. You've only got a shirt—" He didn't seem to listen; he led her down the stairs after the sacristan, who tripped with surprising agility down the steps, and opened a massive carved oak door at the bottom. More electric lights, but hidden in the roof; the walls were yellow stone blocks, the floor marble flags, and down each wall there were the arched recesses where the city's great families had been buried. There were eighteen Malaspiga tombs. The earliest ones, including two effigies of crusaders, all wore armor. The faces were hard and alien under raised helmets, the heraldic dogs slept at their feet; their medieval wives and children lay beside them.

"Now," the Duke said, "look at this. This is what I wanted you to see. This is Alfredo di Malaspiga, the Fourth Duke, modeled by Cellini. It's one of the greatest works of art in the world."

The figure was life size; it rose from a bier in colored marbles, with bronze figures at each corner, so realistic and so beautiful they seemed alive.

"Charity, Chastity, Prudence and Hope," he translated the Latin for her. "Aren't they superb? But it's the figure of Alfredo that takes the breath away."

He had died at the age of thirty-seven, having outlived three wives and leaving five children, all that remained of the eleven his wives had borne him. He lay slightly on one side, an elbow bent, his head resting on his palm as if he were peacefully contemplating, clothed in the rich costume of the early sixteenth century. It was an astonishing face, modeled in bronze. A tracery of veins showed at the temple, the mouth was so mobile it could have moved; the neck ligaments stood out under the stress of the position of the head. In spite of the beard it was Alessandro di Malaspiga, dead and buried for five hundred years.

"It's incredible," Katharine said. "It's you!"

"It's said to be very like me," he answered. "But that's not important. It is the quality of the work that matters. It is a shame that so few people see it; commissioning this statue and hiding it away must have been the only unobtrusive action of his life. The final irony from a man who had always lived exactly as he pleased!"

"He looks like a bad man," Katharine said quietly. There was a stillness around them; the air was colder than when she first came in.

"It depends on what you mean by bad," her cousin answered. "Certainly those four figures have no connection with the living man. He was certainly not prudent. He took, rather than gave, he didn't hope, he made things happen and no one would have insulted him by suggesting he was chaste. But he was a man of his time. A true Renaissance prince, a lover of women and the arts, a warrior, a statesman—what has the modern man to offer by comparison?"

"And that's what you admire?"

He looked down at her and gently laughed. "My dear

cousin," he said. "That's what I hope I am. In my own way. We'll go and have lunch now. This afternoon we'll drive out to Fiesole. It's a charming suburb, and there is a church with some interesting thirteenth-century wall frescoes." She followed him back and up the stairs. She saw him give money to the sacristan and say something that made him smile and glance at her. He had spoken too low for her to hear. When they went outside into the brilliant sunshine, she realized that she was trembling.

As if he knew she was chilled and frightened, he flung an arm casually around her shoulders, drove her off in the Ferrari to a smart restaurant near the Piazza Michelangelo where they were given a table in the garden, and set himself out to be gay. There were no more stories about their ancestors, no reference to the past. The sixteenth-century monument with its beautiful, familiar face seemed to have no connection with the amusing man who talked about his antique business, Italian politics, the coming American elections and made every subject fascinating. She cast about in her mind for some comparison, some simile to describe him, and was defeated. She had never met anyone who had so many gifts; culture, humor, charm, extraordinary good looks, intelligence— And in that gloomy crypt, surrounded by the dead, he had revealed his cold philosophy of life. Pride, ambition, arrogance, power. At any cost. She looked at him, remembering the cost to her brother, and was afraid he would see the hatred in her face. He had said it was expressive.

"You've eaten very little," he said. "I think the crypt depressed you. Why didn't you tell me you didn't like tombs?"

"It's hot today," she excused herself. "Of course I liked the crypt. It was most interesting. But I've been wondering—could we go to Fiesole another time? I'd really like to look through my grandmother's papers again."

"Why, yes—if you'd rather. We can go back and look at them together." He gave a slow, confident smile, as if he knew she was making an excuse to get back into the villa and into the library. To recover the tape from the little recording ma-

chine under the marble table. She thought suddenly that if
he had known what she was really doing in Florence, he
would have smiled in the same way.

"Are you enjoying yourself, Katharine?" The question was
so unexpected that she stammered for a moment, not knowing what to answer. When she did it sounded clumsy and
false.

"Of course—I'm having a wonderful time! Why do you ask
me that?"

"Because you look unhappy," Alessandro said quietly. "I'm
an impetuous man—perhaps I've forced you into coming out
with me. Would you have preferred to spend the day alone?"

"No." She had recovered herself, and she managed to smile
at him. "I'd have been very lonely. You *are* impetuous, you
know, and maybe I'm not used to being rushed off my feet.
But I've enjoyed it. I wouldn't have come otherwise."

"That's what I thought," he said. "If I'm impetuous, you
are the sort of woman who can say no, and mean it. I feel
you've been unhappy. Is that true?"

She didn't want to answer him; she didn't want to discuss
her life or expose her grief which he had inflicted, however
indirectly. She hated him and she especially hated him when
he was gentle. He reached across and took her hand. She
felt her body stiffen.

"Is it your brother's death?"

"Yes," she said slowly. "He suffered very much, and there
was no cure for his disease. I shall never be able to forget it.
We were very close."

"I had a younger sister," Alessandro said. "We felt the
same. We were companions as children, there was no fighting, no jealousy, we just did everything together. After the
war she caught meningitis and died. I was terribly upset; I
can sympathize with your feelings. I suppose you could say
she was the only person I have ever loved." He offered her a
cigarette.

"That's an extraordinary thing to say," Katharine said.

"You must have loved your mother—and your father, what about him?"

"My father also died after the war. I was very young, and he had never done anything to make me love him. He only knew how to make us all afraid. Even my mother feared him, and she had a genius for evading the unpleasant. My father was an autocrat, someone you went to see to be punished. When he died I was relieved. As for my mother—she was just beautiful," he said. "A beautiful visitor who came to my nursery when I was a child, kissed me and went out again. She was already old even then; she had both of us in her forties, after a lot of miscarriages. She lived for her beauty and her love affairs. It wasn't possible to love a legend who belonged to other men. My sister was the only one."

"I thought Italian families were affectionate," she said. "We were all very close—my mother doted on us."

"The Malaspigas are not typical," he said. "We have a reputation for being without hearts. As you will see, when you read some of the letters today. I looked at them myself when I got them out for you. Your grandmother was very brave. I feel you've inherited this quality."

"What makes you think that?" She slipped her hands under the table; she had a habit of clenching them in tension. Brave. Why should he say that? Brave. And foolish.

"It's just a judgment I made when I first met you," he said casually. "I watched you come into that room and find us all sitting there. My mother. Francesca, John, and me. We were strangers, and in spite of our connection we had nothing about us to make you feel at home. Quite the opposite. You were nervous, my dear cousin. I saw your hand tremble and you have a trick of looking long and intently at people when you are not sure of them. As if to show that you don't care. It's very charming. Cowards cannot do it. That's how I know you're brave. Do you want more coffee?"

"No, thanks."

"You are certain you don't want to go to Fiesole instead of

wasting the afternoon looking at those old letters? You've plenty of time to read them."

"I haven't really," she said. "I can't stay here indefinitely. I've allowed myself a month away, and I've already spent two weeks of it. I'd like to go to Fiesole another time, if you'll take me."

"Whenever you want," he said. "We will go home."

When he took her back to the hotel it was dark. She had refused an invitation from the old Duchess to stay to dinner. It was obvious that good manners and not inclination prompted the suggestion. The large dark eyes were cold, even while the mouth smiled. Katharine excused herself, saying she was tired. In the hotel lobby Alessandro paused. He took her hand and kissed it.

"I have to go to the castle tomorrow to look at some imports," he said. "A big consignment has arrived for sorting and pricing before I send it to my shops. I will be away for two days making a list of the best things. When I come back, will you have dinner with me?"

She didn't want to accept. While she was alone in the library she had retrieved the tape and it was safe in her handbag; she wanted to go upstairs and play it over. A big consignment had arrived. If it was the consignment she imagined, then there might, there must, be some reference to it on that tape. She didn't want to go out to dinner with him, and she hated him holding on to her hand.

"Will you come?" he repeated.

"Doesn't your wife mind?" It came out instinctively. She saw a flash of anger in his face. Then it was gone; beautiful, smooth as ivory.

"Francesca wouldn't mind at all. She intends inviting you to dinner at the villa. She wants to give a party for you. I'm not suggesting anything improper."

Katharine felt herself change color. "I never thought you

were. I just thought she might object to staying behind while you had dinner with me. I know I would. That's all."

"American women object to everything their husbands do," he said softly. "Perhaps that's why there are so many divorces. I shall come at about eight thirty on Friday. John has promised to look after you while I'm away."

The voice-activated tape had run for twenty minutes before she heard anything significant. There were conversations between the Duchess and Alessandro, inconsequential and rather formal, several telephone calls which didn't convey anything unusual, long gaps of silence, and then at last a call made by Alessandro himself.

The little machine had picked up every word and nuance with amazing fidelity. He could have been speaking in the room.

"This is the Duke of Malaspiga. When can I expect the consignment of goods? On Wednesday—by the usual route—excellent. I shall go to the castle myself and supervise the sorting. No, certainly not; this is our most important shipment so far. Arrange for Taylor to take delivery. Good, good-bye."

She pressed the button and re-ran it.

The most important shipment so far. The one which concealed the heroin—the one for which Raphael had been waiting. This time there would be false compartments, secret places built into the furniture to carry the plastic bags filled with pure heroin from the laboratory. Carpenter had shown her a sample. It had looked like Epsom salts. It was processed from opium, by a means so simple that the equipment needed to boil it down and refine it could be packed up in the back of a small van. There were laboratories known to be operating in Naples, but their size and mobility made them difficult to track down. The heroin could have come from there. She reached for the telephone and asked for Raphael's number. A woman's voice answered, cool and brisk. Raphael was not available. "But I've got to talk to him! Where can he be reached?"

"I'll pass on your message," the woman said. The voice was flat, monotonous; Katharine could have shouted at her.

"It's terribly important—"

"If it's an emergency, please use the appropriate call sign."

"It's not that kind of an emergency, but it's very important!" Katharine said angrily. "Tell him to call me as soon as possible. It's urgent." She slammed down the receiver. She wondered whether the woman on the other end had answered Firelli's final desperate call.

She switched on the tape again while she was waiting and played it through. After the telephone call there was silence. She reached out to shut it off and looked at her watch as she did so. Nearly half an hour since she had telephoned and Raphael hadn't made contact. Loud and clear on the machine she heard the sound of a door opening and closing. Then the Duchess Francesca's voice.

"Sandro, Mamia sent me to find you." Katharine kept still. She had forgotten in her excitement that the tape had longer to run.

"I was telephoning. I'm coming in a moment." Alessandro's voice, cold and impatient.

"I want to talk to you."

"Not now, I'm busy."

"You're always busy when you want to avoid something. You had lunch with that American girl today, didn't you?"

"And if I did?"

"Are you going to make her your mistress, too?" Katharine froze at the words.

"That's no concern of yours. If you've come to pick a quarrel, you're wasting your time as well as mine. I'm not going to discuss Katharine with you."

"Oh, I've seen the way you look at her!" The disembodied voice was deep with anger and reproach. "You're happy, smiling—a changed man again. It's always the same—God knows, I can recognize the signs. . . ."

"I've told you, Francesca—I will not discuss her!" Now his anger came out, harsh and vibrating through the machine.

"You love to humiliate me, don't you! You've done it for years—you're bored with our friends' wives and the harlots you've picked up. Now it's this girl! Something new, somebody different. . . . I know you, Sandro, I know what you're going to do!"

"You know nothing about me." The contempt was acid. "Nothing. You wouldn't understand what it means to meet a woman who's fresh and honest. A real woman. You say I want her? Well, you're right, I do. I can't think why you should mind."

Her voice was thick with tears. "You can reproach me," she said. "For that one thing—you've never let me forget it."

"I've never been able to forget it myself. Go and do something to your face. It agitates Mamia when we argue."

"Sandro! I warn you. . . ." It was a hysterical cry, tailing off as the door opened and closed. He had left the library. The tape clicked and stopped. It had run out. For some time Katharine sat stiff and horrified, a hot color in her face. There was a dreadful sense of eavesdropping, as if she had been physically concealed in the room listening to that bitter private exchange. The references to herself, the hate and jealousy, the contempt . . . she felt sickened. And afraid. She had been deluding herself that Malaspiga's interest was platonic, ignoring the way he looked at her, the sensuous touch of his hand on her bare arm. She hated him and she was frightened, frightened of the desire which flickered around her like fire. And like fire, it burned. She remembered when he had hung his coat over her shoulders in the crypt and she had wanted to turn and run. A drug smuggler, a murderer. Her brother's murderer. And she knew, with horror, that in spite of everything, there had been times when she responded, when she had forgotten what he really was. *Know the enemy.* Carpenter's advice again. But equally she had to know herself. She looked at her watch. Why didn't her Interpol contact ring back? The silence in the room oppressed her, but she dared not go out in case the call came through.

She put her tape recorder away in its case and locked it in the wardrobe. She wandered downstairs and sat in the lounge, ordered some coffee because she couldn't eat, and waited. *The heroin was hidden in the antiques. This time it must be.* She tried hard to think about that and forget the conversation which had followed.

The reception clerk came in and signaled to her. "There's a telephone call for you, Signorina."

Katharine sprang up. "I'll take it upstairs in my room. Thank you!"

Raphael was full of congratulations. "This is wonderful—you've made tremendous progress, and so quickly! I'll cable the message to New York immediately. They'll make arrangements to search the goods when they arrive. It'll take about three or four weeks before they reach the States."

"Three or four weeks. . ."

"By sea," he said. "First they've got to be crated. It could be longer. But don't worry, your Customs will be ready for them."

"Would you ask them when I can come home?" She hadn't meant to say that—she was surprised when it came out.

"Do you want to make it an official request?"

Katharine hesitated. They'd think she was frightened. Carpenter would say that women weren't suitable as agents because they lacked the nervous stamina. "No," she said. "Nothing official, just ask."

"I'll let you know," he said. "Good night."

She *was* afraid. Perhaps Frank Carpenter was right. But then they hadn't known and neither had she, that she would have to fight on two fronts. She undressed unwillingly and got into bed. She didn't expect to sleep well, and when at last she did, it was a sleep tormented by confusing dreams.

She was awakened by the telephone. She felt heavy and unrested—her head ached. It was Raphael. "I've had an answer from New York. Go to the nine o'clock Mass at the

Santa Trinità Church—it's near the Ponte Vecchio. I'll be in the back row on the right of the Sassetti Chapel. Kneel beside me."

It was a bright morning, warm although still early. She had drunk some coffee and tried to shake off the malaise of a bad night and a feeling of anxiety, but without much success. The Santa Trinità Church was a beautiful fourteenth-century building with famous frescoes by Ghirlandaio, situated on the left side of the Piazza Santa Trinità. It was still too early for the tourists and the church was almost empty. A Mass in the Italian Rite was being said in the Sassetti Chapel; there was little light except for the candles on the altar and a single spotlight directed on the crucifix which was said to be miraculous. The famous frescoes were in shadow. Katharine looked around, and after a few moments, she became accustomed to the dimness. Raphael was where he had said, in the last pew at the back. She moved in and knelt beside him. He glanced at her and smiled.

"Good morning. This is supposed to be good for the soul."

"What did New York say?"

"They said to congratulate you. You've done very well. They believe this consignment will contain heroin, and so do I. Then we'll have them."

The priest began to read the Gospel. His voice boomed through an amplifying system. They stood up.

"What are you going to do?"

"Let the goods go through to the States," he said. "Your people will examine it secretly, find the heroin and then arrest this Mr. Taylor when he takes delivery. They're very excited.

"We'd been tipped off that a large quantity had been processed in Naples and was on its way to a pipeline. This is the one. I have a feeling for heroin. I know it has been sent to Malaspiga."

"I hope to God you're right," she murmured. The Gospel ended, the amplifier crackled, exhorted the Lord to be with them all, and a mutter of response came from the congregation. They sat down.

"Then there's no reason for me to stay," she said. "I've done all I can." He glanced quickly at her; the remaining hair on his head grew in little snaking tendrils over his ears. There were flecks of gray in it.

"New York wants you to stay on," he said. "I mentioned that you'd like to go back, but they said it was very important that you finished your part of the operation. They want you to get a look at the furniture. Mark it for identification later. That way, nobody can say the pieces were switched after they left Malaspiga."

"I can't do that," she whispered quickly. "That's impossible. . ."

"If you don't do it, we may not be able to pin this on the Duke. Remember who he is. This isn't like nailing some dirty little trafficker in Naples or Marseilles. Your cousin is head of a great Italian family. That kind of thing still matters here. We've got to prove that he sent out goods which concealed heroin. And one antique chest or table can be much like another. I've brought something for you."

He passed a prayer book to her and the marker was hidden in the middle of it. It was the shape and size of a small pencil, only thicker.

"It's stain," he said. "And it doesn't come off without re-polishing. All you have to do is make a specific mark, like a T, something which won't immediately be noticed. It works on marble, too. Bronzes are no good—there you'll have to try and memorize what you can."

"But if there are dozens of pieces, sets of chairs—it's not possible to mark them all!"

"The last consignment of furniture was about ten items. Some statuary and some objets d'art. The customs value put on them for insurance was around half a million dollars. Your cousin only deals in the best. This lot will be about the same."

"I don't want to do it," Katharine said.

"Nobody can make you." Raphael's tone was patient. "But if you want to avenge your brother's death it will make all the difference. It's up to you."

"Lamb of God," the amplifiers invoked, "you take away the sins of the world." "Have mercy on us," the scattered worshipers replied.

"All right," Katharine said quietly. "All right, I'll do it." After what she had heard on the tape, she knew that a request to Alessandro di Malaspiga wouldn't be refused.

"I'll let your people know." She saw him smile at her. It was easy for him to be encouraging. The Communion bell had rung; people were filing out of their pews and walking down the aisle to the altar. To her surprise, he moved to join them. She had been brought up a Catholic and lapsed after leaving her convent school. It had never occurred to her that a man like Raphael could still practice.

She bent her head, her eyes closed. It was a thought, not a prayer, a groping in the darkness of doubt. *Help me. I'm frightened.*

She looked up, as he returned to his place. He knelt for a moment, his hands shielding his face.

The Mass was coming to an end. They stood to receive the blessing, and Raphael crossed himself.

"You'll need to go soon," Raphael said.

"I'll try for this weekend. Otherwise everything will be packed up."

"You're being very brave," he said. "But you will have to be very careful. Malaspiga is a little town; you will have nobody to help you if anything goes wrong."

"I know that," she said. "I hope you said one for me just now."

"As a matter of fact, I did."

"It didn't help Firelli much. I have a nasty feeling that the saints are sleeping." They moved out of the pew toward the side door. At the holy water stoup Raphael paused. He dipped his hand in the water and touched hers with it.

"In an emergency you can call me, and whatever happens I'll come. I promise that. But don't do it unless you have to. Good luck."

He hung back, and she went out ahead of him. Outside

the sun was like a laser beam; she shielded her eyes against it. The inside of the church had been cold and musty with the smell of age. Like the tapestries at the villa. It was Thursday; Alessandro had said he would be back on Friday and take her out to dinner. And that was when she would ask him to show her Malaspiga Castle. To take her to the place from which Firelli had not come back. She walked slowly across the Piazza Santa Trinità. There was comfort in the crowds, in the warm sunshine. She took half an hour to get back to her hotel, and when she did, she found John Driver waiting for her in the lobby.

"Hi there," he said. "I thought I'd catch you early. Reception said you were on the telephone when I tried to call. I've come to take you on a tour of the city. Then we can have lunch, if you'd like?"

"I'd love it," Katharine said. "How very nice of you . . ."

"I hate to admit it," he said, "but it was just as much Sandro's idea. He was afraid you'd be lonely."

Then she remembered his remark when they parted. "John will look after you till I get back."

"Yes," she said, suddenly chilled. "He told me you'd be around." Out in the brilliant sunshine and the busy street, she took his arm.

"I have a car around the corner," he said. "They're hot on parking offenses in this city. I thought you might like a tour of the galleries. Do you like modern art?"

"Why, yes," Katharine said. "I do."

"I hate it," he said. "But it has something to teach me, so I go along and study. Then when I've seen enough I go around to the Bargello and look at the Donatellos and the Michelangelos. Just for reassurance. Here's the car."

"You sculpt, don't you? The old Duchess was talking about you. So was Francesca. I'd love to see some of your work."

"You'd have to come to Malaspiga Castle to see that," John Driver said.

"It'll have to be soon," she answered. "I haven't that much time left of my holiday."

"Anyway I don't think you'd like the castle," he said. He took a corner with surprising speed. The Duke was a flamboyant, ruthless driver. John lacked his style but equaled his force. "It's a very gloomy, medieval place. Maybe I'll have an exhibition in the States. Then you can come to that." He found a permitted space on the Piazza San Croce, and they went into the famous Lanzarrotti Gallery to see the exhibition of abstracts by James Ferris, one of the most avant-garde of English sculptors. She found the Canadian a knowledgeable and relaxed companion. There was no suggestion that he found her attractive or had any personal motive in escorting her. He was friendly, but obviously absorbed in what they were seeing.

Lunch was leisurely. They ate in a simple trattoria, quite unlike the smart restaurants frequented by the Duke. The food was plain but excellent; they drank a sharp Chianti which she preferred to the more sophisticated Italian wines.

John Driver asked her about herself, and she gave him the story invented for the Malaspigas. She referred briefly to her brother's death and told him he died of cancer. He looked concerned. "That's terrible. My mother died of it. It must have been hell for you, too. What are you going to do when you go home?"

It was an unexpected question and she had no answer. She hadn't thought about the future. Without Peter, nothing awaited her but a vacuum.

"I don't know," she said. "I'll get myself a job, try to settle down. I haven't made any plans. How about you? Are you going to stay here indefinitely?"

He shrugged. "Alessandro wants me to," he said. "And it's a big temptation. I came here without any money. I did odd jobs to earn enough to keep myself going, and now that I think about it, I guess I starved for about three months. Then somebody told me there was a job repairing some stonework at the villa, so I went along. I met Alessandro—he asked to see my work and, presto! he became my patron. I stayed on at the school for another year, studying, and then they insisted that I live with them and work on an exhibition. So I spend most of my time at the castle."

"And do you like having a patron?" Katharine asked him. "Isn't it a little old-fashioned—"

"Of course it is." He smiled. "But then you must have realized that Alessandro is not a modern man. He's a Renaissance prince, born into the wrong century. That's how he thinks and how he acts. He believes in my work. He'll support me for as long as I'll let him. His ancestors did the same. Your ancestors, I should say."

"That's a very good description of him," Katharine said slowly. "He took me to the crypt to see Duke Alfredo. The likeness is uncanny."

"He showed it to me, too, soon after we met," John Driver said. "I've done some casts of the face. It's superb, beautiful. But then Alessandro is a beautiful man, don't you think so?"

"Yes," she agreed. "Yes, I suppose he is."

"How much do you like him?" She looked up in surprise to find him watching her. He had gray eyes and they were worried.

"Very much. He's been so kind to me."

"Would it make you angry if I offered some advice?"

"It would depend on the advice," she said, "but I don't think so. Go on."

"Don't fall in love with him," Driver said. "If he's making a play for you, and I guess he is, then don't be fooled. Alessandro loves women, but they don't mean a thing to him. You'd only get hurt."

"You needn't worry about me," she said quietly. "In the first place I don't go for married men; in the second, Alessandro's not my type. I'm not likely to take him seriously. I do know something about men."

"I'm sure," he said. "But don't underestimate him. He has a habit of getting what he wants."

"Well, he won't get me," she said.

"Okay." He smiled at her. He was immensely likeable—

there was a gaucheness about him which was touching. "And we're still friends?"

"Of course. It was nice of you to warn me."

"I was thinking of Francesca, too," he admitted. "Much as I owe Alessandro, there are times when I just can't forgive him for the way he treats her."

"She looks unhappy," Katharine said.

"She's miserable," John said simply. "She has been for years. She hasn't had children and you know what that means to an Italian family. And he's the last of the line. He's never forgiven her for it. And she can't forgive herself. There's no question of divorce. Anyway"—Driver managed a smile; he still seemed awkward, as if he couldn't accept her assurance that she wasn't angry—"people have to live their own lives. It upsets me to see them making such a mess of things, especially when they've done so much for me. I wish I could help, but I can't."

"Francesca said you were a genius," Katharine said. She watched his face and saw a sudden change in the expression.

"She shouldn't say that," he said. "It isn't true. I have talent, but I don't have the immortal gift. One time I thought I had—I dreamed of creating something like the beauty I see around me here in Florence. And I can create beauty. That's not a boast. But it falls short. Always—there's something missing. That's when I need Alessandro. He gives me confidence, he builds me up again. He's wonderful that way. Francesca just likes me; she's grateful because I'm nice to her. That's why she talks about my being a genius." He looked at Katharine and grinned. "I don't even have an artistic temperament."

"I hope I'll see your work," she said, and she meant it. He had a human quality she found comforting. She felt he was a man on whom one could rely. An innocent being sheltered by a wolf. She wondered what he would say about his patron if he knew what he was doing. They had lingered over coffee, and he was drinking Strega, which she refused. Her courage had been so low since the previous night. Now she felt stronger, her resolution had returned. She leaned toward him. "Tell me," she said. "Tell me about Malaspiga Castle."

"This is great news," Ben Harper said. "When that consignment comes over here, we'll have them cold. She's done exactly what I hoped she'd do."

"Then why don't you bring her home?" Frank Carpenter said. "The job's finished, and she's still alive. She should be recalled at once."

Harper looked at him, making a bridge of his fingers. He had suspected Carpenter's attitude to Katharine Dexter very soon after he undertook her training. It wasn't as impersonal as he pretended. He wasn't just arguing on behalf of an agent. If it had been Firelli, no one would have suggested he be pulled out at such a crucial stage.

"Frank," he said slowly. "She's got to stay on. She's got to identify that stuff for us. Then she can testify that it's the same as Malaspiga's goods. Otherwise how can we prove it wasn't switched, or other pieces carrying the dope weren't added after it left the Duke's possession? We've got to *prove* this case and smash this whole organization. Just how much heroin could they pack into a load of antiques—Jesus, it could be the biggest haul we've ever made! I can't call the girl home now. I want her to get to that stuff and mark some of it, if she can. *Then* I'll recall her."

"Okay," Frank said. "Okay. I can't argue with that, but I don't like it. It's asking her to take additional risks. I think she's done enough."

"Nobody else can get close without arousing their suspicions," Harper insisted. "She's got herself inside, and they've accepted her. Nobody suspects anything and they won't. She'll come out of it all right. How is your end of the investigation going?"

"I'm flying out to the Coast again tomorrow," Frank said. "I want to check on Eddy Taylor's connections there, and I want a few questions answered about Mrs. John Julius."

"What do the files say?"

"The usual. Wealthy socialite marries star, that sort of guff. Pictures of them getting married, on yachts, at the Oscar ceremonies, at Chasen's . . . pictures of her playing hostess and raising money for charity—the usual. There isn't a single bad smell anywhere. The only gossip item I dug up never came to anything."

"What was it?"

"A piece in Harriet Harrison's column. I brought a Xerox with me, I guessed you'd like to see it."

Harper took the paper from him. A blurred inset picture of one of Hollywood's most feared and venomous gossip columnists was set on the top right hand corner, surrounded by a halo of stars. The section mentioning Elise Bohun Julius had been ringed in red pencil.

"All is not right between the lovebirds in John Julius' luxury nest up on Honeymoon Hill. In between entertaining our Ducal couple, there's been less billing and cooing between the handsome movie idol and his upper-crust wife and quite a lot of angry squawking, according to what other little birds are whispering. The reason? Well, watch little Harriet's column to find out whether the lovebirds have got a cuckoo in their nest."

Harper gave it back to Frank. "So what was the scandal?"

"There wasn't one," Carpenter said. "Harriet never made the revelation. If you look at the date and that line about a Ducal couple, that was written around the time the Malaspigas were visiting.

"There's a later item mentioning a big party given for them, full of bitch and bite as usual, but about the guests—what director was casting what star on what couch. Nothing against the John Juliuses, though. Whatever she was going to say about them, she thought better of it."

"That woman never thought better of anything unpleasant in her life," Harper said. "If she didn't print it, it must have been because it wasn't ugly enough or big enough. So there's no lead to anything there."

"I'm not sure," Carpenter said slowly. "I'm not happy about a vulture like Harrison letting anybody off the hook. I'm going out to see her while I'm looking into Eddy Taylor. She might have something to tell me."

"She's been retired for a long time," Harper said. "I don't know what she's doing now."

"She's in a sanatorium," Carpenter said. "I've got an appointment to see her at four o'clock tomorrow. I'll report back direct if I find anything."

"Nathan hasn't made any progress," Harper said. "Nothing but dead ends. He says Eddy Taylor's clean. Can't find anything on him."

"I know that," Frank said. "But that doesn't tie in with Kate's report. Malaspiga mentioned Taylor, he said he was to accept the consignment of antiques direct. If Jim can't find anything in New York, maybe I'll do better in Hollywood."

The following morning he flew to the Coast, and spent the first part of the afternoon checking on Eddy Taylor's antique business. The shop now sold Spanish rugs and iron work. It was owned by an arty little woman with long hair hanging around an old face, yards of colored beads, and an Indian type dress.

The shop had been selling antiques but of the less fashionable English and French nineteenth century. It hadn't done well and the owner, whom she remembered by name, sold out to her. She talked openly and at length—Carpenter had difficulty getting away from her. There was nothing, in spite of her appearance, to connect her with drug smuggling. Aside from the middle-aged hippie look, which he suspected was deliberately cultivated, the lady was a shrewd, experienced business woman. He had to check on her as a routine, but he didn't feel it would yield anything. Then he took a cab to the Bel Air sanatorium, high up in the hills above Hollywood and about a twenty-minute drive from the residential area.

It was a smart, mock-Colonial mansion, complete with stuccoed front and pillars, surrounded by beautifully kept grounds, where he could see people sitting, some with a nurse beside them. He went inside and asked at the reception desk for Miss Harrison. A bright, pretty nurse directed him to the first floor.

"Room eighteen, sir. She's expecting you."

It faced the back, and when he went inside, he saw the magnificent view of the gardens from a window that reached to the floor, even before he saw the woman sitting up in a chair beside it, a colored rug over her knees.

"Miss Harrison? I'm Frank Carpenter." He shook her hand and gave her his DEA card. She glanced at it and gave it back.

"Sit down, Mr. Carpenter. Pull up a chair near me."

She wasn't as old as he had expected; surprisingly, she showed traces of having been very pretty. Her hair was nicely dressed and was still faintly blond; the eyes were blue and must have been her best feature. It was a petite face, lined with pain and bitterness of spirit. When she smiled, her mouth twisted on one side.

"I'll ring for tea," she said. "I've ordered it, but they're so inefficient here you have to remind them of everything." From what he had seen of the place, Carpenter felt this was unlikely, but he recognized the invalid's malaise. Her left hand was paralyzed; it lay white and clawlike on her lap, the palm turned slightly upward.

A nurse appeared in the doorway.

"You rang, Miss Harrison?"

"Bring tea for two," she said. "And I'll have some of those coconut biscuits." She turned back to Carpenter. "What can I do for you, Mr. Carpenter? It's a very long time since anyone came to see me. People don't like invalids."

"I'm grateful for the appointment," he said. "And I promise not to tire you."

"Oh, you won't do that!" She laughed. "I'm so bored in this crap heap I could scream! If I could walk, I'd be out of here in ten seconds flat—but I had a stroke and I'm not mobile anymore. Four years ago, and I've been shut up here ever since. Dying by inches. When it comes to you, Mr. Carpenter, make sure you go with a bang, not a whimper. It isn't pleasant."

"No," he said, "I'm sure it's not. But I'm surprised you don't have visitors. That must be lonely for you."

She smiled the painful, uneven smile again. "You don't think any of the movie colony are going to come up here and hold my hand, do you? They were so shit-scared of me, that when I had the stroke they all rushed off to order wreaths, just to make sure. I gave them hell, Mr. Carpenter. I made them shake. They could ass around playing the big star with everyone else, but not with me. I was bigger than Louella, Hedda, or Sheilah Graham. Nobody crossed me up and got away with it; and nobody hid anything from me either. That's why you're here, isn't it? You want information."

"Yes," Carpenter said. "Do you mind if I smoke?"

"Go ahead," she said. "And light one for me. How well do you know Hollywood?"

"I don't know it at all. I came up here last week to talk to John Julius."

"Good God." She laughed again—it was a staccato sound that grated. "How is he? Still playing the English gentleman? His father served behind a counter in a hardware store in England. I printed that about him, and he never said a word. But he wasn't a big star then."

Carpenter took out the Xerox of the clipping. "You never followed this up," he said. "In fact you never wrote anything about either of them which was at all unfriendly. You were pretty tough on everyone else, but you left the Juliuses alone. Why, Miss Harrison?"

She drew on the cigarette, watching him with the beautiful, embittered eyes. They were carefully shadowed and mascaraed.

"Who are you investigating—me or them?"

"Them," he said. "And some friends of theirs. The Duke and Duchess of Malaspiga. Italians. They paid a visit to the Juliuses about seven years ago; there was a big Hollywood party given for them. You wrote about it. Do you remember them?"

She stretched out her good hand and gave him the cigarette end. "Put that out for me, will you? They never leave the damned ashtray where I can reach it. Of course I remember them. Newly married, on their honeymoon. Jesus! *That* was a laugh."

"Tell me about it."

"Why?" She shot the question at him. "Are they in the drug racket?"

"We believe so," he said quietly. "We believe that there's a big smuggling organization and that the Malaspiga family is tied up with it. Please help us, Miss Harrison. Tell me anything about them you can remember."

She didn't answer for a moment. She lifted her useless hand by the wrist, and put it higher up on her lap, and she looked at Carpenter while she decided.

"I've kept my mouth shut for seven years," she said. "It was the only time in my life I suppressed news. I don't think I've ever gotten over it. Year after year I wrote about John Julius and that wife of his, Elise—nice things, crappy bits about how they'd given this to charity or she'd opened some lousy flower show. And all the while I was sitting on dynamite."

"Will you tell me about it now?" There was tension in the room; her long association with the film world had given her a sense of theater. She had a big scene coming up, and she was going to play it.

"Another cigarette," she said. He gave it to her. She blew out smoke. "You want to know about Elise Julius and the Malaspigas? Okay, Mr. Carpenter. I'll tell you."

Eddy Taylor's apartment was near the Park Avenue shop. It was beautifully decorated and furnished with seventeenth-century French and Spanish pieces. A superb Flemish tapestry hung on one wall, lit by a spotlight. Taylor was the second

son of a middle-class family in Cleveland, Ohio, and graduated in art, which surprised everyone and disappointed his
father, who thought it effeminate. He had left home to work
in New York with a firm of decorators, where he learned a
great deal about antiques and works of art. Doing up rich
women's apartments didn't really interest him, but he loved
antiques and within two years the decorators were followed
by jobs with several antique shops, always graduating higher
in the scale. He hadn't married, but he was not a homosexual.
His big chance had come in Beverly Hills when he had saved
enough to start in business for himself. It was a big chance in
more ways than one.

He held a drink in his hand, and it was trembling. He was
facing Jim Nathan.

"You're getting nowhere," he said to Nathan. "You say
you've taken the heat off me—how do I know that? And what
about this agent they're planting? What the hell do you think
you're doing?"

Nathan's face was pale; he lost color when he was angry.

"I'm doing all I can," he snarled back at him. "I've given
you a clean bill, and they won't bother looking into you anymore. And I'll get the agent's name—I've told you, it takes
time!"

"Well, time is what we *haven't* got," Taylor said. "I've got
goods coming in—while they're sniffing around me I don't
dare touch them! You've got to get me the details on this
agent—if they penetrate the other end, we're in real trouble; I
told them we could rely on you. I told Lars Svenson we'd have
the details before he left—but what have you given me—
nothing!"

"I'll get it," Nathan said. "For Christ's sake, I'll get it—stop
leaning on me!"

"We won't lean on you," Taylor said. He took a swallow of
his drink and looked at Nathan. His round face was dull and
cruel. "It's your wife who'll be getting the visitors."

Nathan swung around, his fists clenched. Sweat shone on

his forehead. "You threaten that again, you little bastard, and I'll kill you!"

"You can't protect her and you know it," Taylor sneered. They'd been through this scene before and Nathan always threatened to kill him. He wasn't afraid of him anymore. "You cooperate with us and she won't get hurt. That's the deal. I want to know the name of the person they're sending to Italy. And I want it by the end of the week, so Svenson can warn them."

"I tipped you off about Firelli," Nathan said. "I'll find this one. But don't talk about hurting Marie. Just don't talk about that . . ."

"All right." Taylor relaxed. "Have a Scotch."

"Go to hell," Nathan said bitterly. He had often thought of killing Taylor in the last two years. But it wouldn't have helped. It wouldn't protect Marie from the forcible fix that would start the whole nightmare over again. Even if he moved her away somewhere, and busted the whole organization to the bureau, he could never be sure that sometime, somewhere, the hoodlums known as rent collectors, wouldn't find her alone one day. The dealers in narcotics had long memories. Even from a Federal prison, men like Taylor could exact revenge. There was nothing he could do but work for them, and he'd recognized that long ago. He made his threat but it was empty. And every time he was a little more broken.

"I'll get the name for you," he said. "Meantime keep a low profile. I've told them you're clean, but there's a guy named Carpenter working on it and he's no fool. If they hadn't killed Firelli you might not be in this mess! I told you at the time to leave him to me. I could have stalled him."

"He'd gotten too close," Taylor said. "He can't make trouble where he is."

"No," Nathan agreed. "But his boss didn't like it. And Ben Harper never gives up. You should've explained that to your pal in Italy!"

"You get me the name of the agent," Taylor said. "By next Friday. Svenson leaves on Saturday morning. You call me and give me the name." He finished his drink. "Or else," he said. Nathan looked at him, and called him a filthy name. Then he went out of the apartment. Taylor looked at his watch. He had an appointment with the Swede, and he was running late. He'd booked a couple of girls for the evening. They were taking them to dinner and then coming back to his apartment for the finale. He didn't know how Svenson had the stamina. He was exhausted just by watching, and the Swede insisted that he stayed. He knew Taylor got no kick out of that kind of thing, but it amused him to force the other man to participate. Fortunately he was only required to act as voyeur. He sighed, wondered if there was time to pour another quick Scotch, and decided there was. He'd given Nathan four days. Behind the glasses his eyes were narrow with anxiety and rage. Firelli had penetrated the Italian end of the organization. Now another agent was going in. Ben Harper never gave up. He wiped his forehead—it was damp and his stomach felt queasy. The last thing in the world he wanted was an evening of strenuous sexual activity, even as spectator. If Nathan failed him . . . if he hung back. . . . Impotence against men like Ben Harper and the men in the bureau who couldn't be corrupted, made him especially vicious toward his only victim. He'd fix that wife of his. He'd have her filled so full of heroin she'd walk on water . . .

He went downstairs, got out his car from the garage under the high-rise and drove to meet Svenson. The two whores were already at his hotel.

4

Dinner at the villa was at nine. The old Duchess sat at the head of the long marble table in her son's absence, with John and her daughter-in-law on either side. It was a long low room, paneled in rose colored marble and lit by a superb Venetian chandelier. The furniture was painted in the soft colors of eighteenth-century lacquer, pale yellow and gold with touches of green and blue. It was a cool, summer room, designed for the hot months, and in winter they abandoned it for a smaller dining room on the other side of the hall. The old Duchess ate very little and drank watered wine. She was abstemious from a lifelong habit of watching her weight, and it amused John Driver to see her adulterating the excellent claret. He suspected that she didn't really like wine, whereas she had the sweet tooth of old age and had greedily drunk down three of his old-fashioneds before dinner. Her cheeks were flushed and her lovely eyes bright. She looked at Francesca and at him and smiled.

"It always seems strange without Alessandro, don't you think so?"

Francesca didn't answer. Driver was watching the old lady sharply. When she drank, she was inclined to be malicious. She had been very pleasant to her daughter-in-law before dinner, and he hoped her mood wasn't changing.

"He'll be back soon," he said.

"I don't know why he ever goes near that horrible place," she said suddenly. "Poor Alfredo wouldn't notice. It's so gloomy and cold. I always hated it, but his father would spend the summer months there, and Sandro is just the same. He says Alfredo gets lonely. I wish he'd let us stay in Florence."

"It gets too hot," Francesca said.

The Duchess dismissed her with a look. "Not for me," she said. "Old people feel the cold. The castle is like a tomb. I shan't go this year." She made the remark with defiance. She made it every year at regular intervals and nobody took any notice. When Alessandro said it was time to leave the city, the family left. She raised a pretty hand, adorned with an enormous turquoise and diamond ring, and patted her lips to hide a yawn.

"I'm tired tonight," she said. She smiled affectionately at John Driver. "Too many of your lovely cocktails, *caro*. I don't think we need any fruit for dessert." She rang the bell and got up. She put out a hand to John. It was a gesture that had brought men running to her all her life. "Help me upstairs, please, *caro*."

He took her arm, and slipped his own around her. Over his shoulder he signaled to Francesca. Wait for me. Then supporting the Duchess, he climbed the staircase to the first floor.

It was some time before he came into the library. Coffee had been brought in, and Francesca was sitting waiting for him. She raised her head and smiled. He came toward her and their hands reached out and gripped. Neither spoke. He knelt by the chair and put his arms around her; her head went back on his shoulder and they kissed. There was silence.

"Do you want coffee," she whispered, "before we go upstairs?"

"Why not?"

"Why were you so long with her? What were you doing?"

"Talking. She wouldn't let Gia undress her till we'd had a talk. She was tipsy, darling. I'm sorry you were waiting."

"I spend my life waiting," she said quietly. "Waiting for her to go to bed and for Sandro to be out of the house. So we can be together. I love you so much."

"I know," he said. "I know."

"What happened with the cousin today?" she asked him. She smiled, but the pitch-dark eyes were watching his face. "Did you fall in love with her?"

"No," John Driver said gently. "There's only one woman for me. You ought to know that. I took her around the galleries, we spent the morning looking at that rubbish of Ferris's, and then I gave her lunch."

"And what did you talk about?"

"About Sandro," he said. "I told her to be careful, I told her not to take him seriously."

"She won't listen," Francesca said. "They never do. No woman has ever said no to him."

He leaned forward and kissed her. "I know one," he said.

"I hate him," she whispered. "I hate him as much as I love you. I hate them all."

"Shush, sweetheart," John Driver said. "It doesn't matter. Nothing matters except you and me."

"Why do we have to wait?" she whispered. "Why can't we go now? He's away, we could leave tonight—"

"Be patient," he whispered. "You know I love you. When the moment comes, I'll take you away. We'll have the rest of our lives together."

"The thought of the summer drives me mad," she said. "That place where I was so miserable . . . My God, the idea of going there makes me ill. And that mad old uncle, wandering about. He should be shut up!"

"He does no harm," Driver said. "When you think of the castle, try to remember that it's where we came together for the first time. Then you won't hate it so much."

"It's easier for you," she spoke with bitterness. "You have work to do. Sandro likes you, my mother-in-law dotes on you —that old madman follows you around like a dog—they all hate me! And now there's this girl!"

"You shouldn't mind about her," Driver said gently. "You shouldn't be jealous. You have me. You shouldn't care what he does with anyone else." He kissed the side of her neck. For a moment her eyes closed with pleasure, but they flashed open again, tormented by inner visions.

"I'm jealous," she whispered. "I think of how he treated me, how he abused me and humiliated me, and the thought of him making love, enjoying himself with other women makes me mad! I could kill him!" She turned in his arms, and put her hands on his cheeks. "Try to understand," she said. "It doesn't alter my love for you, John. I've stood by while he paraded his mistresses, and it was torture. But this cousin is worse. She's different from the others."

"That's what Mamia said." Driver nodded. "She's worried about it, too."

"Not for my sake," Francesca interrupted. "She despises me; she doesn't care how I feel. All she knows is I haven't had a child—I've failed in my duty to the Malaspigas! If she's worried it's on her own account. And she's jealous. She's been the center of attraction all her life—with Sandro, too. She has to have men dangling after her—her son, you, anyone male. Her vanity makes me sick. She doesn't like the cousin because she's afraid that Sandro will pay more attention to her."

"She thinks he's in love with her," Driver said. "And she could be right." Francesca pulled away from him.

"In love?" She jerked back her head and laughed angrily. "Love? He doesn't know what the word means—he's cold and cruel and selfish . . ." She turned her head away, trying to hide the tears. Driver put his arms around her, his voice was soft, and he soothed her gently.

"Darling, darling, don't cry . . . I thought I'd made up for what happened. When I see you upset like this, I feel I've failed you. We know what love means, and that's what mat-

ters. You and me." He forced her to look at him. She clung to
him.

"Forgive me. Forgive me. Of course you haven't failed
. . . You've given me happiness, you showed me what love
could be like. I owe everything to you." She reached up and
kissed him passionately. "You are my life."

"Come upstairs then," he said. "Let's not waste time talking about him."

In her bedroom on the first floor, so tiny in the enormous
Florentine bed that she was only an outline under the covers,
the old Duchess di Malaspiga lifted her head from the pillows and listened. The cocktails had worn off; she had dozed
for a while and then a noise had awakened her. It was the
sound of her daughter-in-law's bedroom door closing.

For years Francesca and Sandro had slept in separate
rooms. It was an arrangement that distressed the Duchess. A
husband and wife should share the same room and the same
bed; it preserved the *bella figura* which was so important an
aspect of Italian life. Whatever the truth, a proper façade
must be presented to the outside world—one's dignity and
that of the family was the first consideration. Ladies must
always smile in public, however much they might weep pri-
vately. But the old standards were lowered; people discussed
their problems and exposed their shames in a way she found
offensive and incomprehensible. She folded her hands on her
breast and closed her eyes. Her window was slightly open,
allowing a little cool air to circulate. Quite clearly, carried
from another open window, she heard the low murmur of
John Driver's voice and knew that he was in her daughter-
in-law's room. She didn't open her eyes—sleep was too near.
So they had come together at last. Her experienced eye had
seen the furtive looks, the timid gestures over the past months.
She had been grateful for their restraint. Sandro didn't suspect anything, and that was her only concern. Whatever they
did themselves, the Malaspigas didn't like the idea of playing

cuckold to their wives. Her own husband, notoriously unfaithful himself, might have suspected her, but she had never
offended against good taste or caused an overt scandal. He
had no proof and honor didn't demand that he investigate
too closely. She hoped her daughter-in-law and the Canadian
would show equal good sense. Seconds later she was fast
asleep.

Francesca was awake when Driver left her. She lay with
her eyes closed, pretending to sleep, while he dressed and
slipped away to his own room. She stretched, then ran her
hands down her body. Love had been satisfying and beautiful; they had pleased each other and fallen asleep with
tenderness.

She lay alone in the hour before dawn broke and in spite
of everything she thought about her husband. His mother
thought he was in love. She flung herself around as if a whip
had cut across her. Love. Love for the American cousin with
the dark Italian eyes. He had never loved anyone in his life;
he had used the word to describe the ruthless possession of
her when they married. It was the euphemism for lust, the
lust for her which she remembered with loathing, the lust for
the women who came after her—social acquaintances, a
young film actress with a good publicity agent and a marvelous figure, women who drifted briefly in and out of his life.
She knew about them all because she had spied on him; whenever there was a suggestion of a woman, Francesca had applied herself to finding out the details. It was a form of
self-torture she couldn't resist. There were moments of in-
sight which suggested that it was a deliberate punishment for
an old sin, but such revelations were rare and instantly rejected. She had no need to feel guilt for what to her had been
so natural. It was her husband who deserved the blame.
His pride, his condemnation, that terrible year after their
marriage. . .

She tried to turn her thoughts to John, but instead they reverted to Alessandro, dwelling on the idea which caused her such frantic pain. He was in love. The emotion she had found with the young Canadian, the tenderness, the sense of union which transcended mere sexuality—these were things which she couldn't permit him to share with another woman. She sat up in bed, trembling. It was just as if John Driver hadn't held her in his arms that night. Hate blotted out everything else.

Every time they were alone she begged Driver to keep the promise made when they became lovers, and free her from Alessandro. So long as she was in the villa, or living in the castle, she was a prisoner, fettered by humiliation, jealousy and hate. She threw back the covers and went to the window; she was unaware of her nakedness. The relaxation of making love was gone. She stood watching the sun rise over the villa gardens, frigid with loathing of the man and jealousy of the woman. She let the curtain fall back; the room was dark again. She found her nightdress and put it on. There was nothing to do but wait until she could decently get up and go downstairs.

There was a moment when Frank Carpenter was sorry for Harriet Harrison. The ashtray was full of cigarette butts, and the room was stuffy with smoke and the scent of an indefinable decay.

"Why did you keep this quiet so long?" he asked.

"Because they had a habit of throwing acid at people who crossed them," she answered. "Now, I don't give a damn. Nobody sees me anyway. I had plenty going for me in those days." She smiled her bitter smile and held out her good hand. "I hope I've been some help," she said.

"You'll never know how much," Carpenter answered. "I think you've just saved someone's life. Could I come and see you again sometime?"

"Sure." She shrugged. "Anytime you want some information . . ." He glanced back at her as he opened the door; she was staring out of the window at the view of the gardens. He wondered how much longer she would go on sitting there, paying for what she had done to other people. He had kept the cab that brought him from the Beverly Hills shop; he drove back to the city and booked into a hotel. The following morning he had an appointment with one of the smart lawyers who looked after the affairs of the rich. He spent an hour there, looking through the files. Then he telephoned John Julius and asked to see him urgently.

The same Hawaiian manservant showed him in. The reception lounge seemed smaller, less modern than when he had last seen it. Perspective showed it to be out of date, an avant-garde effect of several years ago. He was grateful for the air conditioning; it was hot outside.

John Julius kept him waiting. When he came in and Carpenter saw the look on his face he knew the delay was due to fear. He had been nerving himself for the interview—his breath smelled of whiskey. No champagne and orange juice that morning. They shook hands; he felt that Julius didn't want to touch him.

"Why have you come back here? What do you want?"

"The truth," Frank Carpenter said. "I went to see Harriet Harrison yesterday."

"Oh, God," John Julius muttered. He sat down, his body sagging. "I thought she was dead . . ."

"She told me about Elise," Carpenter said quietly. "I'd like to say I'm very sorry. It must have been tough on you."

"Tough?" He gave a bark of laughter; the whites of his eyes were streaked with red. "Son, you've no idea! Living with it was bad enough, but keeping it quiet— And I could never be sure it wouldn't leak out. Then Harriet dug it up. She's a bitch out of hell, that woman—if you knew the lives she's ruined—"

"I can imagine," Carpenter said quietly. "But you shut her up, didn't you? She didn't dare follow up her story."

"I went to Elise's uncle," John Julius said. "He said to leave it with him. I don't know how he stopped her, and I never asked."

"She told me she had visitors," Carpenter said. "They promised her a face full of acid if she printed anything."

"Too good for her," he snapped. "Two of my best friends here in Hollywood committed suicide because of what she wrote about them. It ruined their careers and their marriages. She's the only really evil woman I know."

"When did you find out your wife was an addict?" Carpenter lit a cigarette. The handsome, haggard face turned slowly toward him.

"Three months after I married her," he said. "I was very much in love. She was a lovely girl—it wasn't just the money. I found the works in her bedroom. It nearly broke me. I wanted her to take a cure. She wouldn't. She said she could cope with the problem so long as she got the heroin."

"And she wouldn't have had any difficulty with that," Carpenter said.

"No," Julius agreed. "It was all laid on for her."

"Harrison told me about the Malaspigas," Carpenter said. "That was true, too?"

"Yes." He covered his face with his hands for a moment. "They change," he muttered. "The drug changes them. She wasn't that way when I married her . . ." He got up; he seemed unsteady. Suddenly he looked like an old man, the façade of middle-aged charm had cracked open, showing the ruin underneath. "I need a drink," he said. "I used to drink a lot at first. Then I pulled myself together. I made the best of it, and I hoped maybe one day she'd try . . . So long as nobody knew . . . You want a Scotch?"

"No thanks," Frank said. "Nothing for me. Tell me about Eddy Taylor—how did he fit in with your wife?"

"He ran an antique business over on Sunset," Julius said. He poured a large whiskey into a glass and swallowed half of it. He turned back to Carpenter. "How did you find out about that?"

"I went to see her lawyer this morning," he said. "He told

me about her business affairs. She owned the shop and set Taylor up in business. When she died the executors sold it." There was a deep frown on Carpenter's face, and it wasn't connected with John Julius. "It didn't take much to find that out. But I want you to tell me how it happened."

"She met Taylor when she was buying antiques. We had an apartment on East Fifty-second in New York, and she was furnishing it. They got on well, and she staked him in a business of his own out here. I thought he was a creep."

"You were right," Carpenter said. "Why was her connection with it kept a secret?"

"I don't know. She was a snob, I told you that. She didn't want anyone to know she was investing in a business right here in town. She never invited Taylor up here or mixed with him socially. Tell me something, Mr. Carpenter—why are you digging all this up? She's dead—what good will it do?"

"I'm not interested in your wife," Frank said. "I want the people she was connected with. I want the racketeers who sell the drug and the smugglers who bring it in. And don't worry, none of this will be made public. You've nothing to fear from that."

"That's good to know." He finished the drink. "We built up a life together. Maybe it was partly a lie, but some of what we had was good. I don't want to see it exposed now. I did care for her."

"And being who she was," Frank said quietly, "I guess you'd have found it difficult to leave her?"

Julius smiled a wry smile—it was one of his trademarks as a movie star. "You don't leave a man with many illusions, do you? Maybe you're right. Maybe I knew I couldn't leave her, so I told myself I didn't want to. Live with a lie long enough, and you end up believing it's true."

"I want to know about her family," Carpenter said. "Not the Bohuns, the others."

"Ah, yes." Julius smiled again. The whiskey was having an effect. "The grandfather, the uncles, the cousins. I can tell you a bit about them. But you'll have to be careful, son. They were very proud of Elise. Just don't let any of them know you're snooping . . ."

Two hours later Frank Carpenter was on the 747 back to New York. He telephoned Ben Harper's office from the airport. His secretary said he had gone to Washington.

"Jim Nathan's here," the girl said. "He wants to see him, too. He won't be back till Monday. Are you coming in?"

"Yes," Frank said. "Put Jim on, will you?"

Nathan sounded cheerful. "Hi, Frank. Where are you?"

"Kennedy," Frank said. "What's new with you, Jim—"

"Nothing." The voice sounded flat. "Dead ends everywhere. How about you? You get anything out in Hollywood?"

There was a small mirror set above the telephone in the booth. Carpenter saw his own reflection in it.

"No," he said. "I got nothing either. I was hoping you'd have had some luck with Taylor."

"Not a chance." The answer was emphatic. "I've checked and double-checked. He's absolutely clean." Frank put a hand to the back of his neck—he was ashamed to feel in clichés, but the small hairs were on end.

"Too bad," he said. "I'll be seeing you, Jim." He hung up. Clean. Checked and double-checked. He'd known Jim Nathan for twelve years, ever since he joined the bureau. He was a straight man; he hated crime and he hated drugs. He had a reputation for being too tough. But he was lying about Taylor, and Frank knew it. He had lied about the Beverly Hills shop. A routine inquiry would have established Elise Julius as the owner. Instead he'd pretended that it belonged to Taylor, and done his best to head Carpenter off. *I've checked very carefully. He bought the place, ran it for a year or two, then sold out . . . No connection there.* Lies, deliberate lies told to mislead an investigation. From the start he had tried to cover for Taylor. He's clean. He has no record. Nothing illegal about it. He could hear Nathan saying it, looking him in the eyes and shaking his head.

Taylor had been mentioned in Kate Dexter's report as taking delivery of the shipment, and because he had used the time before going to see Harriet Harrison by calling on Elise's lawyer, Carpenter had found the second, and equally sinister connection. Nathan hadn't expected him to follow that up; he thought he'd diverted the investigation. Carpenter came out of the telephone cubicle; he stood still for a moment. He'd known about Nathan as soon as he talked to the lawyer, but he had needed time to adjust, to accept that his friend was lying to him. Now there was no doubt—no chance it was mere carelessness. Nathan was going out of his way to keep Taylor clear of the investigation. And that meant only one thing. He was on Taylor's payroll. He got his car out of the airport parking lot and drove toward the city. Ben Harper was in Washington. And Nathan was in his office. Harper was keeping a special file on the Malaspiga case—it included Katharine Dexter's last report. Frank had seen Harper put it in the folder. Everything was there in Harper's office, the plan for using Katharine as an undercover agent, her reports, Raphael's messages. Everything.

He had begun to speed up as he drove. If Nathan was taking money from Taylor, then he was also working for the Malaspiga organization.

If he got into Harper's office he would look in that file. Nathan had been friends with Firelli, too. His foot flattened on the accelerator. There was a siren fixed to his car, to be used only in an emergency. He stabbed at the button and it began to scream as he cut through the traffic.

Ben Harper's secretary was a talkative girl. She lived with two friends over on the East Side in a small apartment that was too expensive but located in a relatively safe area. She was twenty-seven and unmarried, and the agents who came in to see Harper were apt to be waylaid and talked at for as long as she could pin them down. She liked Jim Nathan—the tough types appealed to her. She gave him coffee from the machine and settled down to entertain him.

Nathan played his part because he had to. The insides of his hands were sticky and the coffee tasted like cough mixture, but he kept on smiling and let the flow run over him. She laughed and preened a little, enjoying herself in an innocent way; she wasn't aware of his tension or the brevity of his answers as time passed. Twenty minutes. Nathan used some ugly words in his mind to describe her as she powdered her face and put on lipstick, watching him flirtatiously. He made up his mind. There was only one way to do it. Otherwise she'd sit there till it was time to close the office and he'd never get into Harper's private office.

"Betty." He leaned over the desk. "How about coming out for a drink?" She stared at him in delight.

"Why, that would be lovely! You mean right now? It's not six o'clock yet—but I guess I could lock up and go. Mr. Harper won't be back till Monday morning."

"I'll go inside and leave a message on his dictaphone," Nathan said. "While you pretty yourself up. I won't be long."

"Oh, Jim, you can use my machine—nobody's supposed to go in there—"

"Too confidential," Nathan said as he turned Harper's door handle. "I can't record in front of anyone. Not even you. I'll be through in a minute." He went inside and shut the door.

"You know"—Sandro di Malaspiga leaned across the table toward her—"I missed Florence while I was at home. That's strange, because I prefer the castle."

They were having dinner in a restaurant high up in the hills at Fiesole, seated outside in the garden with a view over the city that was one of the most beautiful Katharine had seen. He had arrived at her hotel to pick her up, and she had forgotten how handsome he was. Thinking about him in his absence had made him appear even more sinister. He had seemed very pleased to see her. She had to fight against her fear and pretend to reciprocate.

"Don't you like Florence? I think it's wonderful."

"I love it," he said, "but I like Malaspiga better. I grew up there, it's my home. Perhaps I was missing you, and that's why I wanted to come back."

The very dark eyes were watching her; there was an expression in them which was intense and frightening. For a moment the easy charm had slipped, showing a man of strong passions, of dominant will.

"Perhaps," Katharine said. She looked away from him. The hand lying across the table, the gold signet ring gleaming on the little finger, moved toward hers.

"You don't like me to say things like that, do you?"

"No," she said. "It makes me uncomfortable."

"You talked about my wife last time—is that the reason?"

"Yes, of course it is." She forced herself to turn away from the glittering panorama of Florence at night and look at him. He laid his hand over hers and held it.

"You're making a mistake, Katharine," he said. "There is nothing between us anymore—there hasn't been for years."

"Is that her fault?" She remembered John Driver's description. *She's miserable. . . I can't forgive the way he treats her.* He could be so cruel, she could see that, so cutting and indifferent. She had heard it for herself on the tape. If she had been his wife and he had taunted her with his desire for someone else. . .

"It is entirely her fault," he said quietly. "I don't expect you to believe that. You're a true American liberated woman, always on the side of your own sex against the male. This time you shouldn't be. I don't owe Francesca anything."

"We're cousins," Katharine said. "Can't we just leave it like that? I don't want complications. I've very little time left before I have to go home."

"I know," he said. "That's why I can't afford to be patient. Normally I'm more subtle."

"Normally?" Katharine asked. Her tone was cool—the word

irritated her with its arrogant assumptions. She longed to be able to walk out of the restaurant, away from him, away from the whole pervasive atmosphere of his desire. She had hated him in the abstract because of her brother and what he was doing to the innocent. Now she hated him because of what he was trying to do to her.

"I don't live with Francesca," he answered. "And I certainly don't live like a monk. Does that answer your question?"

"I don't think I asked one," she spoke quickly. Nervousness made her angry.

Suddenly he laughed. "Do you realize we are nearly quarreling? Maybe that's a hopeful sign—come, I'm sorry. I won't embarrass you and spoil our evening. I brought you here to enjoy the best view in Tuscany. Drink your coffee, Katerina, and don't be angry with me."

It was the first time he had Italianized her name. She felt herself change color. *You bastard,* she said inwardly, *you know all the tricks—*

"I am enjoying myself," she said. She smiled, with a tremendous effort, thinking of Raphael and what she had to do. "You must make allowance for my American prudery. We take things a little more slowly at home than you do here."

"When are you leaving?" He thought how clear her profile was against the garden lights. She had a beautiful chin and neckline, a natural grace in the way she moved and sat still. He had taken his hand away from hers.

"I should go at the end of next week," she said. "There's something I wanted to ask you—as a favor."

"Please," he said, and he made his voice very gentle. "I would love to do something for you."

"Can I come to Malaspiga before I go? I'd love to see the castle."

"But of course! I have always wanted to show it to you. When do you want to come?"

"It should be early next week. Are you sure it wouldn't be a nuisance?"

"You have a delightful diffidence," he said. "You're full of contrasts, did you know that? Very independent, very quick to take offense, and then you ask for something like a shy little girl. We will go to Malaspiga tomorrow. All of us, so you will feel chaperoned—and I shall show you everything. Including a relation that you haven't met. Uncle Alfredo."

"You've never mentioned him—does he live there?"

"Yes," Alessandro said. "Now he does. But when things were difficult for us after the war, he was put in a home outside Massa. It was one of those places run by nuns. There aren't many of them in Italy. We haven't adopted the Anglo-Saxon habit of sending our old people out to die with strangers." He lit a cigarette.

"I brought him back to Malaspiga," he said. "I'll never forget the day I took him out of that place. He was crying, just like a child. And laughing, at the same time. I think you'll like him. He's very eccentric, but quite harmless. I know he will fall in love with you."

She tried not to look at him, because while he was speaking, he had taken her hand again, and she couldn't draw it away.

"Is he your father's brother?"

"Yes. He was always a little strange—childlike. The war upset him. He hated the Germans. My mother was always terrified he would do something to provoke them. One of the first things Francesca suggested before we married was sending him back to the convent. I wouldn't hear of it. But he knew, and he never forgave her. You're looking anxious—you needn't worry about meeting him. He's a sweet-natured old man who loves people who are kind to him. You will be kind. I know that."

"He must love you," Katharine said slowly. "For what you did for him."

"He does," Alessandro said. "He told me he'd be happy to die for me, and I believe he meant it. Even in senility, we're a passionate family." He smiled and squeezed her hand. She tried hard not to imagine the old man, weeping with gratitude and joy, as his nephew brought him home.

"He's known as the Prince of the Hats by everyone in Malaspiga. You'll know why when you meet him. But you'll love the castle. I have so many things to show you, so much history to tell you! Your history as much as mine. And some beautiful treasures. Some of the finest pictures in Italy. My father sold everything, but I have bought most of it back. I can't imagine what their value is now. Bronzino, a Giorgione . . . that was hidden in the cellars, rolled up in sacking. My mother wanted to sell it, but I wouldn't. I knew I'd make money some other way, and that when it was gone we'd regret it forever."

Make money some other way. Katharine said casually, "What about the antiques you went home to sort out? I'm fascinated to see what you sell so successfully."

It seemed to her he hesitated.

"Yes, you can see them. They are sorted and ready for packing, but that won't be done yet. They're going to the States. I have a magnificent Louis XV *poudreuse* which was discovered in a private house in Sienna. It was used for storing records—nobody even knew what it was. That's the prize piece. And you'll see some of John's work too. Did he look after you properly?"

"Yes, he was very kind," Katharine said. "We had a most interesting day going around the galleries. He's very dedicated, isn't he?"

"Completely," the Duke said. "But he doesn't believe in himself, that's the trouble. He is always dissatisfied with what he does. I suppose that is common to all great artists—only the mediocre think they've succeeded."

Katharine was glad to keep the conversation on John Driver. It served as a barrier between her and Malaspiga and all the things she knew he would say if she gave him the chance. And the consignment of furniture was not packed up. She would be taken to see it, shown everything. And then she could come back to Florence, and leave for home immediately.

"You'll love Malaspiga," he said. "The little town is very beautiful, almost untouched by the present day. It's like going back in time to live there."

"And you like that, don't you? John said you were born centuries too late." He smiled; the idea pleased him. She could see that he saw himself the same way.

"I'm not in much sympathy with our modern world," he said. "I find its way of life is very artificial. It's the age of hypocrisy, too. Everybody talks about morality when what they mean is politics. Man doesn't change all that much—he is cruel and greedy and afraid. The only thing that matters is beauty. It's the link between God and man, the imprint of Divinity upon the soul. Otherwise we're just beasts. You're very beautiful. But not in the modern way. You have an old face, Katerina. Bronzino could have painted you, with your hair in a gold net, and a dress embroidered with pearls. The more I look at you, the more I see what a true Malaspiga you are. And I'm not trying to pay you compliments now. When you come home with me you'll see for yourself."

Home. *It's a cold and gloomy place, you wouldn't like it. Firelli had gone to Malaspiga Castle and disappeared. They murdered him. We'll never find his body.*

"Are you cold? I thought you shivered . . ." He was pushing back the chair, calling for their bill.

"A little cold. We should go anyway, it's getting late."

He drove her back to her hotel, and stopped the car. She sensed that he was going to put his arm around her and she opened the door and slid out quickly. He joined her, and for a moment took her arm as they walked up to the entrance.

"I wasn't going to touch you," he said. "I promised I wouldn't spoil the evening for you."

"I didn't mean it like that," she said. She wanted to get inside the hotel, to get away from him. He was much taller than she was and she had to look up. "I loved Fiesole—it was a perfect evening."

"Then you should look happier than you do," he said quietly. "I think a change will be good for you. I'm glad I'm taking you to Malaspiga. The car will collect you tomorrow at five. Good night."

He took her hand and kissed it; before she could stop him he had turned it over and pressed her palm hard against his mouth. She ran upstairs to her room, not waiting for the elevator. The reception desk was closed and the lighting was reduced. Inside, the ugly little hotel bedroom seemed the safest, warmest place she could imagine.

When she got into bed and tried to go to sleep she began to cry.

Carpenter came out of the elevator and down the corridor at a run. There had been a maddening delay while he showed his ID at the entrance. Then both the elevators were on a different floor and he had to wait. Outside the door of Ben Harper's offices he unbuttoned his coat. It was an instinctive gesture, before facing the enemy. That way he could reach the gun in his shoulder holster. He didn't stop to answer Harper's secretary. He had an impression of her half standing up behind her desk saying something in protest, and then he was wrenching at the door of the inner office. The light was on, and he could see a shadow behind it. He knew Nathan was inside.

"Jim!" He yelled, finding the door locked. "Jim—open up!" On the other side, Nathan slammed the file drawer shut.

Katharine Dexter. And she had been gone almost two weeks.

He moved very quickly, grabbed the mike from the dictaphone and switched it on.

"Jim—open this door!"

He unlatched it and came face to face with Carpenter. He looked surprised to see him, and he gave his usual friendly grin. "Hi, Frank—what's the panic?"

Carpenter walked past him. "What the hell are you doing in Ben's office? Nobody's supposed to come in here."

Nathan shrugged. "I wanted to leave a message on his tape. It's highly confidential. So what about it?"

Carpenter didn't answer him at once. He went over to the machine, saw the little red light on for recording, and flicked the switch abruptly to play back. There was nothing on it.

"I didn't have time," Nathan explained. "You were trying to bust the door down, so I opened it. What's this all about, Frank?"

He looked pained and as if he were getting angry. As angry as any innocent man would be at the suggestion he was doing anything irregular.

"Look." Nathan pressed his advantage. "Look, what is this, Frank? I knew the rules around here when you were still in short pants!"

Suddenly Carpenter felt at a disadvantage. He had accused, tried and judged his friend on evidence that was only circumstantial. He just might have turned negligence into guilt.

"I'm sorry," he said. "Maybe I just got uptight. I've had a long day. Ben gets very edgy about anybody coming in here. He's liable to fire Betty for letting you in."

"Forget it." Nathan relaxed. He shrugged his shoulders, mocking himself as usual.

He felt in his pocket for his pipe. The movement turned him slightly, and Carpenter looked past him to the filing cabinets against the wall. He slid his hand in his coat. "Jim," he said. Nathan looked up from lighting his pipe and saw the gun.

"For Christ's sake!"

"What were you doing looking in the Malaspiga file?" Carpenter asked him. "You know that's got a highly confidential sticker on it. What were you looking for?"

"I've never touched anything in this room," Nathan exploded. "You've gone nuts! Pulling a gun on me—"

"You didn't quite shut the drawer," Carpenter said. "The

edge of the file is sticking up. You were looking for something, weren't you—something Eddy Taylor wanted to know."

"Now listen, you crazy bastard—"

"Keep your hands where I can see them," Carpenter told him. "I'm arresting you on suspicion. Go on into Betty's office. And don't try anything."

Nathan walked ahead of him. There was a rigidity to his shoulders that warned Carpenter he was thinking of going for his own gun, but the odds were too high and he did nothing. Outside the secretary saw them both and opened her mouth in amazement.

"Get me Security," Carpenter said. He didn't look at her. He knew Nathan and all he would need was a second's inattention. He had seen the file. Carpenter knew by the look in his eyes that he had got what he came for. *Katharine Dexter.* If he'd seen anything recent on the operation he must have seen that and known she'd gone to Italy. If he got away and passed that message on, she was dead.

"This is Carpenter here. I have a suspect in Ben Harper's office. Send up two men immediately."

"You're making a mistake," Nathan said. He looked white and grim. He spoke to the girl. "He's nuts," he said. "He's gone over the edge. He pulls a gun on me and says I'm under arrest . . ."

"If you're clean," Frank Carpenter said, "you can prove it. And Ben Harper will bust me for what I'm doing. Keep your hands out from your sides, Jim. If you try anything I'll shoot."

"Go fuck yourself!" Nathan turned on him, blazing. He looked like a small violent animal. Betty cringed back behind her desk.

The two security men came in and Carpenter spoke to the senior officer. "I'm booking Jim Nathan on suspicion. He's to be kept in close custody until Ben Harper gets back."

"I want a lawyer!" Nathan snarled. "What about my wife—"

"Betty will telephone her and say you've been called away on a case. You can have a lawyer when Ben says so." Nathan didn't say any more. He looked from Carpenter to the two burly security men and knew he didn't have a chance. Fear made him cautious. Fear for Marie, not for himself. If he got hurt, if he couldn't find a way, some way, of getting that message to Taylor. . . . He blinked once, as if he'd been hit, as the fear smashed at his nervous system. She would be all alone, thinking he was away on assignment. Anybody could get to her. He looked once more at Carpenter.

"You son of a shit," he said. "I'll have your ass for this!" He went out with the two men and down to the security section under the building.

Carpenter turned to the secretary.

"How long was he in there?"

"Oh, just a few minutes, Mr. Carpenter. I didn't want to let him go in, I know it's against regulations, but he said—"

"I know what he said," Frank interrupted. "Did he make any phone calls?"

"Not from this office—not since he spoke to you."

"How about while he was in Mr. Harper's office?"

"I'll ask the switchboard. You can't dial direct—"

The answer was negative. No calls had been made from Ben Harper's office since he had left that morning. Whatever Nathan had found out, he hadn't been able to pass it on. Carpenter went back into the office. The file drawer was jammed open by the right-hand corner of the Malaspiga file, where it had been hurriedly shoved back and hadn't fitted into its slot. He didn't touch it. Ben Harper would need to see what had made him arrest one of the most senior agents in the bureau. If he was wrong and Nathan could clear himself, then his own career was finished.

Ben Harper would never forgive a mistake and a scandal inside his organization. Carpenter turned back to the girl. "Lock up here and leave. Don't talk to anybody about what's happened. You'll have plenty to do explaining to Ben why you broke the rules. Don't make it worse for yourself by talking." He went out of the office and down the passage to his own room.

He wondered whether he would have taken such prompt action if Katharine Dexter hadn't been involved.

Lars Svenson was in a genial mood. He had enjoyed his trip to the States. The girls and the liquor had been provided with liberality and taste. He had found innocent amusement in tormenting the sexless Eddy Taylor by forcing his participation, and he had done a lot of business. In Stockholm he was a respected member of the rich industrial circle, with a wife and two children, a large house in the suburbs, and a cabin where the family spent weekends. He was an importer of antiques and works of art, owned a chain of retail furniture stores where cheap reproductions were sold, and was the head of a heroin smuggling ring. He had operated on a modest scale years ago, after a dubious career with the Swedish Red Cross during the war, where he discovered the purchasing power of stolen morphine. The profits accruing from his activities on the side during those years had set him up in legitimate business. His connection with the Malaspiga organization had begun two years before, through an introduction to Eddy Taylor. He had since made personal contact with the organization in Italy, and was on his way for his annual visit.

He stretched out on Eddy Taylor's sofa and yawned. He reached for a large glass of neat whiskey and swallowed grossly—he had a capacity for drink which was the equal of his appetite for sex, and he was proud of both. He was a big man, very fit, distinguished by a shock of gray-blonde hair and bright blue eyes. A lot of women thought him extremely handsome. He called to Eddy Taylor, who was fumbling in his wallet by the hallway. "Hey—haven't they gone yet?"

"Not yet," Taylor called back. Two tall, busty girls in very short skirts and white kid boots were standing by Taylor, towering over him. He paid them for the evening's entertainment, which had left him feeling sour and irritable as usual, and hustled them out of the apartment. He came back into the living room.

"They've gone," he said. "Pity." The Swede grinned. "I could have done it again."

"Christ," Taylor groaned. "One of these days it'll drop off! You ready for another drink?"

"In a minute." Svenson waved the glass. "Sit down—stop fussing. You make me jumpy." He watched Taylor ease himself into a chair. He was a man who did everything carefully, with an old-maidish economy of movement. He wriggled to get comfortable and crossed his small feet at the ankles. Svenson despised him and enjoyed battening on him for free meals, drinks, and sex parties. In his eyes, Taylor was less than a man. Less even than a practicing homosexual. That he would have understood and accepted. At least it was active. His blue eyes went narrow, and suddenly the broad, strong face was wiped clean of its bonhomie.

"You realize it's Friday night," he said to Taylor. "What's this policeman think he's doing?"

"He should have called today," Taylor said. "I gave him till tonight. I told him you were leaving Saturday morning."

"One thing's for sure," Svenson said. "I'm not taking any shipment at my end if there's a bureau agent on their track. And I shall tell them so when I get there! They won't be pleased with you. You're responsible for the New York end."

"I know that," Taylor snapped back at him. His nerves were raw from lack of sleep, too much drinking, which disagreed with him, and the ghastly evening spent with Svenson and the departed whores. He felt ready to quarrel with anyone. Svenson didn't frighten him; he was only a middleman like himself, although an important one. But at Malaspiga, far away in Tuscany, there was someone of whom he was very frightened indeed. "I'm going to call his home," he said. "Right now." He went to the telephone, dialed the number and almost immediately the other end answered.

"Could I speak to Jim Nathan? Oh, he's not? Who am I talking to?" Svenson watched his back. Under the beautifully cut jacket, the shoulder muscles tensed. "I see. You couldn't tell me where? Okay. No, it doesn't matter. I'll try next week." He banged the receiver down and the phone jangled. His face was contorted. "He's out of town! That was his wife—he's been sent away on an assignment, and she doesn't know where he is, or when he'll be back!"

"He's stalling," Svenson remarked. He finished his whiskey. "He can't get the information, and he's run out on you."

"The bastard." Taylor almost spat. "By Christ, I'll teach him not to cross me—"

"Maybe the call'll come through tonight. It's only eleven."

"He's out of town," Taylor shouted. "He's run for it—you just said so!"

"It looks that way," Svenson said. "Maybe you should have paid him."

"I'll pay him," Taylor said. "I'll pay him just exactly what I promised!" He swung on one foot, neatly like a ballet dancer, and went for the phone again.

"What are you doing?" Svenson asked.

"Mind your own goddamned business!" The Swede shrugged. He got up and went to the cabinet where Taylor kept his drinks. It was a seventeenth-century Spanish Vargueno, beautifully inlaid with ivory. A strong Moorish influence, Svenson noted, fingering the elaborate iron hinges. He poured a massive Scotch into his glass. He heard Taylor's voice, rising with anger.

"You get over there tomorrow. And you fix her good, understand! Don't let this one get away! Okay—no beating up, no rough stuff, just fix her!" The phone jangled again. He turned to Svenson.

"Nobody crosses me and gets away with it," he said. He let out a deep breath. "You have an early start in the morning," he said coolly. "I don't want to be inhospitable, Lars, but I'm worn out myself."

"I'll finish this, and then I'll go. What do I tell them at Malaspiga?"

"Tell them there's going to be a replacement for Firelli," Taylor said. "I can't give them any more details than that, but to be on their guard against strangers. Anyone turning up unexpectedly, no matter what the cover story. Any time in the next few weeks. My guess is it'll be someone posing as a distributor. They won't try another antique dealer again. Tell them I'll try and find out what I can, but my contact inside has gone sour on me." The plump little face was pinched and spiteful. "The bastard," he said, not really speaking to Svenson, "that'll teach him . . ."

"Okay." The whiskey disappeared in two huge swallows. "I'll pass on your messages. And thanks for all the good times, Eddy. I've really enjoyed myself. I'll have to be a good boy when I get to Malaspiga. There's nothing like you have over here." He came and grasped Taylor's hand in his big fist, squeezed it, and thumped him on the shoulder. "Goodbye," he said. "If anything does come through, call me at the hotel. I shan't be moving till I go to the airport."

Taylor saw him to the door. He snapped out the lights in the living room and hallway, and went to his bedroom. He undressed, neatly folding his clothes, discarding shirt and underwear to be laundered, and crawled into bed. He felt sick and tense. It was all very well for that randy Swede to take it calmly—he wasn't in danger, nobody was on his tail. Everything Taylor had built up for himself was in jeopardy— a big bank account in Switzerland, a thriving business, and a beautiful apartment, full of the treasures he loved. Whoever the bureau was sending out to investigate at Malaspiga, must inevitably lead to him if they succeeded. He had already been screened once, but then it was Nathan asking the questions and telling the lies. Nathan, his safeguard, who'd disappeared when he was most needed. Taylor said several obscene words, quite unconnected. It was his way of swearing, and for some reason it gave him satisfaction. He disliked taking any-thing, but he knew he'd lie awake, fretting and worrying all night. A few minutes later he was asleep, his mouth ajar, his hands folded meekly under his cheek like a small boy.

"I want a lawyer," Nathan said. "And I want to talk to my wife!"

"You're not talking to anybody, Jim," Carpenter said. There was a small wooden table between them, its legs screwed to the floor. Nathan faced him, pale and red eyed, snarling defiance.

"I know my rights," Nathan shouted. "I'm not some poor son of a bitch off the street who doesn't know the law! You can't hold me like this!"

"I'm holding you till Ben gets back," Carpenter said. "If I'm wrong, he'll nail my ears to the office wall, and you can swing the hammer. But I'm not wrong, Jim. You're bent and I know it. Why don't you stop yelling and tell me the truth. Why are you covering up for Eddy Taylor?"

"I'm not covering for anyone." Nathan glared at him. "You're out of your mind!"

"I've checked on Taylor," Carpenter said quietly. "He's connected to the people at the head of this smuggling ring. There's no doubt of it. So you aren't helping yourself by lying. He's a pusher, and we've got proof."

Nathan jerked his chin. "You know what you can do with it! You know something, Frank? I thought you were a right guy—I really liked you. Now you turn out to be the biggest bastard I've ever met in my whole life! How do you think my wife feels? Haven't you any fucking decency, any feelings?"

"Your wife was sent a message yesterday," Carpenter said. "She isn't worried. You're the one that's worried, Jim. Why? What are you scared of?"

Nathan didn't answer. He covered his face with one hand. There was no sweat. His skin was dry and hot, his eyes felt as if there were hot coals in the sockets. All he had to do was get a message out. He'd worked out the words, he knew exactly what to say. It was Friday evening. Fear gripped him so tightly it became a physical pain, torturing the muscles of his stomach. Friday. If he didn't get that message to Taylor, Eddy might carry out his threat. If he gave in to Carpenter and confessed, his wife would still be in danger. He wasn't impressed by police protection. A few weeks of surveillance that grew less effective as time passed. A move to a new district, a succession of addresses. And Taylor's vengeance following stealthily behind her, with her husband in jail and nobody to care for her, to stand guard . . .

He looked up. Carpenter waited.

"Okay," he said. "I'll make a deal."

"No deals," Carpenter said flatly. "You're not holding any cards."

"I'm holding more than you know," Jim Nathan said. "A hell of a lot more. You want to bust this, don't you? It means a lot to you. Okay. You make a deal with me, and I'll give you everything you need. And something extra."

"What's the deal?"

"Let me talk to my wife."

Frank lit a cigarette. He looked at Nathan. "You'd spill everything just for that? Just to talk to Marie? Why?"

"That's my business." Nathan was calm now—he had stopped shouting. It was a gamble only a desperate man would have contemplated, a hopeless, crazy million-to-one chance. But he had to take it. If he could get Carpenter to agree. He shook his head suddenly. Twelve years of friendship must count for something. Carpenter was tough, but he wasn't inhuman. In his place Nathan wouldn't have fallen for it, but he had to believe Frank would. That was the first part of the gamble. The second came later.

"I won't let you talk to Marie unless you tell me why," he said. "As far as a deal is concerned, I can't promise anything. That's Ben's decision."

"She's pregnant," Nathan said slowly. "That's why. The doctor says she's due to have the kid at any moment. She ought to go stay with my brother. I want to talk to her, make sure she isn't worried."

"Why didn't you say so before?" Carpenter said. "You stupid clown, why didn't you tell me?"

"Because I was mad," Nathan said. "Nobody likes getting caught. Let me talk to her, Frank. Just for old times' sake. You can stand right beside me and hear every word. For Christ's sake—she isn't strong . . . if anything happened and she was all alone in that apartment—the doctor wouldn't let me tell her in case it got her scared and brought it on . . . I want her to go my brother. Right away. Tonight."

"It's past eleven. Won't she be in bed?"

"She watches the late show Friday nights," Nathan said. "She can call a cab and get over there."

"And then you'll talk about Eddy Taylor?"

"I'll talk about him and a few others," Nathan said. "Just as soon as I've made the call."

Carpenter got up. "Okay," he said. "You can call from my office. The regular switchboard's shut by now."

Two security men were in the office with them. Nathan took his place behind Frank's desk, and picked up the phone; he pressed the switch to give him an outside line. He knew the figures by heart. It was one of the latest push-button machines. He looked up at Carpenter, who was standing beside him; his fingers flew over the tiny buttons as he held the other man's attention.

"Thanks, Frank. I appreciate this." The ringing began.

Taylor was deep in sleep. By the side of his bed the telephone shrilled, impinging on his dream. The sound screamed in his unconscious, clamoring for recognition. He threw himself on his side, fighting the noise.

In Carpenter's office, Nathan waited. Now he was sweating, trickles were running down his neck and flooding his armpits. It seemed like hours instead of seconds while the ringing went on and on, and there was no answer. This would be the final irony, the kick in the groin delivered by a malicious fate. He had got to the telephone, dialed the number undetected, and now Taylor wasn't in . . .

"She must be asleep," Carpenter said. Nathan cupped his hand over the mouthpiece.

"Sometimes she has the set on loud," he said.

Finally the ringing triumphed over the mild barbiturate Taylor had taken. Groaning, he rolled over to the side of the bed where the telephone stood, and fumbling in the darkness, unhooked it. "Hello—"

Nathan could have shouted with relief.

"Honey? This is your husband, Jim Nathan—remember me?" He couldn't hear anything but a mumble, and he didn't dare hesitate. "How are you? Sure, fine, fine. Just for a few days. Listen, I want you to go over and stay with Bud . . ."

Holding the receiver, Taylor dragged himself up in the bed. Nathan. It was Nathan on the line, talking gibberish . . . He fought off the comatose feeling and tried to concentrate. The voice went on. "Look after you, honey. Sure. I'll be home soon." For a moment he thought it was a crossed line and that the conversation was taking place between Nathan and his wife. Then he realized there was no answering voice. Nathan was talking to himself. Taylor cleared his throat. "Nathan—what the hell is this?"

"Yeah," Nathan went on talking. "I wanted to call you before, but I was busy. Listen, honey. I know it's going to be a girl. Understand that? A girl. And we'll call her Katharine." He paused. Frank Carpenter saw that he was smiling. Something in his head went off like a rocket. He reached out for the phone, but Nathan was quicker. He hung up. "Thanks," he said. "I feel a whole lot better now. She'll be okay."

Taylor clicked on his lamp; the receiver hung crookedly on its cradle where he'd replaced it in the darkness. He put it straight. Now the sensation of drowsiness was clearing. As he appreciated the significance of the last exchange in that garbled telephone call, he jerked upright. *I know it's going to be a girl. Understand that. A girl. And we'll call her Katharine.* That was the message he'd been expecting. Nathan's tone had been precise, emphatic. He must have made the call under great difficulty. A girl. The agent was a woman, and the name was Katharine. Taylor got out of bed. He felt slightly dizzy, and there was a thick taste in his mouth. He poured some more mineral water and drank it. Damn pill. They were the weakest prescribed, but it was still confusing him. He repeated the message to hold on to it. There were two things he had to do. Contact Svenson. And something else. He yawned, and sat down on the edge of the bed. Svenson. He would be at his hotel. He looked at his watch, and found it difficult to focus. It was a Piaget with a lapis face. He had given it to himself the previous Christmas. He thought good accessories were important. It was almost midnight. Svenson would be asleep, but that didn't matter. He was leaving very early in the morning. Taylor wanted to go to sleep himself, but he had to make that call first. Svenson was staying at the Plaza. He couldn't remember the number. He got out the directory, found it, and dialed.

"Who did you call?" Carpenter had Nathan up against the wall. He hadn't hit him, because he knew instinctively that the truth couldn't be beaten out of him.

"My wife," Nathan said.

"I've just spoken to her. She had no call from you. Who was on the other end of that line? It was Taylor, wasn't it?"

Nathan made the same obscene suggestion as he had when he was first arrested, and Carpenter smashed his fist into Jim's face. He sagged but didn't fall. Blood oozed from his nose. He wiped it with his hand.

"You'll have to do better than that," he said. Carpenter took him at his word. Before he finally lost consciousness, Nathan's last thought was that no matter what happened to him, his wife wouldn't be harmed.

Taylor heard the doorbell ringing just as he was about to make a second phone call. He had remembered what he had to do after speaking to Svenson, who sounded sleepy and irritable when he woke him. Nathan had come through. He had to call the "rent collectors" off his wife. The doorbell rang long and stridently, and was suddenly accompanied by loud knocking. Taylor hesitated. Instinct told him what was outside. He had no way of escape. But they wouldn't find anything. There was nothing in the apartment, nothing in the shop below. He never kept anything or wrote anything down. His nerves were dulled by the sleeping pill, and he stayed calm. He put on a red silk dressing gown, slid his small feet into Gucci slippers and went to the door. "Who's there?"

"Federal agents. Open up!" The door, like all entrances in New York apartments, was on a bolt and a chain. He slipped the bolt back and opened it until the chain caught and held the door.

"I want to see your identification," he said. "How do I know you're FBI—" The ID card was thrust through the opening and then withdrawn.

"You open the door," a voice said, "or we'll break it in."

Taylor opened it. Twenty minutes later he was in Carpenter's office, demanding to call his lawyer and refusing to answer any questions. He had never made the telephone call to reprieve Marie Nathan.

5

Malaspiga was a fifteenth-century town about a hundred and fifty kilometers from Florence. It clung to the skirts of a massive hill, green with olive trees and spiked by clusters of the tall cypresses that abounded in the area. The little town had grown around its base—pink and dusty yellow houses, roofed in Tuscan red tiles, with the church and the long finger of the Campanile housing its bronze bell dominating everything. The car drove through narrow streets, rough-paved and without sidewalks; the houses leaned toward each other, closing out the light. There was a little piazza with a statue, a man in armor on a stylized prancing horse. Katharine didn't need to see the inscription to know that it was a Duke of Malaspiga. The Duchess Francesca was with her, John Driver drove. A second car with a uniformed chauffeur in front, preceded them through the winding streets. The Duke and his mother sat together in the back. Katharine sensed that a return to the castle was part of a ritual. It was a procession of a feudal lord, and it moved at an appropriate pace. She saw people saluting the front car, and sev-

eral of the children waved and called after it. Whatever they
were to the outside world, the Malaspigas were popular among
their own. They left the town behind and began a steep
climb up the side of the hill. It was a wide road, and im-
peccably surfaced; the drop on their right became more pre-
cipitous as they went higher. She turned to Francesca, who
had been silent for most of the journey. "Is the castle at the
top?"

"Yes. You could have seen it from the substrada. I should
have pointed it out."

John spoke from the front. "I feel like Jack climbing the
beanstalk every time I come here. Wait till you see it—"

"I hope you brought some warm clothes." The kohl-painted
eyes looked at her with blank hostility. "It gets very cold in
the evening."

"Thanks, I'll be all right." Katharine turned away and
looked out of the window. She had never been in close
proximity to her cousin's wife before. During the two-hour
drive she had an impression of coldness and bitterness which
was unpleasant even if it was excusable. The woman hated
her, and Katharine understood why. But it was a chill hatred,
the emotion of someone who felt in ice rather than fire.
Whereas there was fire in Alessandro—hot pride, temper,
sensual passion. She thought suddenly that he must have found
it impossible to love such a woman, and then reproached herself angrily for making this excuse. Far below she caught
sight of the town and realized how high they were; it looked
like a doll's village.

"Don't you like heights?" She saw John watching her in
the mirror.

"I don't mind them. I don't like looking over the edge, but
otherwise it doesn't bother me."

"I thought you were looking a bit sick," he said. "We're
nearly there." A few moments later they rounded a sweep
in the road and came upon a massive stone arch which was
part of a wall. She saw the Malaspiga arms carved above
the dark mouth of the gateway. The wreath and the malev-

olent spike growing out of the corn. It was stark and cruel in the ancient stone. Impulsively she covered the ring on her own finger with her left hand, as if she could ward off something evil.

Out of the darkness of the gateway and into a huge courtyard. The castle itself rose like an illustration from a history book, so huge and tall, with its square turrets and cliff-high walls, that she exclaimed. The Canadian looked around and grinned at her. "I told you! It's quite something—"

Francesca di Malaspiga turned toward him. "It's a place where the stones cry out," she said. "I hate it."

A manservant in a dusty black suit had come toward the car. He opened the door for the Duchess. Katharine followed; the sun was going down, staining the sky above the battlements with red. Alessandro's car was parked ahead of them. Nobody came to her or said anything. She stood for a moment looking around her at the great fortress of her ancestors, its stones bloodied by the sunset, and a sense of cold fatality came over her.

"Katerina," his voice said by her side. "Welcome to Malaspiga." She turned and saw him standing close, smiling down at her. He slipped his hand through her arm. Raphael had warned her he would kill her without mercy.

Something very old woke in her heart, a sense of dignity before danger, of the contemptuous acceptance of death. It did not belong to Katharine Dexter and the New World across the ocean. She smiled into the face above her.

"It's magnificent," she said. "But if I wasn't a Malaspiga myself I think I'd be afraid." Still holding his arm, she went inside. The old Duchess had gone upstairs to rest before dinner. She had complained angrily about having to leave her comfortable villa, but her son had insisted. He never raised his voice to her or showed any sign of anger, but she knew that she would give in and do what he wanted. It was inevitable, and she didn't feel anything but a fleeting resentment. All her life she had been bending to the dictates of men; at the same time as she was working to have her own way whenever possible. When he explained why they were going, she had tried to protest.

"Why does she have to stay—couldn't she go down with John for the day and come back again? Surely all this inconvenience isn't necessary just to show her the castle . . ." He hadn't listened. He had reminded her, in his courteous way, of the hospitality they owed a blood relation and the need for his family to chaperone her. As a result, they were all at Malaspiga, and after the car journey the old Duchess was exhausted. She rested on her bed for half an hour, wrapped up in a warm woolen gown, edged with a thick border of swansdown, and fastened with a diamond pin. Her pink rose was propped in a glass on the dressing table—a fresh one for the evening was wrapped in wet tissue and foil. She turned her head on the pillows; everything she used was embroidered or edged with lace. It had been so all her life. Delicacy was part of a gentlewoman's equipment. Nothing rough or coarse must touch her, unless it were a man. She had thought of her daughter-in-law and the sculptor while she dozed. Her mouth curled with sensual memories from her own past, induced by remembering the voices in Francesca's room. She couldn't imagine her daughter-in-law as a man's lover. She couldn't see that cold face upturned to a hungry kiss. But then nobody knew or understood the girl, or had ever taken the trouble to find out what she was really like. She was childless and abandoned by Alessandro, and that was all anybody thought about her. Perhaps now that she had become the young man's mistress, she might achieve serenity. A knock at her door awoke her.

It was her son. She moved upward on her pillows and smiled at him. She had always smiled at men, even if she wasn't particularly pleased to see them.

"Mother. I hope you're not too tired. Did you sleep?"

He sat beside her on the bed, and took her hand. It was unlike him to be demonstrative, and she was surprised. She didn't much like holding his hand, but she refrained from drawing it away. And she was curious to know what he wanted.

He knew perfectly well that she was tired, because she had said so when they arrived, and he also knew she always slept if she lay down.

"A little tired." She gave him a lovely smile. "It was sweet of you to come and see. You're already changed."

He wore a dark blue velvet coat, with a silk scarf around his neck. Perhaps Francesca's jealousy wasn't so silly after all. He was a remarkable looking man. "Where is the cousin?" she said. "Americans don't like changing their clothes before dinner. They think it's old-fashioned."

"I explained it was our custom," he said. "It didn't surprise her. I want you to promise me something, Mamia."

"Yes?" This was why he had come, of course.

"Be very nice to Katerina," the Duke said. "Make her feel happy and at home. I particularly want this. I want her to relax."

"Then you shouldn't have brought her here," she said. "This is no place for seduction, my son. You ought to know better."

He let her hand go. "You shouldn't talk like that," he said quietly. "It's not becoming."

His mother shrugged; the diamonds on her wrapper glittered in the light. "I'm too old to be a hypocrite," she said. "And much too old for family scenes. You've formed some plan for this girl, Sandro. If it isn't seduction then what is it? You've never behaved like this with any of the others. Why bring her here, to the castle? Why come and ask me to be nice to her, as if I didn't know how to behave in my own home? What is between you—are you already lovers?"

"No," he said. "We are not. I just want her to enjoy her stay. I hoped you'd help."

"Sit down," she said quickly. "Don't go away angry. I'll do what you want, *caro*. I like you to be happy. If you want her, then I'll make it easy for you. But I must warn you. This girl isn't like the others. They understood the situation. She doesn't. She could be very troublesome. Think very carefully before you get yourself involved."

"You don't understand, Mamia," he said gently. "But it

doesn't matter. Just do as I ask. Be very nice to her. Because I ask you. I'll see you downstairs."

When Katharine came into the small salon, she thought at first that nobody else had come down. She felt nervous and expectant, as if something significant were going to happen. Her bedroom was filled with flowers. The hand of Alessandro was unmistakable; they were all roses and out of season. As she came into the room, she heard a noise behind her and turned quickly. A tall old man was standing directly in line with the door. He had been sitting in an armchair placed to the left of it, so that when anyone entered the room he was invisible. Almost as tall as Alessandro, with a beautiful head, crowned by thick white hair, and perched on top of it, an ancient fez with a black silk tassel. He didn't move; he stood and looked at her, and on the patrician face there was the shy expectancy of a child. Katharine came toward him and held out her hand.

"Uncle Alfredo?" He nodded. "I am your cousin, Katharine. I am so glad to meet you."

The smile was like a sunburst. He put his head back, with the incongruous Eastern hat, its tassel swinging, and gave a loud laugh of delight.

He took her hand, bowed, kissed it, and then shook it.

"The pleasure is mine, my dear! All mine. Alessandro told me about you. But he didn't say how beautiful you were! You remind me so much of someone . . . I can't remember who. No matter. No matter. Will you sit down? Excellent! Excuse me. I shan't be a moment. Then we can have a little talk. Before the family comes down. Before *she* can try and send me up to my room."

The smile had gone. He scowled, but it only made him look pathetic. "I hate her," he said simply. "But Alessandro protects me. I shan't be long!" Katharine walked to a chair by the fireplace and sat down. When the door opened a moment later, the old Duchess came toward her, swathed in dark green velvet, and behind her was John Driver. In the background, hovering near the doorway, she saw Alfredo di

Malaspiga. She understood the local nickname. He had replaced the fez with a British solar topee.

Dinner was a long, formal meal, taken in a small stone room untouched since the fifteenth century. The only concession to the present was the strip lighting over a superb Gothic tapestry. They ate by candlelight; the manservant who had met them on arrival was wearing white livery and gloves, and he served the food with a slowness that grated on Katharine's nerves.

She looked around the table, and the faces seemed to belong to people from another age. Francesca, so pale and dark, seldom speaking and never seen to smile; her mother-in-law, beautiful as a girl in the dim light, Alessandro, seated like a medieval prince at the head of the table, watching over them, paying special attention to her, the bland, senile smile of Uncle Alfredo as he chattered to John Driver; the sense of unreality was sinister, as if she were playing her part in a charade. The conversation was general, and trivial—much of it referred to local people and affairs she didn't understand. She saw that the eccentric old man was watching her, and pretending not to. While he talked to Driver he kept glancing quickly at her and then away if she looked up. She got the impression he was much less unbalanced than he appeared. There was a furtive intelligence he couldn't quite hide, a look that was at variance with his parade of senility. When they left the table he came up to her; his vacant smile was ready, and she responded, waiting for him to speak. "How do you like my hat?"

"I think it's very unusual," Katharine said. He nodded.

"It was given to me by an Englishman, years and years ago. He knew I liked collecting different kinds of hats. I have over sixty—what do you think of that?"

"Marvelous," she said. They were the last to leave the room, and she could see her cousin waiting for her just beyond the doorway.

"You're nice," the old man said in a suddenly low voice. "I like you. Be very careful here. I'm not such a fool as people think." Then he bowed and stepped back to let her pass. The warning was repeated in a whisper as she went toward the Duke.

"Be very careful . . ."

Ben Harper had been called back from Washington. He took over the interrogation of Taylor, and found he was having no more success than Carpenter. He had a brief interview with Nathan. Nothing hit him as hard as a crooked agent, and what he said was short and bitter.

"You'll get the maximum," he told him. Nathan jeered, his bruised face full of ugly defiance.

"You've got nothing on me," he said. "You can threaten till you drop dead!"

"We'll prove it," Harper promised him. "We'll prove it because we'll break Taylor. He'll end up hanging you to save himself."

But Taylor was unexpectedly resilient. He knew his rights and he insisted on them. Neither Carpenter nor his chief could get him to admit to any connection with the Malaspigas or to knowing Nathan. Unlike many engaged in pushing heroin, he was not frightened by the sentences involved in turning state's witness and betraying his fellows. He sat in Harper's office, very pale and agitated, insisting that he see his lawyer and refusing to say anything.

Carpenter was called into Harper's office as Taylor was taken away. "Any luck?"

"Nothing. He's clammed up tight. We can't hold him much longer without getting a lawyer—the same goes for Nathan. You shouldn't have beaten him up, Frank."

"I should have killed him," Carpenter said. "If you'd stood there and listened while he passed on the message about Kate, and seen the smile on his face when he'd done it. Why don't you let me try Taylor? Give me half an hour alone with him and I'll get it out of him! We've got to know if that message has gone one stage further and got to Italy!"

"He couldn't have called, there wasn't time between Nathan's tip-off and his arrest. We checked with International, there was a three-hour delay in calls to Italy at that hour. Relax, Frank. I don't think there was any way he could have got a message through."

"I didn't think there was any way for Nathan to pass it on, either, but there was," Carpenter said. "They'll kill her, just like they killed Firelli!"

"Give it time," Harper said. "We'll use one against the other; somebody will crack. My money's on Taylor. I'll wait ten minutes till he thinks the heat's off and I'll bring him in again. You can sit in on it, if you like. But no heavy stuff."

"I think we should contact Interpol; somebody should get Kate out of there!"

"And wreck what she's doing? You'd have Raphael up there with a squad of *carabiniere,* and there wouldn't be a grain of heroin in any shipment—they're not fools. There's nothing we can do about her till we know whether that message stopped with Taylor. If it *was* Taylor he called. Let's hope so."

"I know it was." Carpenter lit a cigarette, the knuckles of his right hand red and puffy. "If anything happens to her—"

"You shouldn't have got involved," Harper said slowly. "It's going to make it very rough for you if we have to let Taylor walk out of here. And so far there's nothing we can charge him with—the same goes for Nathan. We know they're in it, but we haven't any proof. We're stretching the law by holding either of them. Stop thinking about Kate. Get us both a cup of coffee, and then we'll give Taylor another workout."

He looked at his watch as Carpenter went out to the coffee machine in the corridor. It was ten twenty-eight. They could stall on the lawyer till late afternoon. It didn't give them enough time and he knew it.

Over on Eastern Parkway, Marie Nathan was ironing her husband's shirts. She had finished cleaning the apartment and done some shopping for herself by ten fifteen. She made coffee and set up the ironing board. She laundered everything for him by hand—she wouldn't allow him to wear drip-dry shirts.

She didn't understand why Frank Carpenter had called her so late the previous night asking if she'd heard from Jim. She didn't understand why she hadn't heard, because if he was ever away from home he always telephoned her. Carpenter had been reassuring. There was nothing to worry about. He must be very tied up. She tried not to worry and woke up early the next morning. She cleaned the apartment extra carefully, and comforted herself by doing his laundry. She loved housework and enjoyed a routine. So much of her life had been spent in shiftless wandering and casual jobs—no settled home, no future, no background. Only heroin to offer an escape route. The glow at the end of life's dark tunnel had been the entrance to hell. Nathan had made her see that. He had loved her and saved her. She would have laid down and died for him.

The bell rang at ten forty-five. In reply to her question through the door, a man said, "FBI, Mrs. Nathan. We've got a message from your husband." There were two of them—medium height, lightweight suits, soft hats they didn't remove. She looked at them in turn.

"Jim? Has anything happened to Jim . . ."

One of them closed the front door, and the second one said quietly, "Now don't be alarmed, Mrs. Nathan," before he grabbed her around the shoulders and slapped adhesive tape across her mouth. He was very strong, and her resistance was pathetic. She kicked and flailed while he pulled her into the bedroom and threw her on the bed. He sat on her legs and held her down. The other man had a leather wallet open on the dressing table. Marie's eyes followed him, and behind the stifling tape she tried to scream and scream as she saw the hypodermic. They dragged her arm out, and the second man tied a rubber band around it to raise a vein.

They held her for a moment or two until it was ready. Then he put the needle in. She gave a violent jerk, and the man holding her down laughed. "Baby," he said. "You're going to love it." He got up and they looked down at her. She didn't try to move; she lay as if she were dead. Her eyes were closed and tears were creeping under the lids and running down her face. The man who had injected her reached down and pulled off the tape from her mouth. He packed up his hypodermic and put the wallet away.

"I guess it's hit her already," he said. "Let's get the hell out of here." Somewhere in her mind she heard them go. The slam of the front door registered.

She crawled up on the bed. The sensation was familiar, terrifying in its intensity. *Jim.* She heard her own voice, a whisper, coming from lips that were raw. She was very thin and the rough handling had bruised her. She didn't feel anything. *Jim.* She had to get to him—she had to get help. She fought the inertia as far as the front door. When she got it open and started down the short stair to the street, she had forgotten where she was going and why.

Lars Svenson arrived in Rome at three o'clock in the morning Italian time. He enjoyed flying, although long journeys bored him, but he had found a congenial companion in the next seat, a director of a textile firm who was also going to Rome. He had tried telephoning Florence from the airport, but there was no connection through the exchange. Svenson was due to take the route via Pisa, and then on to Florence by car the next day. But Taylor's message couldn't wait.

The agent would be a woman named Katharine. He roused a sleepy telephone operator at his hotel and tried again. This time he got through to the exchange, but there was no reply at the villa. He slept uneasily for a few hours and then made another call—a call frustrating even by Italian telephonic standards. The phone was eventually answered by a servant who didn't understand his accent and kept repeating that the

Duke was not at home. It was some time before Svenson could persuade him to tell him where he had gone.

The Duke was expected at the castle later that day. He could telephone then. Svenson didn't need the number. He had been to the castle twice before: the inspection of furniture and sculpture had been accompanied by an invitation to stay the night.

He ordered an enormous meal, a combined breakfast and lunch, which the hotel provided after a considerable delay, and then began the difficult assault on the Tuscan telephone exchange at Massa, through which calls were passed to the town and the castle at Malaspiga. Through a storm of crackling, and a fade-out on the line he heard that the Duke and his party had gone out. A voice suggested that he ring before dinner. Cursing the apathy and inefficiency of all things Italian, Svenson slammed down the phone. With no hope of reaching anyone for several hours, he went out into the afternoon sunshine of Rome.

Katharine woke early. Her room was on the first floor overlooking the range of the Apuane Alps at the rear of the castle.

The mountains were snow white in the morning sunshine; jagged peaks reached six thousand feet into the blue sky, their summits hidden by clouds. There was a grandeur about mountains which had always appealed to her, but the dazzling range at Malaspiga was cold and dangerous, glittering with the sheen of the famous Carrara marble. Michelangelo himself had come to the marble mountains to choose the materials for his greatest works. Below them the countryside was green, swollen with hills; the castle was on the top above the little town, a monument to the arrogance and power of the family that had built it. Who held Malaspiga was master of the plain and the Versilia, that narrow strip of land running parallel to the sea.

The air was very clear. When she opened the window it

was cold and she shivered. They were much higher up than appearances suggested. She had slept unevenly, waked by ugly dreams; she couldn't forget that hurried whisper as she left the dining room. *Be very careful.* The old Prince, with his mania for hats, was certainly eccentric, but in his own words, not nearly the fool he was supposed to be. *I like you.* She believed that, too. The little attentions she'd paid him had been appreciated. And he had tried to warn her, even as her cousin stepped toward her, and took her by the hand. After dinner they took coffee in the small salon; she had avoided Alessandro and managed not to sit near him. She had been aware of the young Duchess watching her with a hatred that couldn't be concealed, and of Driver, hovering between them, trying to distract Francesca's attention. At one moment he had come up to Katharine on the pretext of lighting a cigarette, and whispered to her.

"If you want to go back to Florence tomorrow, I'll drive you."

"Thanks," Katharine had murmured back. "I'll be all right."

"I wasn't thinking of you," he had answered. "He had no right to bring you here." He had turned away, and she found the Duke looking down at her, smiling. She wondered whether he had heard. When she went upstairs she turned the key in her bedroom door. There had been a look on Alessandro's face that made her fear she might wake to find him in her room.

She had listened very carefully to all the conversation, noting the names of the servants, hoping to hear that single clue left behind by Firelli. *Angelo.* It was such a common Italian name, but finding out about it had caused his death. She had heard nothing. The bedroom was furnished with a seventeenth-century walnut bed, massive chests and a ceiling-high cupboard, its doors painted with the coat of arms. A mirror in a gilt Florentine frame showed her the reflection of a woman in a white dressing gown who looked like a ghost in the dark background. She didn't want breakfast, and nobody had mentioned any plan for the morning. She dressed in slacks, a silk shirt and a long cardigan, and went downstairs. She found Francesca waiting in the hallway, dressed in sober navy blue with a hat framing a face that was even paler and more expressionless than the day before. She glanced at Katharine.

"We are going to Mass," she said. "I think it would be better if you wore a skirt. They're very old-fashioned here."

"That won't be necessary, as I'm not going," Katharine said. "I don't go to church anymore."

"I see." The Duchess turned away and picked up her gloves and a Missal. "Sandro won't be pleased. He likes the family to go."

"I'm sorry about that," she said. "But he'll just have to excuse me."

"And what will I have to excuse you?" He had come up behind them; he moved very quietly. He came to Katharine and put a hand on her shoulder. He bent down and touched her cheek with his lips.

"I hope you slept well," he said. "You looked tired last night."

"Your cousin doesn't want to come to Mass," his wife said.

"I'd rather not," Katharine said to him. She was prepared for a struggle of wills. He dominated the women in his family so completely that he wouldn't expect anyone to say no to him. "I haven't been for years. I'd feel a terrible hypocrite."

"Then there's no problem," he said quietly. "You shall do exactly as you like. John isn't a Catholic, but he comes with us. He can go this morning, and I shall stay and keep you company."

"If you're staying at home, then why can't I?" Francesca spoke suddenly. There was a flush on her cheeks like two bright smudges of rouge. "You make me go when you know how I feel about it!"

"I know all about your feelings," the Duke said. "But you are my wife and you cannot parade your atheism to the town. My mother has never missed Mass in sixty years."

"Good morning." They turned as John Driver came up to

them. He glanced from Alessandro to Francesca, and his smile grew tight. He stepped near to her.

"I'm coming to Mass with you. Is everybody ready?"

"Katharine and I are staying behind," Malaspiga said. "Would you go and call Mamia and Uncle Alfredo?" There was no mistake about his tone. She saw the look of hatred that crossed Driver's face before he turned to do as he was told. "We'll see you off," the Duke said, as they assembled in the hall. The old Duchess looked frail and exquisite in misty blue, a tiny spotted veil over the brim of her hat added to the illusion of youth. A huge star sapphire gripped her pink rose to her shoulder. The uncle seemed glum and abstracted. He wore a simple panama hat and carried a cloth cap in his right hand. The old Duchess gave Katharine a smile and kissed her hand to her as they drove away. For a moment she and the Duke stood side by side in the courtyard. The sun was hot and high even at the early hour. She shielded her eyes against it.

"You shouldn't have stayed with me," Katharine said. "You're making it so obvious. It's upsetting your wife terribly." Suddenly something broke the restraint she had put on herself. She swung on him. "How could you be so cruel to her! I shouldn't have come here!"

"You asked me to bring you," he said. For a moment, blinded by an emotion that was struggling to evade control, Katharine had forgotten that. Forgotten why . . .

"And I'm not cruel to Francesca. In Italy it is the custom for the women of the family to go to Mass. On all important feasts and many Sundays I go with them. If Francesca stays away, it causes scandal. She knows that as well as I do."

He took her arm and she stiffened. "Don't be angry. Let's enjoy our morning together. There are some lovely walks, if you'd like that."

She didn't want to walk. She didn't want to go through the silver-gray olive groves and climb the terraced hills with him beside her, knowing that in some secret place they would stop, and he would try and take her in his arms. She couldn't be free of the sweet air and the blue skies. They were part of the heritage which was fighting for her recognition, as deadly as the desire which flowed from him, drawing her like a magnetic force. She turned to face him, forcing herself to smile.

"I don't feel like going outside," she said. "Why don't you show me the antiques? I'd love to see this famous *poudreuse* you've discovered."

Once again he seemed somehow reluctant. Then, "Of course," he said. "If it would amuse you. I'd like to look at it again myself. It was a fantastic find."

The coolness inside the castle made her shiver after the heat outside. If they were going to the storeroom she would need the marker. He gave her the excuse to get it. "You're cold," he said. In a man so ruthless, his solicitude for her was almost frightening. "Go and put on something warm. You'll catch a chill." She turned, grateful for the excuse and fled upstairs to her room. She put on a long cardigan and hid the little marker in the pocket. Alessandro was standing exactly where she had left him, his hands in his pockets watching the stairs for her return. They crossed the entrance hall, proceeding to the left and through a low stone archway which had once been closed by a door, into a long vaulted passage, its walls lined with suits of armor, weapons arranged in geometric patterns above. Some of the workmanship was so fine that she paused. Chased in gold and silver, the empty shells that had protected the Malaspigas in the wars of long ago and glittered on the jousting field stood hollow sentinels along their way. He told her names of those who had worn them and the battles which were part of Italian history. Florence against its old enemy Pisa, whom it finally subdued, against intractable Lucca which was never conquered, quarrels with Rome, with Venice, whose power was threatening the might of the Medicis. Their voices echoed—her questions, his answers. There was something frightening about armor, with its suggestion of a vacant body, something sinister in the closed visors and the grotesque shapes made for the human head.

"After the war," Alessandro said, "when the anti-Fascists came here, looting and destroying in the name of liberty, they broke up the armor. It was damaged and scattered. Parts of that suit over there, which is from Cellini's work-shop and almost unique, were found around the walls outside, and some of it was recovered in the town itself. This is a fine collection now. But it took a long time and a lot of money to restore what they had tried so hard to ruin."

"So the creditors never got any of these?"

"They weren't thought to be of any value," he said. "Only now, when art is reaching such an investment peak—now money couldn't buy that suit of Cellini's or many of the others. Come through here. This is the banqueting hall. All the best things are in the rooms upstairs. We're living in what used to be the old servants' quarters. I had them all modernized after I married Francesca. Look at the tapes-tries—there's nothing better in the Uffizi."

The hall was a staggering size, the stone flagged floor covered by a green carpet, scrolled with crimson and black, the arms of the Malaspigas woven into a ten-foot center piece. A huge refectory table ran down its center, flanked by twenty-four superb gilded Florentine chairs, upholstered in faded crimson velvet, with the wreath and the spiked ear of corn embroidered in gold thread on their backs. But splendid and rich as the furniture was, imposing by size alone, the tapestries were indeed the principal treasures. Katharine, re-membering the afternoon spent in the Uffizi, compared them with the priceless series depicting scenes from the court of Catherine de' Medici, and couldn't disagree with the Duke. These were a series, the seasons, each twenty feet high by sixteen feet long, the colors as true and brilliant as when they had come from the looms. Pure gold and silver thread was woven into the designs of beasts and flowers, birds and foliage, with an allegorical group symbolizing the four sea-sons in the center, and the arms of the family woven at the top. They were not the familiar device.

"Our own were torn down from here," he explained. "They

were sold very cheaply for a few thousand dollars. I had to buy these to replace them."

She looked at them and said, "They must have cost a fortune." Probably as much as a single consignment of heroin would buy.

"Not quite," he said. "I've had them for about three years. But I couldn't afford them now." She didn't want him to see her face, to see the bitterness, the contempt for his hypocrisy. A millionaire many times over, so Raphael had said. Trafficking in suffering and death.

"Where is the *poudreuse* stored?" She asked the question quickly, stifling a wish to turn and run, to run out of the castle with its treasures and its history, from the man standing so close that when he turned their shoulders touched.

He reached out and opened a small paneled door. "Down here," he said. "I'll switch the light on, and be careful. The steps down are very steep." They began the descent into the room below. It was a big storeroom, a quarter the size of the banqueting hall above, brilliantly lit by fluorescent lighting. Katharine slipped her hand into her pocket, gripping the marker. With her finger and thumb she eased off the cap.

There were a dozen pieces of furniture, stacked neatly at the end of the room. A superb Italian *cassone,* its front and lid painted and carved, two Florentine chairs of grotesque shape and form, their arms shaped as nubian boys, a crest rising from the center of the backs; two tables, including one small *scagliola,* its colored marbles creating an exquisitely intricate design of birds and flowers and fruit, with a classical motif. On the table there stood a small marble bust of a child, and a Renaissance bronze inkwell in the form of a nest of serpents. A Venetian console table, another *cassone,* simpler and smaller than the first, an ebony cabinet, inlaid with ivory and silver, and the *poudreuse* itself. The ormolu mountings were like gold; they embellished a gem of eighteenth-century French craftsmanship. Katharine stopped in front of it.

It was made in tulipwood, the top, drawers and sides marquetried in a pattern of scrolls and wreaths of flowers, the center depicting a pair of doves with an olive branch between their beaks.

"It's magnificent," Katharine said. She stepped close to it, and pulled out the drawer. Alessandro was behind her; she had the marker in her palm and she pressed the tip of it along the inside of the polished wood. Her hand was shaking as she closed it again.

"Lovely things," she said. The chairs were next; she sat in both of them, again the marker slid along the edge of the seats. She went on making comments, moving among the pieces, pulling out drawers, lifting the lids of the *cassoni*.

Even the ornaments, Raphael had said. Bronzes had to be memorized. The sinister nest of serpents wouldn't be difficult to identify. She was touching the marble bust of the child when Alessandro said suddenly, "What do you think of that?"

"It's charming. It has such an innocent expression. But it looks modern."

"It is," he said. She hid her hand in her pocket, gripping the marker tightly. "It's John's work. There is a pair. I sell them for him, and he makes a little money. They don't command much, three thousand dollars will buy both of them, but he likes to feel he's independent."

"The more I look at it," she said, "the less I like it. It's sentimental and after the first impression it cloys a bit. He shouldn't do things like that, even to make money. It can't help his reputation."

"It's sentimental because it's commercial," Alessandro said. "I'm glad you weren't taken in for more than a few minutes. All our family have good taste. He did a fine male nude, last year. I sold that to Sweden, and it fetched quite a lot of money. One day, he'll make a great name. In the meantime he must work hard and save what he earns."

"And you'll go on supporting him?"

"Of course." He smiled at her. "He creates beauty, and that is one of God's great gifts to men. We have always promoted the arts and looked after artists. It's a Florentine tradition. The treasures of the Renaissance only came into being because the Medicis and people like our ancestors commissioned most of them."

"Where does he work," she asked. "He told me he spends a lot of time up here."

"He has a workshop on the northern side. I've given him the ground floor of a big storeroom where he can keep his marble and work in peace. He is very sensitive, you know. He lacks confidence in himself, and he won't let anyone see his work until it's ready. I have to build up his confidence. I've seen him come out of that room weeping sometimes, when he wasn't satisfied. There's the companion to that bust." He lifted the little head and shoulders of a boy and stood it next to the girl. They made a charming pair, a study in innocence with a disturbing superficiality about them. Katharine saw a picture standing on an easel. It was covered by a green cloth.

"That must be something good," she said. "What is it?"

This time his hesitation was unmistakable. He concealed it quickly, but he caught her arm, holding tightly to keep her from moving toward the picture.

"A landscape," he said. "One of those dull Venetian views of the Grand Canal. I detest Canaletto, and I doubt this is genuine. But your Americans love those sort of pictures. Let's go upstairs now and out into the sunshine. There's nothing more to see down here. I want to show you some of the gardens."

There was nothing she could do. He guided her firmly away and toward the stairs, stepping aside to let her go ahead of him. She took her hand out of the cardigan pocket. She hadn't marked the marble children, and most important of all, he had steered her away from the picture. She had seen one corner of a Florentine frame. They were heavily carved and often massively out of proportion to the painting. Hollowed out, such a frame could contain a large quantity of heroin. They crossed the banqueting hall and through the long passage with the armor, walking quickly. She sensed his mood was a happy one, that the danger was past from his point of view, since she hadn't been allowed to approach the painting. And unless she could see it and positively identify it, the whole purpose of her coming to the castle might have been defeated. As they came into the hall they heard the car coming into the courtyard. The entrance door was open, hooked back on a thick iron ring. The sunlight outside was blinding. Alessandro caught her by the hand.

"Come to the gardens with me," he said. "We can go another way . . ." She hesitated just long enough, and then his mother walked through the door, assisted by John Driver; Prince Alfredo and Francesca following. The Duchess freed herself of his arm once she had climbed the few steps and came toward her son. There was a look of gentle determination in her eyes. The smile she gave to Katharine was especially warm.

"Sandro," she said. "I want to steal you away for a few minutes. Poor Father Dino spoke to me after Mass. He's so worried about the new heating system . . . you will excuse me, my dear?" She slipped her hand through his arm. It was covered in a pale gray glove and buttoned to the elbow.

Mother and son moved away, leaving Katharine alone with John Driver—the uncle and Francesca had disappeared. She saw the Canadian turn and look for her. And then reluctantly turn back.

"I'd like to talk to you," Katharine said quietly. "Let's go outside." He took her to the little formal garden at the side of the castle wall. It was a sheltered place, hewn out of the rocks, protected from the winds which could sweep down from the mountains, shaded by cleverly planted olive trees. A beautifully carved marble seat with griffin arms was set under a clump of mimosa in brilliant yellow bloom. Above them the eastern keep soared into the sky, stark and gray, with arrow slits above the level of the first floor. It was still and airless, the heat beating back off the stones. Katharine sat down under the trailing yellow rachmese. She reached up and pulled a long tassel of mimosa off and began picking the little yellow buds off one by one.

"What's happened?" Driver asked her. "I guess he made a pass?"

"No," she answered. He came and sat down beside her. He seemed worried and irritable, as if what the Duke was doing were her fault.

"Why don't you go back to Florence?" he said. "I offered to drive you. The situation's going to blow up, and he couldn't give a damn. He's such a bastard! He forces Francesca to go to church every Sunday when they're up here, and he has the gall to stay behind this morning and play the lover with you—right in front of her!"

"I said so myself," Katharine said. "He told me people would be scandalized if she didn't go." He didn't answer; his hands were gripped between his knees and he rocked slightly backward and forward, staring at the ground and frowning.

"You're in love with her, aren't you?" She hadn't meant to say it.

He glanced at her slowly. "She's a wonderful person," he said. "And he's a bastard." He looked at the ground again. There was silence—there were no more mimosa buds left. They lay scattered by Katharine's feet.

"I saw the busts of the boy and the girl," she said. "They were beautiful."

He turned and looked at her for a moment. "They're crap, and you know it," he said. "I had a beautiful idea. Youth and innocence—pure innocence, the soul without Original sin, shown through the medium of the purest stone in the world. White, white marble. I thought about it for months. You know something? It's almost impossible to portray the better side of human nature, lust and greed and fear and hate—they're easy. But try love, or courage, or purity . . . those two heads are just crap, like I said. They'll end up in some apartment decorated by a smart fag, and people'll hang their hats on them at cocktail parties."

"You shouldn't run yourself down," she said quietly. "Sandro says you have a great talent." He surprised her by turning around and smiling. It was a painful thing to see.

"He's damn right," he said. "I have. I have a very great talent indeed." He straightened up; his hands came loose from each other. He made a visible effort to relax. "I get discouraged," he said. "Maybe I do have the artistic temperament after all. Why did you want to talk to me?"

The first time she had met him at the villa, she had felt he might turn out to be a friend. He was unhappy, frustrated, working on things that dissatisfied him, suffering the torment of the artist who has not yet found his goal or realized his true capacity. Katharine sympathized with him, even more because he was forced to stand helplessly by while the woman he loved was humiliated.

He could have been a friend, but now he blamed her because of Alessandro. He blamed her for coming, for encouraging her cousin, for not taking his offer and leaving the castle. "I'm very anxious to leave here," she said. "You said you'd take me."

"And I will." He didn't hide his eagerness. "We can go right after lunch. Everyone rests. We won't be missed till this evening."

The temptation to tell him the truth almost overcame her. If he knew why she was there and why she couldn't run away . . . if she told him what Alessandro really was—the sun slid behind a little cloud. He wouldn't believe her. The Duke of Malaspiga a heroin smuggler, a murderer. It was too fantastic. She could imagine the disbelief on his face. He would be sure to tell her cousin. She got up, buttoning the cardigan. "I can't go till tomorrow," she said. "I promised to stay today. But tomorrow morning. Early. Will you take me?"

"Sure," he said. "But it ought to be today. For Christ's sake, try and keep out of his way when Francesca's there. It's the least you can do."

"I will," she promised. They turned and began to walk back toward the castle. There was only one way to obtain the proof Raphael needed. She had to get back into the storeroom and see the picture. And mark it.

Outside the shelter of the garden, the sun escaped its cloud. For a moment Katharine paused. They had reached a low part of the outer wall. Below them there was a chasmic drop of many hundreds of feet onto the roofs of Malaspiga below. "It's even higher up than I thought," she said.

"It's a very exposed place," Driver answered. "But it was built to dominate the countryside. You couldn't attack it with an army up this hill. Close the outer gates and you'd have to be a bird to get in."

Nathan was dozing in the detention room. He had his tie off and his shoes, and he stretched himself out in the chair, his head leaning against the back, and within a few minutes he was asleep. He was sore and bruised from Carpenter's assault, but his mind was at peace and because of this he slept. *Marie was safe.* Even if Taylor had been picked up, he knew Nathan had kept his bargain. His chief was convinced the antique dealer would crack under pressure. Nathan didn't think so; tired and aching, at that time he didn't really care. His only motive was love for his wife and determination nothing should harm her. He would have connived at anything, including murder, to protect Marie. His department had no proof against him; circumstantial evidence wouldn't hold up if they brought charges. So long as Taylor kept his head and waited for the inevitable sharp lawyer to get him out, the worst Nathan could expect was to be fired from the bureau. He could survive that. One of the less particular detective agencies would be happy to employ him. They paid better than civil service. When the door opened he was instantly awake. He saw Carpenter standing there. He reached down for his shoes and put them on. He wasn't going to take another beating. He got up and stood ready, his fists swinging lightly at his sides.

"Ben Harper wants to see you. Upstairs." An armed security guard was behind Carpenter. Nathan knotted his tie back on, picked up his jacket and walked out of the room.

They closed him in on either side. They took the elevator eight floors up to Harper's office. The secretary was hiding behind her typewriter as they came in; she didn't look up. There was a patrolman in Ben's office. Nathan was surprised to see that. Harper's face had a blank look. He was turning a pencil in his hands, around and around between his fingers.

"Sit down," he said to Nathan. Nathan didn't move.

"I want a lawyer," he said. "You've held me for eighteen hours without making a charge. That's illegal."

"This is Patrolman Regan from the Seventy-fourth Precinct. I'm afraid we've got bad news for you."

Nathan looked at them, at Harper, the policeman, who was young and looked uncomfortable, at Carpenter, stony-faced, and then back to Harper again. He felt as if he'd grown a lump inside his throat and couldn't speak.

"What bad news?" Suspicion flared in him. This could be a game, a trap to get him off guard. He'd played that kind of trick on a suspect many times. "What are you trying to pull? I've sat on that side of the desk too often—I know the score."

"Your wife's dead," Harper cut in. "Regan will tell you about it. He was on duty when it happened."

Nathan didn't move. Now there was a lump—it was swelling up, choking him. "Marie . . ." The croak became a shout. "Marie? You say my wife . . ."

"She was hit by a car," the patrolman said. "Right outside your apartment. I wasn't more than twenty feet away and she came staggering out like she was drunk or something. She just walked into the road and the car struck her. She didn't have a chance."

Nathan was staring at him. *A trick,* his mind screamed, *a lie . . . she isn't, she couldn't be* . . . Regan was saying something else. "I was the first to get to her, and she was still conscious. She said something. It didn't make sense, but it was meant for you, I guess. I told Mr. Harper about it."

"What was it?" Nathan said. His throat was clear now, he could speak, but a hammer was beating in his chest. "What did she say?"

"'Tell Jim I didn't take it . . . they fixed me.' That was all. She died a couple of minutes later, before the ambulance came."

When he began to cry Ben Harper looked away. He didn't have Carpenter's private motive, and human agony distressed him. He had known the man for many years. *I didn't take it. They fixed me.*

"It looked like she'd been drinking," Regan said. "She wasn't walking straight." She wouldn't be, Nathan's reeling thoughts supplied the answer. She wouldn't be coordinated if they'd pumped her full of heroin. Fixed. Taylor had done it. He hadn't phoned in time and Taylor had carried out his threat. He'd sent the rent collectors around to see her. He was hardly aware he was crying. He found a handkerchief in his trouser pocket and wiped his face roughly.

"Where is she?" he said.

"In the city morgue. There'll have to be an inquest. I'm sorry, Nathan." That was Ben Harper. Carpenter said nothing. It made sense.

"Where's Taylor? Are you still holding him?"

"No," Harper said. "His lawyer came around half an hour ago and we had to release him. But we'll get him back. You'll be glad to know he sprung you, too. Considering he says he's never seen you before, that was a mighty friendly thing to do. It won't do you any good. We'll get you back, too."

"Maybe," Nathan said. "Maybe not. Then I'm free to go?"

"Yes." Harper stood up. "Unless you want to talk to us. You're in this and I can't believe you haven't got a reason."

"I'm not in anything," Nathan said. He blew his nose and shoved the handkerchief back in his pocket. "You've made a big mistake." He turned and walked out of the office. Harper looked at Carpenter and shook his head.

"We blew that one, Frank. I thought for a moment he was going to crack."

"You think he'll contact Taylor?"

"There's a twenty-four-hour watch on both of them from now on," Harper said. "Taylor's telephone's been tapped, and

I had the apartment bugged this morning. If they so much as whistle at each other we'll know it."

"And Kate?" Frank Carpenter said. The patrolman had gone out after Nathan. They were alone in the office.

"Okay." Harper nodded. "Now Taylor's loose, we'll have to pull her out. Cable Raphael. She's to come home."

Out in the street Nathan stood slowly fastening his jacket. His gun and his badge hadn't been returned to him, but he was a free man. Free except for the bureau agents who'd be watching him. And Taylor's men. He stood on the crowded sidewalk, jostled by people passing by, and a small smile twisted his lips for a moment. Taylor had got him out. Having murdered his wife, he had sprung Nathan to freedom. So that he could be shut up before he talked. Nathan had figured that as soon as he heard about the lawyer. There'd already be a contract on him. He stepped forward and hailed an empty cab. He had let two go by without calling them.

He settled back against the seat and found that he was crying again. He gave way and sobbed with his hands covering his face. His imagination kept showing him pictures. Marie opening the door, being grabbed, strong-armed inside. Knowing what they were going to do to her, fighting as they put the needle in. Her terror communicated itself to him as if she were with him in the cab. As if he had been there and been forced to watch. He sat up and looked out the window. He had told the driver to go to the morgue. They were drawing into a block at a traffic light. Harper's men would be following him. And very soon the others. Maybe just one. A contract killer—a crack shot. A man with class, not the punks who'd manhandled his wife. The light turned green and at the same moment, Nathan opened the cab door and jumped out. Within seconds he was lost in the crowds on the street. He took the subway to East Fifty-ninth and Lexington; he was a native New Yorker and had never wanted to live anywhere else. He liked the hustle, the crowds, the tension that was said to be so wearing on the nerves. Nathan couldn't have spent more than a few hours in the country without the silence grating louder than the traffic belting up Park Avenue. It was late afternoon in the city; the cars were creeping bumper to bumper, tempers were short, people pushed and grunted, the shutters were going up on the luxury store windows and the regular commuter exodus had begun. He walked among them, his head slightly bent as if he were battling a strong wind, gripped by pain and hate and loneliness. She had been typical of the city, typical of the frail and the lost who wandered through it and were tossed away like withered leaves. She would be with him as long as he lived—the little girl face and the big scared eyes, warm with love and trust whenever they looked at him. Brown hair soft and straight, a laugh she'd forgotten how to use till after they were married. The hammer was smashing away in his chest, every stroke a pain. His hands were damp and they trembled; he felt hot and cold in turn. Taylor lived midway on Park. He switched his route down a side street that brought him out on the block behind the shop. There was a side entrance to Taylor's apartment. It worked on an answer system after the janitor had gone home. He didn't want to get there after the man had gone. He began to walk faster. There would be bureau agents watching the building, waiting for him to contact Taylor. That didn't bother him. He didn't care what the agents saw. They wouldn't stop him getting inside; knowing the way Harper worked, the apartment would have been thoroughly penetrated while Taylor was being held. He wouldn't be able to sneeze without a bureau recording device putting it on record. He paused before a jeweler's window—full of expensive, useless costume pieces. Rabbits, bears, a grotesque cat with diamond eyes and tail. There was a mirror at the back, and he could see himself. He carried a comb in his breast pocket; he used it to smooth the short, graying hair sticking up on his head. He straightened his tie and pulled at his jacket. He looked respectable enough for the doorman. They had become a nervous breed, subject to the nightly muggings and attacks that tormented the law-abiding.

He crossed the street to the unobtrusive entrance to Taylor's building. There were two more apartments and a penthouse on the top. Taylor lived on the floor over the shop. Nathan walked up to the door and pressed the bell. There was a pause and then the doorman slid back a panel. Nathan grinned at him. "Hello," he said. "Mr. Taylor's expecting me."

"What name is it?"

"Mr. Lars Svenson," Nathan said.

When the name was phoned through from the hallway Taylor panicked. Svenson. He was due in Rome. He should have been there by now, contacting Malaspiga. For Christ's sake, he wailed out loud, why hadn't the fool gone—what was he doing hanging around . . . All the bureau needed was to pick him up and establish another link in the chain of coincidence. For a moment he shook with nerves, then his stubborn coolness reasserted itself. For a man of his type, he was extraordinarily tough. He'd set up the contract on Nathan as soon as he got home. Nathan had to be released before he started answering any questions. Then he could be eliminated before there was any risk of re-arrest and further investigation. That was his first reaction. The second and more pressing, was his terror of what Nathan would do when he discovered what had happened to his wife.

Taylor had been cowering in his apartment ever since he checked with the two hit men who'd been given the job. Frantic for his own safety he had ordered them to watch Nathan's apartment and get him fast. He didn't care how. He'd be going home after his release. Taylor had drunk a lot of whiskey to steady himself. It had only given him a headache and upset his stomach. When the intercom buzzed, he'd jumped with fright and spilled some of the Scotch on his favorite Persian rug. Svenson. Christ almighty. He told the doorman to send him up.

Eddy Taylor was completely unprepared when he opened the door. There were moments of blind confusion while he tried to batter at the body of the man whose hands were around his throat. He choked and writhed, groping for Nathan's face, but thumbs were pressing relentlessly into his neck and his vision grew dark. His head felt as if it were swelling, his eyes started out and froth foamed on his lips. His face turned blue. He made a last effort to tear the throttling hands away, ripping at the skin with nails he had kept rather long. Nathan gave a final, savage squeeze, using all the strength in his arms. Taylor gurgled horribly and his whole body jerked upward. Then Nathan felt his body go slack. He didn't ease the pressure. He went on pressing, using his weight, until Taylor's eyes had turned up and his face was a dark, blotchy purple. Slowly, reluctant to let go, Nathan opened his hands. He climbed off the body and stood looking at it. It looked grotesque, sprawled with its legs apart, the arms flung out and the discolored face half-hidden as the head rolled to one side. Nathan flexed his fingers; he straightened his jacket, and seeing blood on the backs of his hands where Taylor had torn him, wiped it on his sleeve. He went to the Spanish cabinet and poured himself a neat Scotch. Standing over Taylor's body, he swallowed the drink straight down and after a moment, he spat on the dead man. Then he let himself out of the apartment and the doorman let him into the street. The atmosphere was hot and sour with exhaust fumes; the traffic on both sides of Park was a motionless stream. He saw an empty cab and, slipping between the cars, he got inside and gave the bureau headquarters address. He groped for his pipe and lit it; he felt calm and numb. His wrists ached and he rubbed them. Taylor had fought hard. There were sore places on Nathan's body which were just beginning to hurt. He wasn't really aware of physical feeling. His wife was dead, and he had murdered the man who was responsible. His career was finished, after twenty-two years. The men who'd trusted him and worked with him were his enemies. He had put the finger on Katharine Dexter, and Frank Carpenter had heard him do it. There was no forgiveness for him, no redemption possible. Nothing to live for but revenge. Taylor was dead, but there were others. Hate was fighting the numbness, setting the hammers in his chest to work. He had hated the thugs, the pimps, the racketeers, despised the humanists who argued that they were society's victims, and dealt as harshly with them as he could. When they corrupted him he had become a part of them with a speed that showed him truly to himself. He was no better, turned out of the same mold. He recognized that now, sitting in the cab on his way downtown, thinking while the meter ran up money, and the traffic moved like sludge. Marie was the only good thing that had ever happened to him. She had brought him gentleness and love. Tears crept down his face, and he wiped them away with his scratched hand. Choking the life out of Taylor had preserved his sanity and satisfied his lust for vengeance, but it couldn't bring her back.

Even if every member of the heroin ring was caught and jailed, there was no future for him. Twenty minutes later he was in Carpenter's office.

Frank got up from his desk when he saw him.

"Get a stenographer in here. I want to make a full confession."

"Ah," Alessandro said. "I wondered where you were. I didn't realize John had carried you off." He was waiting in the hall when they came in from the garden. Although he smiled at Katharine, the Duke's expression was irritated when he spoke to Driver. "You shouldn't take my cousin sightseeing —that's my privilege. Come, Katerina. We shall make a little tour before lunch." He took her by the arm and led her to the staircase. At the top they passed Uncle Alfredo. He was wearing a tall silk hat, and walking toward them with a look of purpose on his face. When he saw them he paused, raised the silk hat to Katharine and shook his head at his nephew.

"You should have been at Mass," he said. "Dino preached a sermon that sent me straight to sleep. You should care for your immortal soul, Alessandro!"

"I do, Uncle," the Duke said gently. "I don't need Father

Dino boring me to death in the meantime. I hope you didn't snore?"

"No, no!" the old man protested. "I didn't give offense— I just dozed for a moment. Where are you going?" His gaze had fixed on Katharine. He took off the hat and suddenly collapsed the crown into the brim like a conjurer.

"To the main gallery," Alessandro answered. "I'm going to show Katerina our pictures."

"Ah, that's all right then. If you'll excuse me, I won't come with you. This hat won't do—my ears are quite cold."

"Hurry and change it then," the Duke said. "We will see you at lunch."

"Yes," the old Prince said. He hesitated for a moment. "You will take good care of her, won't you?"

"Very good care. I promise," the Duke said. He pressed Katharine's arm. "He has taken a great liking to you," he said. "You have a disturbing effect on your relations. We go through here; take care, the doorway is low."

They passed under a narrow arch and out into a vast gallery, lit by windows high up in the wall and extending to the level of the ceiling. The light fell downward as if they were in a church. "This was where our family and their household used to walk and gossip and amuse themselves. The Duke heard petitions here. I use it for my collection of pictures. And this," Alessandro said, "is the Giorgione. Don't you think it's beautiful?"

Katharine said simply, "Yes," because anything more would have been superfluous. It was a Madonna and child with St. Anne and the infant St. John. The colors were as fresh and brilliant as if the artist had just finished the picture. There was a serenity about the faces and a grace in the composition which could only be appreciated in silence. She thought wildly, *Why does he do this dreadful thing—there's more than a million dollars hanging there in front of me.*

"If you were so poor after the war," she said suddenly, "why didn't you sell this?"

"Because it was supposed to be a copy," her cousin said.

"My father sold what he could, but this picture wasn't thought of any value. I had it authenticated afterward. I told you, nothing would induce me to sell such a masterpiece. I was thinking of keeping it for my son, if I had had one."

He lit a cigarette, and she took one from the gold case. "You must be making a fortune out of your antique business if you can afford to keep pictures like that."

He laughed. "I am—I'm very successful. All Florentines are good at trading. Why do you always look so disapproving when you mention it? Our ancestors were moneylenders—it's just a euphemism to talk about bankers. There's no disgrace in it."

"Of course not, I didn't mean that. You know the pieces you're sending to America," she tried hard to sound casual, "I didn't really have enough time to look at them again . . . Perhaps I could go again . . ."

"I'm afraid not," he said. "They're being crated and the men are coming in the morning. And this afternoon, I have a plan for you. We're going to the Villa Romani!"

She looked away, afraid to let him see her face. Tomorrow— The furniture would be packed up by tomorrow. And he wouldn't show it to her again. Now there really was no choice. She had to see that picture . . . It could be the biggest cache in the whole shipment. He had some excursion planned for the afternoon. She looked around for an ashtray, the cigarette tasted rank. "Give me that if you don't want it," he said. "I'll put it out. Come and look at the view from this window. Then I'll show you the portrait of Paolo di Malaspiga, the most wicked of us all."

She followed him to a wall embrasure; a little flight of steps brought them up to the level of the window and as they stood there, their bodies touched. He put his arm around her and it was like a band across her shoulders.

"You can see right across the plain to the coast," he said quietly.

She stood stiffly beside him, staring ahead, hating the feel of him so close to her.

"We held the whole countryside around here for five hundred years," he said. She felt him turning, moving imperceptibly downward toward her, and with an effort she drew back. His arm slipped away, releasing her. There was no change in his expression—friendly, charming, mocking rather than angry.

"Show me the wicked Malaspiga," she said.

"Aren't you looking at him?" the Duke asked.

"If you say so." Katharine hoped her voice was steady.

"He's here, in this corner. There's no record of the artist; there have been several attributions, but they were all fake. Nobody knows who painted him. I want you to look at the interior very carefully. There's an interesting story."

There was nothing remarkable about the portrait. It showed a thick-set man with a sallow complexion, a hooked nose and small black eyes, wearing the loose red surcoat and cap of the fifteenth century. As far as she could see he was standing in a stone-walled room with a crucifix in the background. There was a small arched window, no wider than an arrow slit, high on one wall.

"He built the eastern wall and the turret," her cousin said. "He was the second son, and tradition says he poisoned his brother. And his nephews. He married off his nieces for political alliances. He had only one wife, but she was known as the captive duchess. She was the daughter of a nobleman who held lands over by Bocca di Magra, and Paolo kidnapped her and married her as a hostage against her father. People who didn't pay his taxes were roasted alive. But he's really remembered for one of the rooms in the eastern turret. He was so pleased with it, he had it painted into his portrait."

"He sounds delightful." Katharine shuddered. "What was so special about the room?" She had a feeling of discomfort —vague panic signals were flashing in her mind. There was something about Malaspiga Castle she knew was very frightening. It had frightened her so much as a child that she had made herself forget it.

"I'm keeping that a secret," he said. "It's part of the grand tour we will make tomorrow."

"Tomorrow's Monday," she said. "I have to get back."

"There isn't any hurry," he said. "Already you're beginning to like it here. I think you'll stay for Monday, too. Now we'd better go to lunch." He caught Katharine by the hand and swung it as if he were holding a little girl. "Don't worry," he said. "I shall be discreet. And this afternoon, after we've been to the Villa Romani and walked through the gardens, we will have a little talk. I can see, my dear cousin, that you are not going to accept me without an explanation."

It was a strangely gay party that set out that afternoon. The old Duchess had laughed her pretty laugh, and promised Katharine she would love the Villa. John immediately said he would like to come too, and perhaps Francesca would enjoy it. Uncle Alfredo giggled and nodded his head. It was a fabulous place. And the gardens! They were unique. There was more laughter at this remark, and Katharine began to feel bewildered and ill-at-ease. Whatever the joke, it was going to be at her expense. There was a light in Francesca's cold black eyes that told her so. She saw Sandro di Malaspiga watching her, and a sense of fear welled up in her, mixed strangely with pain.

She felt helpless and on the defensive—it wasn't a feeling she liked. It made the circle of smiling faces with their expectant looks into something sinister. "Whatever the joke is," she said lightly, "I hope it's a pleasant one."

"Very pleasant." That was John Driver. "You'll love it," he said.

Carpenter went down to the detention cells with Nathan. He went inside and waited, while Nathan sat on the cot, and bent down to undo his shoes.

"Is there anything you want? Coffee—"

"No." Nathan shook his head. He straightened, kicking his shoes off, and grimaced. Under the ugly naked light, he was sickly white, with a sheen of sweat on his skin.

"Why don't you tell me?" Carpenter said, repeating Harper's question over the past hour. "Why did you do it? Why did you get mixed up in this? You were the last guy in the world to go bent."

Nathan looked up at him. "You got what you wanted," he said. "You got your confession. I murdered that bastard because I knew he was going to put a contract on me to stop me talking. So I've talked. You've got his contact in Sweden and the connection in Italy. The next assignment coming from there is going to be full of junk. I can't give you any more, and my motives are my own business. Now I'd like to get some sleep."

"There must have been a good reason," Carpenter said. "It could make a lot of difference to you if you'd say what it was."

Nathan lay back on the cot. The hammers were breaking down the walls of his chest. He didn't care if they gave him life for killing Taylor. He was not going to dissect Marie with anyone . . .

"You've got your testimony," he said. "Now get lost, for Christ's sake." He heard Carpenter go out and the locking mechanism on the door snap into place. He lay with his eyes closed, feeling the pain in his chest increase. Blow after blow, melting into one another until it was a single agony, running like fire down his left arm. Sweat ran down his face and he groaned once before the embolism burst through from his heart and exploded in his brain. A few minutes later when the security guard looked through the peephole in the door he thought the prisoner was asleep.

Frank had the file out in his office. He wasn't going home that night until he had confirmation from Raphael that Katharine had been withdrawn from the mission. He kept reminding himself that in a few hours she'd be out of danger. Nathan's evidence would give the Italian authorities enough to justify the arrest on suspicion of the Duke of Malaspiga, of his associate Lars Svenson, and the general roundup of all his business partners. From past experience, there was no loyalty among smugglers. The prospect of thirty years in prison always produced two or three states' witnesses. Katharine would be coming home. Harper had sent an urgent message telling Interpol the facts disclosed by Nathan in his confession, and emphasizing the need to get her out of contact with the Malaspigas as quickly as possible. He knew "Raphael"—he had met him with Ben Harper before Firelli went on his mission, and he respected his ability and judgment. He wouldn't delay. There was a thermos of coffee on his desk. Carpenter poured some and sipped it, reading through the file.

Harriet Harrison's revelation—the morbid scandal of seven years ago, hushed up by threats—the much-publicized figure of Elise Bohun Julius, gliding through the society columns, hosting her famous Hollywood parties, and the reality behind the pose. A drug addict, the daughter of a Blue Book Pennsylvania lawyer, whose fortune came from an obscure Italian girl he met in college. A fortune founded on bootlegging, prostitution and the protection racket. Elise Bohun was the granddaughter of Angelo Zappone, one of the most feared and powerful of the syndicate that operated nine-tenths of organized crime in New York State. A hidden figure, never photographed, a name without a face, Zappone moved in shadow, and there was nobody brave enough to try and subject him to the light. His daughter had taken her mother's name. When his granddaughter married Richard Bohun, there was no connection with the gangster who was credited with over forty killings and ran a criminal empire of a hundred million dollars. His power and money had made a judge out of Richard Bohun, reestablished the couple in the family house, previously sold because of debts, and introduced his granddaughter as a beautiful, accomplished debutante in the best American society.

But after her much-publicized marriage to John Julius, in Hollywood where money and degeneracy mixed, she had quickly fallen victim to the craze for drugs. The influence of Zappone moved quickly to protect her. Since no cure was possible, the family supplied her, and in consequence they had used her to set up Eddy Taylor.

A number of Hollywood stars and producers were ensnared, and the domain of Zappone had extended to the movie industry. Carpenter could imagine the opportunities for blackmail, for obtaining options on big film deals, for the purchase of shares which wouldn't otherwise have been available. And Harriet Harrison had stumbled on a part of it. He had heard of the practice of gossip columnists' bribing servants in the star's employ—several of the biggest used the method and Harrison had freely admitted it. From one of the Juliuses' maids she had obtained a used syringe Elise had neglected to clean out and hide, after a particularly rapid-acting fix. A doctor who owed Harriet a favor for not reporting his very profitable sideline—aborting unlucky starlets—ran an analysis of the syringe showing heroin, and immediately the hunt was on. Harrison had in her hands one of the biggest stories in her career. As a prelude to the final revelation, she had published the hint about the Malaspigas. Apart from the hypodermic, the maid had discovered something else. He remembered Harrison's pretty, pain-lined face as she looked at him, the mouth twisted in its perpetual sneer.

"It must have been some honeymoon! And then the husband caught them at it. The maid said it was a real Grade B Hollywood scene. But I never got to print it."

Zappone's emissaries had made sure of that. So the friendship between the Malaspigas and the John Juliuses should have ended when the Duke and Duchess left the next day. But it hadn't. Julius had assured him that on two occasions, Elise paid private visits to Italy. Carpenter had forgotten his coffee, and it was tepid.

Perhaps Malaspiga had been blackmailed. There were so many pressures people like the Zappones could exert on somebody with a public image to protect. The Duke might have been unwilling to start with, until the fantastic profits from the sale of heroin provided their own motive. Angelo Zappone had died three years ago; Carpenter remembered the wide press coverage given the funeral. The unknown king of crime. And the usual speculations as to who would assume his crown. Zappone's organization was part of the Mafia although he was a Neapolitan. Drug smuggling was a Mafia enterprise and jealously protected.

The young Duchess di Malaspiga had given him the means, by force or persuasion, to involve the head of one of Italy's great families in providing cover. It was ironic, in Carpenter's opinion, that the Tuscan Prince should have learned so quickly from the Neapolitan peasant. Zappone's business interests, if that was the right description for extortion, protection and prostitution, had been dissipated among rivals—the kingdom disintegrated. Nobody had imagined that it had transferred the most profitable enterprise of all direct to Italy. There was a knock at his door and one of the night staff secretaries came in. "Cable from Florence, just come through," he said.

Carpenter grabbed it.

MESSAGE RECEIVED. UNFORTUNATELY COUSIN ROSE LEFT FOR MALASPIGA CASTLE TO COMPLETE MISSION AS INSTRUCTED. IMPOSSIBLE PROCEED AGAINST MALASPIGA FAMILY WITHOUT HIGHEST AUTHORITY. THIS CANNOT BE OBTAINED UNTIL AFTER WEEKEND. ATTEMPT TO CONTACT COUSIN ROSE WILL BE MADE WITH INSTRUCTIONS FOR HER TO ABANDON MISSION. RAPHAEL.

Carpenter threw the cable on his desk. She had gone to the castle to carry out Harper's instructions. To get to the consignment of furniture and identify it. She was shut off from all but a doubtful telephone link with any kind of help, in exactly the same situation as Firelli. And Firelli had been a tough, highly trained agent, a man who could take care of himself in most circumstances. A judo expert, a crack shot. He put his hands to his head and let his body drop into the chair. If Raphael got a message to her she might still get out. But if Taylor had passed on his warning via Svenson, and Nathan seemed sure that he had, then they were already many hours too late.

When Nathan first confessed, he had felt confident, thinking in terms of American procedure, where an arrest would have been made in a few hours, no matter how important the suspect. He'd forgotten the slowness and the inequality of European judicial systems. The police did not break in on a Malaspiga and haul him off to jail without making sure they had official backing.

By the time they got it, and went to Malaspiga Castle, Katharine would be dead. He picked the cable up and read it again. Raphael would *try* to contact her, tell her to get out. Firelli had spoken to Florence but it hadn't helped him. He had never been seen again. He got up and went along the corridor and up in the elevator to Ben Harper's office. Harper was gone and the office was locked. There was nothing to keep him on watch all night. Nathan had confessed, the case was opening out, and he could afford to go home and sleep. He wasn't in love with Katharine Dexter. Carpenter went back to his office. It was after ten o'clock. He dialed Ben Harper's private number.

"This is Frank," he said. "Sorry to call at home, but I want permission to go to Italy. Tonight."

There was a pause, and then Harper's voice said, "Sorry. I know how you feel, but it can't be done. This is an internal Italian matter, in liaison with Interpol. We have no right to interfere. I can't send you, Frank. You ought to know that."

"I've had a return cable from Raphael," Carpenter said. "Kate's gone to the castle. He can't be sure of contacting her, and he can't go and get her out. Nothing can be done to pick the Duke up till they have their goddamned authority. They'll kill her, Ben. I know it. For Christ's sake, I've got to go out there."

Harper's tone was sympathetic. "I know how you feel," he said. "But I can't break the rules. Even if you went, from what Nathan told me, it's probably too late. If it's not, Raphael will get through to her. There's nothing you can do."

Carpenter held the phone, and for a moment he didn't speak. *Too late.* While they were holding Taylor that morning, the Swede was in Italy carrying the message to Malaspiga. Katharine could already be dead, while they were sending cables and talking about how to save her.

"I'm going," Carpenter said. "I'm taking leave, and I'm going. On my own time and unofficially." He didn't wait for an answer. He hung up. He dialed TWA and booked a seat on the last flight to Rome; it left at eleven o'clock in the evening, and there were two first-class cancellations. All he could think of as he went to his apartment, packed an overnight bag, and drove out to Kennedy, was that it might all be a waste of time, a useless gauntlet flung in the face of fate. As Ben Harper said, he was probably too late.

It took an hour to drive to the Villa Romani. The old Duchess decided that it was too hot and she preferred to rest, and at the Duke's suggestion John drove Francesca separately. There was nothing Katharine could do about the arrangement; she was as helpless against his determination to be alone with her as his wife was in trying to prevent it. Her murmur that they could all go together in one car had been completely disregarded.

"What is so special about the villa?" she asked him as they drove. He stopped at the toll on the autostrada, paid one thousand lire, and the car shot forward.

"Wait and see." He turned slightly and she saw the cool, arrogant smile that held warmth only when it was for her. Her head ached, and she hated the speed at which he drove.

"You have a passion for secrets, haven't you? First it's that horrible man's room you won't tell me about, and now it's this villa. You make me feel like a naughty child."

For a moment his hand left the wheel and pressed hers where it lay in her lap. "It's because I feel like a child myself,"

he said. "Free and happy and excited to be showing you the
things I know and love. Bear with me, Katerina. I haven't
felt like this for many years." And there was nothing she
could find to say to that. They stopped at the end of an avenue of cypresses, tall and dark against the brilliant blue sky,
having left the autostrada behind them for some seven miles.
The Duke got out, paid the custodian who shuffled out from
his house in the walls surrounding the villa, and took her
through the door in the massive iron-studded main gates.

Fronted by a green lawn, encircled by a blazing mass of
camelia trees in full bloom, the Villa Romani gleamed like a
fantastic wedding cake. White and pink stucco, a façade of
classical statues, an imposing frontal coat of arms in mosaic,
pillars and arches and curves, it only lacked the figures of the
bride and bridegroom and a giant sword to cut it into slices.
It wasn't beautiful, it was stunningly pretty in a ridiculous
way. He took her arm and turned down a side path. "It was
built in the eighteenth century by the Count Romani," he
said. "The family has lost all their money and only live in a
small part of it. They open it to the tourists. But it's hideous
and we haven't come to see that. This way. To the gardens."
He gave her a sly, mocking glance and hurried her on.

The gardens were sunken, and even by the standards of the
Villa Malaspiga, with its landscaping and sumptuous trees,
they were superb. The descent was from a balustraded staircase in mellow gray stone, guarded by life-sized statues,
flanked by a pair of nymphs holding conch shells on each
shoulder. There were low clipped hedges and the brilliant
dwarf plants beloved by Italian gardeners, and everywhere
there were statues—centaurs, goddesses, satyrs with leering
faces, nymphs with open mouths. Another custodian, dressed
in the faded blue of the peasant came toward them and
seemed to recognize Alessandro. The Duke went up to him,
murmured something and the old man laughed. He shuffled
away and disappeared behind the staircase. He came back
to Katharine and she saw him glance up. John and Francesca
were at the top of the steps, leaning over the balustrading

and looking down at them. Her cousin didn't wave or call to them. He took her arm and slid his hand down until it closed over her wrist. "Let's walk," he said. "Down this way."

She thought at first there had been a cloudburst. There was a sudden rushing noise, and then water rained on them from all directions. It spouted from the steps, cutting off their retreat to the top, and jetted from the ground, the flower beds and the statues. Every statue was a fountain—water spouted from the mouths, the eyes, the conch shells. She heard Alessandro laughing and felt him pulling her. They began to run, as the garden came alive with a series of water jets, until only the way ahead of them was clear and behind there was a glittering fountain. There was a tall archway, built under a bridge at the far end. Even though they ran they were caught by some of the sprays. "In here," the Duke gasped. "Quickly . . ." Under the archway there was a grotto; for a moment Katharine couldn't see in the dim, almost green light. They stopped inside it. At the back there was a massive stone statue of Neptune with sea horses rising from waves which had been crusted by water. There were stalactites hanging from the roof and water had misshapen the sculpture till it looked leprous.

"Now! How do you like the Romani gardens? Have you ever seen a *Giocchi d'Aqua* before?" There was water on his face, and his coat—she could feel drops in her own hair. "My darling," he said, "you're wet—"

She knew what was going to happen but she couldn't move. He had his arms tightly around her, and the kisses she had been dreading were being pressed on her mouth. She saw a great double cross spray of water shoot up at each side of the grotto entrance, sealing them off completely inside. She began to struggle with him; he was very strong. He didn't hurt her, but he didn't let her go. For a brief moment her mouth was free. "Stop fighting yourself," he said. Her eyes closed, and she opened her lips to him. She felt his grip tighten and then relax. She wrenched her head back, and the wetness on her face came from tears.

"Don't do that! Let me go—"

"I love you," he said. The fountain outside the grotto sank and stopped as suddenly as it had sprung up. A wide pool of water gleamed at the entrance. He was still holding Katharine, looking at her with an expression she had never seen before.

"I'll never let you go," he said quietly. "You belong to me. I knew it the first time I saw you."

She stepped back, pulling his hands away. "I don't want to hear any more! You've played your trick with the water joke and it's time to go home." She walked out through the puddle, pushing her damp hair away from her face. She felt her body tremble; the grotto had been cold and damp. He was behind her and then alongside.

"You kissed me, Katerina," he said. "Nothing you say can change that. But I made a mistake. I should have talked to you first."

"There's nothing to say," Katharine answered. She could see John Driver and the Duchess watching them from the top of the steps. "I'll drive home with them."

"You'll come with me," he said.

"I'll ask John to take me," she said. He stopped, catching hold of her wrist.

"You do that," he said quietly, "and I'll throw him out into the street. If he's in love with my wife, he's welcome to her. But don't let him try to interfere with you!"

They mounted the steps together. She saw them waiting at the top, the Duchess very pale, Driver looking embarrassed.

"Well," he sounded false in the attempt to be cheerful. "Quite a surprise, isn't it? Great fun—"

"You should take Francesca there," Alessandro said coldly. "I can recommend the grotto." He walked so quickly away and toward the gates, pulling Katharine with him, that she almost had to run. He opened the car door for her and slammed it. He got in and started the engine. "I should fasten the seat belt," he said, then he swung the wheel and the car roared back down the avenue of cypresses and onto the autostrada. It seemed to Katharine that they drove for a long time. She sat tensed up against the speed, hating it and determined not to ask him to slow down. She glanced quickly at him. His face was set, his mouth narrow. The speedometer trembled at 170 kilometers. She didn't recognize the road when they swung off the autostrada through the last toll gate. She felt very near tears.

"Where are we going?" she said. "This isn't the road we took from Malaspiga."

"We're not going to Malaspiga," he said. "We're going somewhere where we can talk." When she tried to object he didn't hear, because at that moment they crossed a bridge and everything began to rattle and shudder as if they were in a train. The noise was so loud it was impossible to speak. Then it was over and they were on the road again, a narrow road running along the edge of a river mouth. "This is the Magra," he said. "The proper bridge fell down last year. We haven't got around to building another because that one we've just crossed happened to be there. It's a Bailey bridge, left over from the war, when the Allies marched through here. Not very efficient, I'm afraid, but that's Italy."

"You don't have to be sarcastic," she said angrily. "And you didn't have to drive like a maniac to frighten me."

"I'm sorry," he said stiffly. "But I always drive fast when I'm angry. You should have told me to slow down." She didn't answer him. They were climbing now, leaving the Magra below them, driving along a mountain road that wound and twisted upward through the pines and cypress-covered hills. He was driving slowly and she knew it was a concession to her. "Look up," he said. "That's where we're going."

It was a village, growing out of the top of the hill, dominated by a little sugar-pink church with its Tuscan bell tower; the streets were narrow, and roughly paved in places. Children played in what passed for a piazza. Two old women, clothed in black, walked slowly by, holding each other's arms. The sun was warm but a soft pink was coming into the sky at the horizon's edge. He turned once more, leaving the village and drew up by the side of a road. "This is the most beautiful place in Northern Italy," he said. "Monte Marcello." He leaned over and opened her door. Reluctantly she got out; he came and stood beside her. He took out his cigarette case and lit one for her and another for himself.

"I'm sorry," he said quietly. "I shouldn't have frightened you by driving like that. I suppose I hoped you would ask me to slow down. I wanted you to give to me a little . . . It was childish of me. I apologize."

They were standing at the rise of a hill. Below them the ground sloped away for many hundreds of feet to the valley, where the Magra was a stretch of silver, dotted with tiny boats, and the pink and ocher-colored houses of the villages of Ameglia and Bocca di Magra looked as if they had been painted into the landscape. Behind them towered the great Carrara mountains, the same mountains that had seemed so cold and sinister with their white marble sides when she had seen them from the castle. Now they only suggested grandeur and peace, brooding over the lovely scene of river and valley at their feet. As if he understood how the view had affected her, Alessandro put a hand on her shoulder and turned her toward him.

"It is the most beautiful place I know," he said. "I was planning to bring you here so we could share it. But not like this, not with anger between us."

"I'm not angry," Katharine said. "You don't understand."

"No," he admitted, "I don't. You say you don't feel anything for me; but when you kissed me you proved that was a lie. You think I'm just a callous Italian who humiliates his wife and makes a public show of his affairs?"

"I think you treat her abominably," Katharine said. "And I'm not in love with you, whatever you say."

"Then why won't you look at me when you say it?" He held her at arms' length. "Why are you afraid of me, Katerina —it isn't just Francesca. What is the real reason you fight against me and yourself? All right," he said. "You won't answer. Very well." He let her go and turned away, facing the magnificent view. "So we will talk about Francesca first. About my marriage and why our relationship is what it is."

"I don't want to hear," Katharine said slowly. "I don't want to know."

"Because it helps you hide from the truth," he said. "But I won't let you hide. You're going to hear about Francesca. You owe me that at least." She looked at him. "Please," he said. "Listen to me, and then judge." She couldn't answer him —she only nodded. She had never imagined someone so inherently proud could bring himself to plead.

"I told you we were poor after the war," he said. "I told you I married Francesca and that her money was a consideration. That offends you, because you're American, and marriages have to be made in heaven, although most of them end in divorce after a few years. We're not a sentimental people, my darling. I knew my duty to my family, and I chose a girl who had the right background and a personal estate which would help restore ours. But I also loved her. I find it very difficult to admit that now, but at the time I did. She wasn't beautiful; I've known many women who were more elegant, more sensually appealing. But she had this cool quality, this reserve. She reminded me of a Giotto painting, secretive and somehow out of reach. I wanted her very much. I wanted to be happy and have children and rebuild, with her beside me. I was thirty-five when I married her, and I had had a lot of women. I felt sure I could make her love me."

A light breeze had sprung up, and the olive trees on the terraced slopes below were gently fluttering their feathery leaves. Katharine looked down, gripping the parapet.

"She was a virgin," Alessandro said. "I thought it would take time. I was patient. When I held her in my arms she shivered; for the first few days of our honeymoon she was in tears. When we went to America, she pretended to be ill on the boat to keep me away. Something was wrong, but I didn't know what it was. I thought of myself as very sophisticated, but when I look back on it now, I was just a fool. I just thought she was afraid of sex. I didn't realize that she hated men."

He paused. She saw him drop his cigarette on the ground and slowly tread it to pulp.

"We stayed with the film star John Julius—I told you that. It was a relief to be with people. I thought it would help Francesca, amuse her. It didn't. She avoided me even more. There were parties given for us, a lot of interesting things to see. I hoped she'd change. I wondered whether I was being soft and stupid with her. But when I saw the loathing in her eyes, how she'd stiffen when I came near or tried to touch her . . . You would never understand what such a thing can do to a man. I think I could have compromised in some way, if I hadn't found out the truth," he said. Now he was looking at Katharine and she saw the disgust in his face.

"I found her with Julius' wife," he said. "I went into the bedroom and saw them together. Naked. They were kissing, like lovers."

"Oh, God," Katharine said. The wind was rising, the trees below were swaying in agitation. She felt cold and sick.

"I took her home," he said. "I left her in Florence with my mother, who could never be told what had happened, and came to Malaspiga. My life was ruined. I was married to a lesbian. There was no divorce in Italy at that time, and even if I tried to get the marriage annulled, the scandal would have killed my mother. I was helpless. I tried to make excuses for Francesca—the American woman was a very sophisticated degenerate. She had known how to seduce an inexperienced girl. It wasn't her fault. I said all the right things to myself, and they didn't make any difference. I stayed at the castle for some days. It was empty, Uncle Alfredo banished to the monastery, the furniture gone, no servants, the village thought we had abandoned them and gone to live in Florence. Everything seemed over. And then I made up my mind. Fate, God —whatever name you like to give the force that rules our lives —had tried to give the Malaspigas a death blow. I wasn't going to accept that."

Looking at him she saw the face of his ancestor, the ruthless Prince of the Renaissance, defying all that God or man could do, cast forever by the genius of Cellini into a mask of pride.

"I went back to Florence," Malaspiga said, "determined on two things. I would have a child with this woman, a son—and I would see my family restored to everything they had lost. No matter how I had to do it."

He threw his arm around her suddenly, taking her by surprise. It was a hard grip which she couldn't have resisted. She felt him press her close against him and for a moment, she closed her eyes, fighting with all her strength not to give in. *No matter how I had to do it.*

"I forced her," he said. "I was without pity. For a year we lived together like animals, hating each other, pretending to the world outside. I made love to her and I hated it as much as she did. But there was no child. Francesca won in the end. She was barren. I am the last of our line."

They stood together, locked side by side. His hold seemed to be tighter, as if he would never let her go. The sun was going down and a gray line showed on the horizon of the pinkish sky.

"I built up my business," he said. "I studied hard, I became an art expert, an authority on Italian furniture and bronzes. I drove myself, building a reputation, making contacts. Now I am a rich man. A very rich man." His voice dropped a little. "Perhaps I have done things you wouldn't admire, my darling. Things I may regret. But they had to be done. For seven hundred years the Malaspigas have been part of Tuscan life. They aren't going to die out with a whisper of self-pity. History can be my judge."

He turned her to him, and she made no resistance. Her arms went around his neck and her body fitted into his.

"I love you," he said at last. "We belong together. And you have told me that you love me, without any words."

"Take me back," she said. "Please, Sandro."

He brushed his fingers over her cheek. "Tears," he said softly. "I'll make them tears of joy."

The flight to Rome was an hour late. There was an agonizing delay over the airport due to stacking. Carpenter hadn't even dozed during the eight-hour flight. His mind was savaging the problem, planning a single assault, unsupported by Interpol or the Italian authorities, on Malaspiga Castle. He was not a man ruled by emotions. He seldom lost his temper or his sense of proportion. But he had made up his mind that if Katharine Dexter had disappeared from Malaspiga, he would kill the Duke. A month teaching her his own particular skills, days spent close to her, deliberately ignoring what was happening to him, his antipathy to her mission based solely on professional objections. Now he no longer pretended. He had beaten Nathan like any precinct heavy, defied Harper and walked out of his job to rescue her because he had fallen in love. There was a gun in his shoulder holster: going through security at Kennedy he'd shown his DEA card, and they had cleared him before the other passengers. Rome—he saw the city swing out beneath the aircraft and then slide out of sight as the jet banked for the turn and the run in.

Nathan. Nathan and Taylor. The whole rotten, crooked alliance had killed Firelli. He had gone out to Italy without a chance because there was a spy in his own organization, who had sold him out. All the care, the preparation had been for nothing. And the same was true for Katharine. The message had gone from Nathan to Taylor, and from Taylor to the Swede. They had many hours' start on him. He gripped the sides of his seat as they slid down to the runway and then bumped once on landing. From Rome he had to catch a connecting flight to Pisa. He hurried off the plane, pushing against the stream of passengers. He showed his card and asked to go through without customs clearance. A lieutenant in the *carabinieri* accompanied him. He went to the ticket office for the internal flight and asked when the next plane took off for Pisa. There was a delay while two of the assistants argued whether the next flight stopped at Pisa or went straight through to Milan. Finally they told him he would have to go to Milan and get a connection back to Pisa. He grabbed his one bag, cursed because it meant still another few hours lost on the trip, and hurried off to board the plane. Milan, Pisa. Then by road to Malaspiga. If there were time, he'd call Raphael from Milan airport. He could use reinforcements. He might even hear that Katharine had been contacted and was out of danger. But he didn't dare hope for that. He had an instinct trained by many years of hopes being disappointed. People in danger were seldom plucked to safety; miracles were only miracles because they never happened . . . In the plane he fell asleep for part of the flight, waking with a feeling of despair just before they landed. At Milan airport, a notice informed transit passengers that there was a fifty-minute delay on the connecting flight. He went to the telephone and dialed Raphael in Florence. The girl in his office answered and promised to deliver his message. Raphael, she said, had gone to Rome. No, the distant voice said, she couldn't give Signor Carpenter any information about Signorina Dexter. Raphael was expected back next morning.

"Tell him," Frank said, slowly and carefully so that she couldn't misunderstand, "tell him that I've gone to Malaspiga. He can follow or not, as he likes." He hung up and went outside to wait for the plane to Pisa airport. He could guess where Raphael had gone. It was Sunday. He couldn't get the authority necessary to force a way into Malaspiga Castle with a warrant until after the weekend. And that kind of authority didn't come from Florence. Raphael had gone to Rome. They must have crossed each other in the air. And that meant, without question, Katharine had not been reached in time.

6

It was the hour before dinner and everyone had gone to their rooms. They had driven back from Monte Marcello in silence. Several times during the journey he quietly pressed her hand, and once he kissed it, as they waited by the toll on the autostrada. It was the most intimate silence she had ever known, a communication deeper than words. She went upstairs to her room and closed the door. She saw her reflection in the mirror and was shocked. Her face was colorless, her lipstick gone, dark shadows under her eyes. The wind on the mountain at Monte Marcello had whipped her hair. She combed it, her hand unsteady. She had had two love affairs —one lasting two years with a boy too young to marry her when they were both at college, and a brief and unhappy respite from nursing Peter, which was over after a few weeks. She couldn't remember a moment during either, when she had felt as she did in the arms of Alessandro di Malaspiga. She dropped the comb and turned away. She had cried in the grotto at Romani, and again on the ridge of that windswept hill. Now there were no tears left. He had wiped them away with his fingers, not understanding what they meant. Tears of joy, he had promised her, because he was thinking of the future. He had been happy, triumphant. She poured herself some water and sipped it slowly. She felt drained and weary.

She loved him. She faced the reality with a strange calmness. From the moment they met, the day she saw him in the long drawing room at the villa, something had sparked between them, some terrible chemistry had begun to work.

She had fought hard against it. Katharine gave herself credit for the struggle. Even though she had weakened in the early days, when Raphael told her the truth about her brother's death she could protest that from that moment her purpose hadn't wavered. She had hated Alessandro di Malaspiga and feared him; nothing altered that. But now she knew she also loved him. Ruthless, a murderer, enriching himself by the most evil traffic in the world, responsible for the final extinction of hope for her brother. He talked of being judged by history. He spoke with the arrogance of a man who doesn't accept the standards of common humanity. It wouldn't be history who passed sentence. It would be the woman who loved him. Whatever he was and whatever he had done, nothing could alter that love or change its consequences. The modern-minded, self-sufficient American girl who had left on Harper's mission had been taken over by another self, a stranger, with alien feelings and traditions that were very old.

Italy and her heritage had claimed her. The New World had not been proof against the power of the Old. The respectable, conventional Dexters, with their sensible values were a blur. Her whole life before she came to Florence was indistinct, as if it had been lived by someone else. She was a Malaspiga, in love with one of her own kin, and she knew by instinct the course that must be taken.

She could never destroy that love, but she had to destroy him. Not because of what had happened to her brother, still less for any moral reasons, but because she felt they were predestined to destroy each other. It was a decision based on a sense of fatalism, the same instinctive knowledge that had overcome her when she first came to the castle. No human beings could escape their destiny. Theirs was to find each other and to be destroyed. She was going back to the storeroom that night, to see that picture and to mark it. Through her, justice would overtake her cousin, and whatever part of her survived, it would be purged.

She changed into a plain black dress, painted her pale lips and went downstairs.

Francesca di Malaspiga was getting dressed when the door to her bedroom opened. She ran to meet him and flung her arms around his neck.

"*Carissimo*—hold me!" John kissed her, stroking the smooth black hair hanging down her back.

They held each other, kissing hungrily. "Make love to me . . ." she whispered. "Make me forget this afternoon!"

"There's nothing to forget," he comforted. "And anyway we have each other. What do you care what he does with her? I love you!" He moved her to the bed and began stripping off her dress. For a moment she stood naked in front of him, her white body shrouded by the long black hair.

He reached out for her. "One day I'm going to sculpt you like this. That will be my masterpiece."

Later he dressed her. She took his hand and kissed it. "You're so gentle with me," she said. "So tender. I can't believe what's happened to me. I never thought it would be possible for me—"

"He didn't know how to love you," John Driver said. "You only needed patience . . . you're wonderful, don't you know that?"

"With you I am," she said simply. "Only with you. God, if only we could be together all the time! I've waited so long!"

"You won't have to wait much longer," he said. "I have a feeling that pretty soon we're going to have our life together. I promised you that a long time ago. Remember that I love you." He kissed her lips and then her forehead. She bowed her head submissively. "Do up your hair, my darling," he said. "And hurry down. I'd better go now."

Alessandro was walking in the garden. He had changed his clothes and come down early. His mood was exultantly happy, and yet he wanted solitude.

From the top terrace, the view stretched out over the Tuscan plain, turned golden by the setting sun. As he walked in the gardens, a lizard streaked for safety along the gray stone wall and vanished down a crevice. He climbed a flight of rough stone steps, their borders crowded with the graceful blue plumbago that grew everywhere like a weed, and at the top he lit a cigarette. It was a perfect evening, warm and peaceful—the scent of flowers and shrubs was strong.

She loved him. He blew smoke into the air, his happiness enlarging like the smoke ring. There was a step behind him and he turned. John Driver stood there.

"I've been looking for you," he said. "They told me you'd gone for a walk."

"It's a beautiful evening," the Duke said. "I wanted to be alone for a few minutes."

John didn't respond to the hint. He sat on the edge of the wall.

"Sandro, I've got to talk to you. This is crazy!"

"Wanting to walk in my garden before I spend the evening with my family?" The expression on the Duke's face and the tone of his voice should have silenced the younger man. Driver scowled at the ground, crushing the feathery plumbago flowers in his hands.

"Bringing that girl here," he said. "You know exactly what I mean. It's crazy. You've never brought anyone here before. I don't understand why you're taking the risk."

"There is no risk," Alessandro said impatiently. "You're talking nonsense. Katharine is my cousin—naturally, she comes to the castle. I brought her here because she wanted to come and because I wanted to invite her."

"All right." Driver spread both his hands. "All right. You bring your cousin here and show her the family home. Okay, fine. But you took her to the gallery and down to the store-room. For Christ's sake, why did you do it? She's not a fool —she could notice something . . ."

"I didn't know you were so nervous," the Duke said, and his smile was momentarily cruel. Then it became friendly, and suddenly he put his hand on Driver's shoulder.

"Don't worry," he said. "I'm not a fool either. Just because we know what we are doing, we imagine it must suggest it-self to everybody else. This is nonsense. Why should Katha-rine suspect anything? Haven't you heard it said that love is blind?" Driver moved, and the Duke's hand slid off his shoulder.

"You should keep that kind of thing for Florence," he said. "Maybe I'm just a middle-class Canadian, but I wouldn't bring it home to my family."

"Be careful," Alessandro said quietly. "We work together, and we are friends. But there are certain limits. I don't want to remind you of them unless I have to do so. If you have come out here to complain that I am jeopardizing our opera-tion, then I can assure you there is nothing to fear. But any personal matter concerning my cousin is nothing to do with you. I hope you understand?"

"You know how to express yourself," Driver said slowly. There was a red patch on the middle of his forehead, like a blush. "But we're in this thing together. I'm a partner, not a bloody lackey. I say you should send her back to Florence. Take her back yourself and let me get on with sending the consignment out."

Alessandro trod out his cigarette. He looked at Driver calmly, with disinterest. "You're not a partner, my dear John. You share in the profits, but there's no partnership. I shall do exactly what I like regarding my cousin, and you will keep quiet. Otherwise it is you who will go back to Florence." He turned and walked away toward the castle. Driver watched him, the patch deeper on his forehead. It looked like a skin allergy. Alessandro had turned a corner out of sight.

"You bastard," Driver said.

The Duke and Uncle Alfredo were drinking champagne in the salon. The old Duchess came in, making an entrance out of lifelong habit, and both men came toward her. She looked a frail, exquisite figure in pink lace, her corsage of roses nestling in a ruby and diamond spray.

Alessandro took her hand and kissed her on the cheek. "You look beautiful, Mamia," he said. The Duchess smiled.

"Lovely, lovely," declared Alfredo. "Bella Isabella!" He swept a low bow, at the same time removing an embroidered velvet smoking cap. The Duchess took a glass of champagne. She would have preferred a cocktail, but since her son was apparently celebrating something, she decided it would be tactless not to join him. She looked at him and wondered whether she should ask him what had happened at the water gardens that afternoon.

He was teasing the old Prince, evidently in a gay, relaxed mood. The trip must have been a success. The gardens at Romani were a family joke, a trick that had been played on their guests since she had come to Malaspiga as a bride. One of the Count Romani's brothers had been an admirer of hers. She remembered that isolated grotto with its effective screen of water. He had been very gallant, although a little stout and short, with a wife who was perpetually pregnant. The Duchess drifted for a moment—it was becoming a habit, to slip away into the past, where one could choose one's memories. Her son was not himself that night. She had always thought him as cold and controlled as his father, devoid of deep feelings except pride and ambition. As a child he had occupied a minor place in her life, reared by a nurse, educated by a tutor. She had been aware that he admired her and enjoyed dazzling the child in the nursery by displaying herself in evening dress. When he became a man and the head of the family, he was a stranger, and she treated him with the same respect she had given his father. But she had never really known him at all. She had never seen him so happy, and she knew with a sad, jealous pang, that the cause was love for someone else. When Katharine came into the room, he hurried to her. Taking her hand he kissed it.

"I've opened champagne for tonight," he said. "I want to celebrate. I'm very happy—you look a little pale. Drink that, it's a fine vintage. I chose it specially for you." Over the glass he toasted her silently. There might have been no one else in the room. Katharine saw John Driver come in; he glanced across at her and then away. He took a glass from the butler and wandered across to the old Duchess. Some moments later Francesca came through the door. She must have seen them standing together from outside because she didn't look, she moved quickly to a chair near the fireplace. When the champagne was offered, she shook her head and turned away.

"Katharine," the old Duchess said, "how pretty you look tonight." She had never called another woman beautiful in her life. It was a word she reserved for herself. She gazed at Katharine for a moment, her head slightly on one side. "You know, you look quite different from when you first came. Don't you think so, Sandro? Doesn't Katharine look different? You look more Italian than American. Perhaps it's the way you've done your hair."

They were all looking at her—Driver with disapproval, Francesca with blatant hatred—but she wasn't aware of anyone but the Duke. The magnificent black eyes, blazing their message of love and pride, the chiseled lips curved in a tender smile. For a second her hand crept to her breast and touched it. She had never believed that love could be a physical pain.

"My mother is right," he said. "Your Italian blood is coming out. You must always wear your hair brushed back like that. It makes you even more beautiful." At that moment the telephone began to ring. John Driver moved across to answer it.

"When can I come to you?" Alessandro said quietly. "Will you let me come tonight—"

"Sandro," John called across to him. "The call's for you."

"When?" the Duke whispered. "How long must I wait for you—"

"Tomorrow," Katharine said. "Not tonight. Tomorrow." His lips formed a word she couldn't understand and then he went to take the call. She could hear Driver murmuring on the telephone in the background.

"He's right here." He turned to Alessandro. "It's Lars Svenson. He's in Rome."

The old Duchess went to bed soon after ten thirty. They had been listening to Vivaldi on a stereo built into the room used as a general sitting room, and she had begun to doze in her chair. Katharine watched her gradually drifting away, her head on one side, cushioned into the enormous wingbacked chair, with her little feet crossed on a footstool. She felt envious of the peaceful withdrawal from life that was the solace of old age. No pain, no desire, no convulsions of the spirit could trouble Isabella di Malaspiga. If she felt, it was on a scale of trivia—comfort, admiration, the cocktails she loved, the choice of her dresses. Her vanity was her only vulnerable point. She had to be beautiful and to be told so. In the semi-shadow, there was a ravishing quality about her face in repose that fascinated Katharine. Looking at the miracle of bone structure and the graceful sweep of hair against the old woman's cheek, she thought how well the image fitted with Vivaldi's gracious music from a different age. Fear and death and the pain of loving were held at bay for a brief moment. Then suddenly the Duchess slipped into a deeper sleep and her jaw fell open. It was like looking at a corpse. "Mamia." Alessandro had seen it too, and he was beside his mother, gently waking her. She opened her eyes, looked startled for a second and then smiled up at him.

"I think you should go upstairs," he said. "Francesca will take you." He bent and kissed her cheek, helping her to stand. "Good night."

John Driver got up, yawned slightly and excused himself. "You know, I'm tired, too. I'll take Mamia up to her room."

Immediately Katharine was on her feet. "I'm going with you," she said. She looked at her cousin. "It must be the air here," she said. "I can't keep awake."

The disappointment in his eyes was quickly hidden. He gave his lazy smile and said lightly, "Stay for five minutes. Till the record's finished."

"Why don't you? The finale's the best part," the old Duchess encouraged. "John and Francesca can look after me."

"I'm afraid I'd fall asleep," Katharine said. She didn't look at the Duke. She knew what had to be done and she had made her decision to do it. She couldn't trust herself if he made love to her a second time. Betrayal. The word came into her mind and shocked her. She loved him, and she was going to betray him, but being what he was, there was no other course. She turned back and came to him. He caught her hand. "I won't stay," she said quietly. "But it's been a lovely evening. Thank you." She reached up and kissed him on the cheek. A Judas kiss, with the same mixture of love and hatred that condemns to death . . .

When she got to her own room, she took off the black dress and changed into a skirt and sweater, with slip-on shoes. She put the marker in the skirt pocket, pulled the window curtains back so that there was light in the room and sat on the bed to wait. It was a brilliant clear night, with a full moon. It turned the marble mountains into snow, showing the clouds floating past on what must be a keen wind. Below, the lights in the town of Malaspiga were going out, until the houses and the church were eyeless in the silver light. She lit a cigarette, watching the tip glow in the semi-darkness from the curtained bed. Her room and everything in it was brilliantly illuminated by the moonlight.

It was her good luck that it should be such a perfect night; finding her way to the banqueting hall in the dark would have been very difficult. She had gone over the plan many times during the evening, looking around her to memorize the way. It was eleven thirty by her watch. The old Duchess was down the corridor. She didn't know where Alessandro slept, or where the servants were, but she suspected that it was on a higher level. Eleven forty-eight. It was superstitious to wait for midnight. There was no magic in the hour, no guarantee that he would be asleep, and that she wouldn't meet him on her way downstairs. She got up, pulled her bed curtains closed and went to the door. It seemed to creak when she opened it. She waited, feeling her pulse leaping, and very carefully looked out into the corridor. There was a light at the end, near the Duchess' door—the rest was shadowy and silent. The stairs to the main hall, which had to be crossed first, were at the opposite end and very dark. She came outside, gently eased her door shut and began to walk very quickly and lightly to the stairwell. It was so dark she couldn't see beyond the first step. The stairs curved in a wide spiral downward to the lower floor. A rope guiderail ran down the inside of the wall. She felt for this, held tight to it and stepped down. Feeling her way and following the curve of the rope, Katharine climbed downward. Once she slipped on the edge of the stair, and saved herself by grabbing the rope with both hands. At a turn in the stair she suddenly saw light.

The hallway was only a few steps below; the light came from two electric sconces set in the stone wall on either side of the iron-studded entrance doors. She waited by the bottom step, listening for any sound that might indicate another human presence. There was nothing. Slowly she stepped down into the hall; it was cold and she shivered. There was very little furniture in it, except a massive iron-bound wooden chest, so old that it was black, two chairs on either side of the fireplace which was so wide and tall that, according to Alessandro, it burned a wagon-load of wood, and a huge marble urn filled with potted plants. It looked larger and bleaker than she expected in the gloomy light. She walked across, raised on her toes with the instinctive tread of the intruder, opened a door leading into the armory, fortunately lit by the bright moonlight through the arched windows, and hurried past into the banqueting hall. It was silver and gray in the light from its great central window, a place of deep shadow where the tapestries moved imperceptibly against the walls, stirred by some secret draught, and the long table could have been the feasting board of ghosts. The silence, the atmosphere, heavy and moist with the sweat of ancient stone, made it seem larger still and full of menace. She crossed at a run and came to the wall and the door to the storeroom. There was a small iron loop, and she pulled. The door opened. Here it was impossible to see. Katharine felt with her hand to the right, up the wall, and when her fingers touched a switch, she snapped it on and there were the stairs she had gone down with Alessandro that morning. She pulled the door closed behind her and hurried down to the room below. Fluorescent lighting flooded it—for a moment she blinked at the contrast. There was the furniture, ready for packing. She shouldn't have run, but she did, hearing the sound of her shoes on the stone floors and not caring, because in a few moments she would have uncovered the picture, marked the back of the canvas and be on her way upstairs again. The picture stood on its easel, shrouded in the green cloth. Someone had been back and covered the corner of frame which she had noticed. The marble children stood side by side on a table; they too had been moved since she had seen them that morning. She took the marker out of her pocket, slipping the cap off, and as she did so, she dropped it. It rolled under the table. She bent to pick it up, and decided that she had better mark the little marble busts, since they were part of the consignment. She lifted the girl with both hands and slowly turned it on its side. She made a cross on the base, and as she did so, a hand fell on her shoulder and a voice behind her said,

"I thought I'd find you here. . . ."

She turned with a cry of terror, knocking the marble off balance, and she was face to face with him.

Pisa was a very small airport. There was none of the streamlined bustle common to the big air terminals of Carpenter's experience. He came down the steps and hurried across the runway toward the main building; inside he was swallowed by a throng of people. It was late at night, but the plane had been full. There was a Hertz office with a dark-haired girl sitting behind the counter. Carpenter rented a car, watching in a sweat of impatience while she filled out the forms. It was a Fiat 127, small and fast. He checked the tank and found it was full. He had begun to expect any factor which could cause delay. The night outside was warm and windless, bright with moonlight. Over his head the Milky Way swept in a shimmering arc across the sky.

He started the Fiat and swung out onto the Pisa road. There was a lot of traffic leaving the airport, and not until he had reached the perimeter of the town was he able to accelerate toward the outlet into the autostrada. He calculated that Malaspiga would be twenty minutes' drive if he went top speed; and then at last he saw the way clear, and his foot went down on the pedal until it was slammed against the floorboards. He blessed the straight two-lane highway, remembering from somewhere that Italians were said to be the best engineers and builders in the world. In the opposite lane cars flashed past him, their headlights blazing. There was a distant howl of a horn that was like a phantom wailing, only to fade out seconds later. He was touching 180 kilometers, and the little car was shuddering under the strain. A glance at his watch showed that it was close to midnight on the luminous dial. A big blue and white sign said MASSA 2 KILO-METERS on the right, with an arrow for the turn off. He began to slow down. The back of his shirt was sticking to him with sweat, and his hands were greasy on the wheel. He wouldn't consider what he might do if he didn't find Katharine at the castle. It was the first time in any operation when he hadn't planned ahead. The gun in his shoulder holster was fully loaded. He brought the little car around and out through the exit lane; he stopped at the toll booth, flung a five-thousand-lire note at the duty officer, who shouted after him to collect his change as he drove on. Now it was difficult to drive fast. The country road was narrow, and twice the lights of other cars bisected the darkness from a crossroad and he had to halt. There was a sign saying MASSA, but no indication of where Malaspiga lay. He pulled into the side, and looked at the road map he had bought while he was waiting for the car. Massa lay close to the autostrada on the line of the coast. Further inland and up a rising gradient of mountain roads, he found the town of Malaspiga. He had miscalculated the time. Five kilometers on roads that wound as sharply upward as the road to the castle and the town, could take as long as twenty on the arrow straight highway. He let in the clutch and set off. He could only trust that no truck or slow-moving vehicle appeared ahead of him. Years of experience had warned him that murders were usually committed at night.

Alfredo di Malaspiga couldn't make up his mind to go to bed. He had undressed, putting on pajamas and dressing gown, examined himself for some time in the looking glass to make sure he hadn't forgotten anything, and then began sorting through his collection of nightcaps. There were a dozen little round ones, some made in linen, others in wool—plain, decorated, with tassels and without. He tried on several before he made a choice. His earliest memory was of seeing his grandfather, Duke Piero, sitting up in bed with a satin cap on his head, and the child had been enchanted to find that men wore hats in bed.

Alfredo had always considered the head the most important part of the human body. The soul must surely be inside the skull, allied to the brain. Hair was one of God's miracles and Alfredo considered that it must be protected against climate and changes in temperature. His obsession had sound reasoning as a base. He cared for the most vital part of himself and adorned it at the same time. It seemed perfectly sensible to him, and when the well-meaning monks had tried to regulate his changes of hats and caps, he had reacted, first with violence and then with miserable apathy. He didn't think of the monastery, except when he saw Francesca. She had wanted to send him back; he knew that, and he had never forgiven her.

He had enjoyed his dinner. He felt stimulated by the company, instead of relying solely on looking at his hat collection for amusement and trying everything on a dozen times a day. He was quite happy during the time his family was in Florence, which he detested—the noise and bustle confused him —but he was happier when they were all together in the castle. He sat on the edge of his bed, and wondered for a moment whether a yellow woolen nightcap might not be a better choice. He liked the beautiful blond cousin. Hats had not been his only interest in youth. He gave a sly little grin. He had liked blond hair; there was a girl in Malaspiga who had true Titian coloring, the golden red made famous by the painter . . . Long, long ago. His mind flitted, restless, touching on one subject and then another. He frowned. He did like the cousin, not just because she was beautiful to look at, but because she had made him feel important. And most of all because she had admired his hats. He was worried about her. That was why he hadn't gone to bed. She should go away from the castle. He didn't want anything to happen to her . . .

He re-tied the cord on his dressing gown and wandered to the door. He was not supposed to leave his room at night. Alessandro would be angry. There was a danger he might trip and fall. He opened the door; there was light in the corridor. Once, some time ago, he had left his room and pattered through the empty passages, creeping downstairs. He had been going to the kitchen. He remembered that. He wanted something to eat, and the maid had forgotten to put biscuits by his bed. He had gone out and downstairs and he had seen . . . He stopped, one hand cupped to his mouth. He gave a little groan of fear and distress. Never mind what Alessandro said. He hadn't found out about the last time. He had to go and tell the nice girl with the lovely hair, that it wasn't safe for her to stay at Malaspiga. He wasn't such a fool as everybody thought. He knew things he wasn't meant to know. And he had seen things. He began to creep down the passageway toward the stairs.

Alessandro stayed on in the little drawing room, listening to the end of the Vivaldi concerto. He felt at peace, his spirit soothed by the music. Closing his eyes, he thought of Katharine. His mother had been right when she remarked on how much she had changed. She seemed to have grown older, not in the context of age but of the indefinable wisdom and experience that denotes a mature woman.

It had begun as an attraction. Listening to the mellow cadences of the oboe concerto, he analyzed the progression from wanting to have an affair with her into the consuming need to have her with him all the time, to possess her mentally as well as physically. When he said that before marriage he had had many women, it was not a boast. He had believed himself in love several times during his twenties, but never with the serious conviction that would suggest marriage. That had come with Francesca. The disillusion, the revulsion he had experienced, and then the bitter sex which he had forced on his wife to make her pregnant, had twisted his capacity for feeling anything but lust for any woman. And if he had indulged in love affairs before Francesca, he couldn't have counted the mistresses who followed after they ceased to live together. And there was the supreme irony, the illogicality of the female mind. His wife, with her shrinking from the crudity of lovemaking, became the prey of violent jealousy as soon as he announced that he would never live with her again. She wept, she reproached, she made scenes that would have done credit to a woman genuinely in love with an unfaithful husband.

When he no longer wanted her for any reason, she couldn't endure the thought that he was finding happiness with anybody else. Some part of her nature, not entirely perverted, cried out against being rejected as a woman. Perhaps she too had matured, perhaps the adolescent instincts seeking pleasure and fulfillment from her own sex had grown to normality. Alessandro didn't know and didn't care. He sensed that John Driver was attached to her and that in her chilly way she was responding, but this aroused no jealousy or interest. He was too deeply involved with Driver to make scenes about his emotional fumbling toward Francesca. He wouldn't have cared what they did. He needed John. Until John came into their lives, his business had been profitable by standards that didn't include restoring and refurnishing Malaspiga Castle. The castle had become an obsession with him. And the need to leave it for posterity, to erase the scars of war and poverty began when he went there after his return from Hollywood, when, as he had told Katharine, he took shelter in his home without hope for the future, with his life ruined. He had found it a forsaken shell, the weeds from the once splendid gardens creeping up to the outside walls. He had gone to the turret on the west side and climbed onto the battlements. Below him stretched the plain of Tuscany, green and silver with olive trees, the blue shimmer of the sea cut into by the sweep of the Magra, once the seaport for the great inland city of Sarzana, now marooned inside its medieval walls. Below the castle, the little town of Malaspiga clung like a child to its mother's skirts. He had been born there, grown up with the view that had pleased the eye of generations of Malaspigas since the fifteenth century. He knew the people of the town by name, just as he knew the little paths and secret places in the olive groves where he had hidden as a child and played with the children of a poor *contadino* who lived in a hovel on the hillside. Malaspiga was more to him than a historical heritage. He had lived through the loss of his family's power and the night when the partisans searched the castle looking for his father. The old Duke had already escaped to Florence; he had lived the rest of his life embittered and withdrawn, dissipating the family treasures to pay his debts.

His last words to his son were regret that he had only ruin to bequeath him. He had died without hearing Alessandro's promise that he would devote his life to restoring what had been destroyed. The first part of that promise had been to marry Francesca—money and continuity were what the Malaspigas needed.

By the time he met Katharine he had built a school and a pediatric clinic for the town of Malaspiga, brought modern drainage and electricity to its people, and was enjoying the selfish, hedonistic life of a rich man with no one to love but himself. He was the master of his household and his family: His mother obeyed him and deferred to him, exactly as she had done with his father, and he had come to terms with Francesca in his own mind. His solution was to ignore her completely. The memory of the degenerate Elise Bohun's hands caressing his wife's naked back was something he could never forget. He had been offered a small Poussin painting of two nymphs embracing in a landscape. The suggestion of lesbianism had so disgusted him, that he refused to buy it.

He rang for the servant on duty; he told the man to put out the lights and close the main doors for the night. He went upstairs to his bedroom. It had the finest view in the castle, with windows that looked out over the Tuscan plains and the line of the coast. It had been a dark room, stiff and oppressive, unchanged for centuries since it was first used as the lying-in room for the unhappy wife of his ancestor Paolo. She had died there, in the huge oak tester bed, leaving twin sons. He himself had been born there. The bed was hung with velvet and damask, its headboard painted with the Malaspiga arms. It looked like a dark cave, vast and uninviting for one person.

He didn't want to sleep. He wanted Katharine Dexter. He wanted her with physical pain, with passion, with tenderness. He understood the fire in the loins only too well—now he accepted that the ache in his heart was not a cliché. He had almost despaired, until the moment in the grotto when in spite of herself she had responded. Again, she had tried to escape him, slipping out of reach at the last moment. When he told her the truth about his wife and held her in his arms again, he knew he had won. He had never been so happy in his life. Or so in need. He wanted to hear her say she loved him, he wanted to wring the promise out of her that she would never leave . . . She had refused him that night. "Tomorrow." Besides the passion in her, he had sensed a fear and a resistance to him. Perhaps it was a fear of love itself. If so, he knew the cure for that. But impetuosity was a mistake; the impulse to go to her room that night must be resisted. When tomorrow came, he would remind her of her promise. And he knew that she would keep it.

7

"Oh, God," Katharine said. His hand was still on her shoulder, he was looking down at her and there was a slight smile on his lips. "Thank God," she whispered. "It's you—I thought. . . ."

"You thought it was Alessandro, didn't you?" John Driver said. "What are you doing down here?"

He had pale gray eyes—in an ordinary, even ugly face, they were his best feature. Katharine saw the look in them and under the hand pressed on her shoulder, she went stiff with terror. There was murder in his eyes, although he was smiling at her.

Her reply was incoherent, stammered out wildly before she had time to think. "I lost something—this morning . . . I was looking for it. . . ."

"You were looking for the stuff," he chided her gently. "I know all about you, Miss Dexter, so you needn't try to lie. You've been very clever, I congratulate you. You deserve to solve the mystery. There's what you were looking for right by your feet."

She looked down, and there lay the little sculpture of the girl. Its nose had broken off and a stream of white dust lay on the ground.

"It's made in two halves," Driver said. "You'd never see the join—it's in the carving of the hair. That's clever too, don't you think so? I'd say there was twenty pounds of heroin inside that one head. The other one's full of it too."

For a moment Katharine thought she was going to faint. There was pain in her shoulder where his fingers were pressing harder and harder into the skin.

Angelo. Firelli's clue. But only half of it, misheard down a crackling telephone line. *Michelangelo, the sculptor.*

"Don't pass out on me," he said. With his free hand he slapped her face. "Don't faint." The blow shocked her. She raised her arm to defend herself, and immediately he caught it, twisting it savagely up and backward. "What were you doing besides looking?" he asked. "How much did you find out. . . ."

"Nothing," she gasped, fighting the pain as he bent her arm backward. "I thought it was Alessandro. . . . Oh, God, you're breaking my arm!"

He let her go so suddenly she staggered. She reached out for the table to steady herself, and the marker fell out of her clenched hand. He looked at it and the smile widened. "Ah," he said. "You were identifying the pieces—that's very clever, too. But since my little children won't be going now, it won't do any good. There's nothing in the other things. Only in my sculptures." He gave her a little push. "They may not be great works of art, Miss Dexter, but they've made me a millionaire. That's surely something for a poor hick Canadian who learned to carve by whittling sticks on a farm—"

Katharine didn't want to look at him. The plain face with the frank expression had become cruel and watchful. His right hand was opening and closing as if he were going to hit her again. She had almost confided in him in the garden, asked him to help her. . . . It was like a nightmare. "Why did you do it?" she whispered. "Why did you work for him? You could have been a great artist. . . ."

"Work for him?" He suddenly snarled at her. "The arrogant bastard thinks he owns me! He figures he's some kind of twentieth-century Medici. . . . You talk about talent!" He reached forward and seized her arm—she shrank back, held by the table. He stepped close to her, so close she could feel his breath on her face. He was hurting her, but almost unconsciously. "I wanted genius," he said, "not talent. The world is full of talented people, crawling with mediocrities who can paint and sculpt. I've seen work exhibited that I'd have smashed up with a hammer! Rubbish, daubs—I didn't want that! I wanted to create beauty. Great art. When I was a kid I borrowed a book on Michelangelo from the traveling library. I saw what he sculpted, what he painted. I knew that's what I had to do." She tried to pull away from him, but he gave her arm a brutal twist. "I have the vision," Driver said. "I have it here, in my head. But not in my hands. I can see it, but I can't create it! Do you have any idea what it means to spend your whole life reaching toward something and to fail? To be so full of beauty that you could burst because you can't get it out?"

His eyes were feverish, blazing. She thought in terror and confusion that in some part he was insane.

"No," she said. "I don't know what it means. I don't know how anyone could smuggle drugs and make money out of murder. You had a talent, even if it wasn't the great thing you wanted. What you've done is obscene."

"You're pretty brave," he said. "You don't whine when you're caught. I'll give you that much. You thought it was Alessandro who'd followed you, didn't you? I was coming along to your room when I saw you come out. What am I going to do with you, Miss Dexter?" He put his head a little on one side. "When Lars told me on the telephone about you tonight, I was shocked. I liked you. I really did. I hoped you'd go home and get out of Alessandro's hair, but I never sus-

pected for a moment what you really were. A narcotics agent.
A spy.

"I'm going to have to shut you up somewhere while I think
what to do." There was a second when he seemed off guard.
He wasn't looking at her, he had let go of her arm, which
was numb from the pressure, and there was a space between them. Fear made her incredibly quick. She flung herself
sideways, eluding his sudden grab by inches, and began
to race across the floor toward the stairs. Once out of the
underground room, in the banqueting hall or the anterooms,
she could scream for help. She had the advantage of surprise, and she was faster than he was. She heard him bump
into something as he followed and swear fiercely. She reached
the stairs, and on a quick impulse, snapped off the light in
the room below. She raced up them, gasping, trembling with
fear. Once she slipped and fell to her knees, only to scram-
ble up again. She could hear him behind her, and then she
had reached the door into the banqueting hall. It opened as
she pushed it. Silhouetted clearly against the brilliant moonlight, blocking her path, stood Francesca di Malaspiga. She
held a gun in her hand, pointed at Katharine.

"Don't move," she said. "I would love to kill you."

Driver was behind her then. He spoke to the girl. "We'll
have to put this one in a safe place," he said. His hand came
and covered Katharine's mouth, pulling her head backward.
"You go ahead, my darling, and be sure there's nobody
around. I'll see she doesn't make any trouble."

Francesca looked at him—she held the gun down by her
side. "Upstairs?"

"I guess so," Driver said.

Alfredo moved very slowly. He shuffled in his slippers, and
it seemed that he was making a lot of noise. He paused to
listen and look around in case he had been heard and anyone
was coming. The corridor was empty. He came to the head
of the stairs, and remembering he had gone that way on the

other occasion, took a cautious step down the stairs and then another. He had forgotten his intention to warn Katharine. Memory was confusing him, reminding him that like that other time, he hadn't had his biscuits and was hungry. He liked going to the kitchens, enjoyed opening the cupboards and finding odd delicacies. Like a child he enjoyed the feeling of innocent theft. He never opened the big modern refrigerator or went near the deep freezer. He hated the cold air which had chilled his whole head when he once opened the door by mistake. Slowly, feeling his way down, Alfredo came around the corner of the stairway onto the bottom step. And there, crossing the hallway, he saw the same scene as the last time. Only now it was the cousin who was being taken . . . He didn't make a sound. He held his breath and cringed against the stairwell, watching as they forced her to the same door, leading to the same place. They went inside and he gave a little gurgle of alarm. His legs were trembling; they almost gave way under his body as he turned and stumbled back up the stairs, clutching at the guide rope that ran down the steep stone wall. He couldn't think of anything but getting safely back into his own room and hiding his head under the bedclothes.

With Francesca gliding ahead of them, Katharine was hustled through the banqueting hall, her arm wrenched up behind her back, Driver's hand tight on her mouth. When they left the armory and came into the entrance hall, she tried to resist; he jerked her arm upward. The pain was so intense she nearly fainted. He gripped her tightly against him and half lifted, half dragged her after Francesca to a door on the right of the entrance. It was partly hidden by a leather screen. It led into a long stone passageway, lit by the moonlight. He eased the pressure on her arm and pushed her to walk forward. At the end of the passage they passed through another large room, filled with furniture shrouded in dust sheets; at this point Francesca switched on lights. Katharine stumbled on, propelled by Driver, following the slim figure ahead still holding the gun. If they turned on lights they must be very confident that there was no one near to see them.

Out of the room, which was musty smelling with disuse, down another corridor, shorter than the first, and up a small winding stair which ended on a landing.

"Why don't you wait here?" Driver called out, and Francesca turned back. He took his hand away from Katharine's mouth. "You can scream your head off now," he said. "Nobody will hear you here."

"Go on," the Duchess said coldly. "Scream. See if anyone comes!"

Sick, and feeling her strength failing, Katharine shook her head. They would have derived some sadistic amusement if she'd taken them at their word. She wasn't going to satisfy them.

"You make a pretty couple," she said. The Duchess stepped forward quickly, and Driver snapped a warning.

"No! Leave her alone— You stay behind, darling. It's a long climb. I'll take her upstairs."

Katharine turned her head to look at him. "Where are you taking me? Why didn't you let her shoot me?"

"I'm taking you to a place where you can't make any trouble," Driver said. "Just till we decide what to do with you. Come on, through here." There was another door. Francesca opened it for them, dragging the heavy iron latch up with difficulty. She reached inside and switched on a light. Rising ahead of them, Katharine saw a spiral stair, so steep and narrow that unless she had both hands free she couldn't hope to climb it. From the shape and the angle of the curve, she knew they were at the foot of one of the castle towers.

"Uncle Alfredo!" Alessandro caught the old man by the hands. He had rattled the door handle and then flung it open; he stood leaning against the lintel, gasping for breath. Somewhere on the way to his own room, he had changed direction. He was extremely frightened, but in spite of his

mental infirmity, he possessed a simple integrity. His generation used to call it honor. He couldn't run and hide a second
time. Even if Alessandro were angry with him for leaving
his room, he had to go to him and tell what he had seen. The
Duke brought him inside and closed the door. He tried to
steer him to the bed and sit him down, but his uncle resisted,
pulling away from him.

"Are you ill, Uncle . . . what's the matter?"

"They're going to kill her!" he said. He caught the Duke
by the shoulder and feebly tried to shake him. "They're going to murder her! Stop them—for the love of God!"

"You've been dreaming," Alessandro said gently. "Be calm,
Uncle, you've just had a nightmare. I'm going to take you
back to bed and send Stefano up with a hot drink. A little
brandy in it and you'll go to sleep again."

"No!" The Prince turned on him, suddenly furious. "I
wasn't dreaming anything—I haven't been to bed! I went
downstairs . . . I wanted a biscuit! And then I saw them.
Taking that poor child to the East Tower! Just like the other
one. It wasn't my business what happened to him. . . . But
I like her—she's our cousin! Stop them, Alessandro, stop
them!" He turned away, shaking one fist in the air. "You
mustn't blame John," he said. "It's all *her* fault—she made
him do it—she's the wicked one . . ."

"Katharine? What are you talking about? Who's taking
Katharine to the East Tower? Uncle, if you're making up some
story . . ."

The old man grew calm, and said quietly, "Your wife and
John—I saw them dragging her across the hall. He was holding his hand over her mouth. They went into the eastern
wing. This is the second time I've seen them do it. It was a
man they took there the last time, and John was pointing a
gun at him. You were in Florence. I never saw him again.
They are going to take her up to the tower, and kill her. They
didn't see me; I was hiding by the stairs." He opened his
mouth to explain in more detail, but his nephew brushed
past him and was running down the corridor. Alfredo low-

ered himself onto the bed and sat down. Alessandro had
believed him. He hadn't reproached him for wandering about
at night, and he would know how to stop them hurting the
cousin. Also the enemy who had wanted to return him to
the monastery would be punished at last. His head drooped
onto his chest and he dozed.

"Go on up," Driver said. He had released Katharine's arm;
it was aching right into the shoulder. Looking up at the
narrow, tortured stair, she felt a sense of horror. It came
over her with such force that she leaned against the gray
stone wall, trembling. She had never been a prey to neurotic
fears. Confined spaces, none of the manifestations of nervous phobia so common in the agitated society of the modern world had ever troubled her. But she couldn't bring herself
to climb that curving cliff of stair into the turret. Something terrible was at the top of it, something so evil that it
couldn't be imagined . . .
    "I can't," she whispered. "I can't go up there."
    "You don't have to be afraid," he said. "I'm not going to
hurt you. I'm just going to lock you up." He squeezed in
front of her; the space was so narrow that his body brushed
against her. He took her right hand in his and gripped it
tight. He might have been doing her a kindness. "I'll go first,"
he said, "and help you up." The next moment she was almost
jerked off her feet as he started up the stairs. Pulling and
dragging her, forcing her to climb, although she stumbled
and began to cry, unnerved by a fear that was getting beyond
her control, Driver led her higher and higher through the
throat of the turret. The walls pressed in on her, her arm
felt as if it were being torn out of its socket. Each time she
pulled backward, he wrenched her up with all his strength.
She had no idea how long they had been climbing. "Careful," he said. "There's a defensive step here." She didn't understand the reference to a step built specially higher than the
rest in medieval times as a deterrent to attackers coming from

below. She misjudged it, slipped and fell. Taken by surprise, he was unprepared for her full weight and he let go. She hit her head against the wall and lay in a cramped, unconscious huddle. He stepped down to her, satisfied that she was knocked out, and swore long and angrily. It was a bump, no more. She had fainted as much from fear . . . He would have to carry her the rest of the way. He pulled her up and lifted her over his shoulder. She hung slack against him, her arms dangling. He began very slowly and with great difficulty because of the constricted space, to climb the rest of the stairs to the top.

Alessandro leaped down the last of the steps and into the hall; it was empty and silent, dimly lit by the wall sconces. This was where his uncle had seen Katharine. "Your wife and John. Dragging her across the hall . . . They're going to take her up to the tower . . ."

He had known immediately that this was no figment of the old man's imagination. He had seen Katharine, just as he described. And there was only one reason why she should be taken by force to the eastern tower. For a moment he felt physically sick with fear. God knew how long it had taken Uncle Alfredo to collect his wits and come to tell him. God knew how long he had been hesitating— He crossed the hall at a run, and opened the door behind the screen. The passage was in darkness, but well enough lit by the moon through its windows for him to see his way. He didn't pause to switch on lights, he ran the length of it, and through the door into the room at the end. Here the lights were on. He didn't even need that proof that his uncle was telling the truth—the open door at the other end confirmed it. At the foot of the staircase leading upward, he paused. It was a short flight of stairs and it ended on a landing. He heard somebody cough. He began to run up the stone steps, lightly, making no noise. At the stair head he paused, and looked around the corner. He saw Francesca. She was standing with her back to him. She coughed again, and leaned against the wall. There was a gun in her right hand, held loosely by her side. She was alone and she looked as if she were waiting. *Katharine.* His lips formed the word. *Katharine.* There was only one door on the landing and he knew where that led. It was open.

Francesca di Malaspiga shivered; she felt cold. She wore a sweater, but it didn't protect her from the chill in the atmosphere. She hated stone, hated the bleakness and the feel of it. Her earliest memory of the castle was one of revulsion, even before she came there as Alessandro's wife. She associated it afterward with the torment of her life with him, although they had spent their first six months in Florence. Since she had become John Driver's mistress, she avoided that memory, unless it was to bolster her hatred of her husband. She had spent the first part of her honeymoon frigid with fear and disgust at the desire of a virile man who insisted he was showing how he loved her. Elise Bohun. She only remembered her with gratitude. To the frightened, unhappy young girl she had been comforting and kind, interposing herself between her and Alessandro as if she understood the situation. Motherless, yearning for the sympathy of her own sex, Francesca had responded to the older woman's solicitude and affection. There was nothing wrong in being embraced, in having Elise smooth her hair and tell her how pretty she was. When the moment of seduction came she was subconsciously prepared. She had let herself be petted, soothed, felt the relationship assume a different role and found that it was satisfying something which recoiled from Alessandro.

She had never shared a secret like the one that existed between her and Elise; it made them allies against both their husbands, her own demanding tormentor and the cardboard film star Elise had married. They clung, they whispered, they communicated silently. And Elise had told her of the delights of heroin, its capacity for wiping out pain and anxiety, for heightening the senses in every exercise in pleasure. If Alessandro hadn't discovered Elise in her room, she would have tried it for herself.

She never had. Even when Elise came out to Italy, and they met in Rome, where Francesca used her sister as an alibi, and resumed their relationship, she had hesitated about following her friend along that path.

In the sun-filled Beverly Hills house, with hothouse lilies in the room and the glamor of a different world to influence her, Francesca had been tempted. But not in Rome. She hadn't taken it herself, but she saw nothing wrong with anyone who did. And then there was the money. Alessandro was poor, and her fortune was modest. She liked beautiful clothes and jewels, she loved to indulge herself in feminine sybaritic ways. Elise was generous, tender, a mother figure who could release her from her tense frigidity. When John Driver came to the villa with his prearranged introduction as a student of sculpture, Francesca welcomed him. She owed it to Elise to do this favor. And her husband, for all his arrogance and his increasing wealth, had not been able to resist the pressure put on him.

She balanced the gun in her right hand. It belonged to John; it was as well he had asked her to follow him down to the storeroom. Katharine Dexter had almost escaped. She looked at her watch. They must be at the top of the stairs. In a few minutes it would be over. Then they had to pack her clothes, drive off in John's car, and establish an alibi on the autostrada. When paying the road toll he would call attention to her, using Katharine's name. It could be done all along the route, making certain some of the attendants on duty would remember their passage. Once in Florence, they would buy a single railway ticket to Pisa for the early morning train, and slip back behind the barrier, driving along the old coast road on the Via Aurelia to Malaspiga before dawn. Driver had worked out the story since receiving Svenson's warning. Katharine had come and asked him to drive her away from the castle. She was distressed by her cousin's attentions and didn't want to stay till the morning. He had left her at the station en route for Pisa. There would be witnesses to prove he had been with a woman. Late at night and wearing a deep brimmed hat, who could identify her clearly afterward— It was clever and with a different variation, it had been worked before. And before the full repercussions came from America, she and Driver would have vanished. They had amassed enough money to buy them privacy anywhere in the world. Enormous wealth deposited in Switzerland. His share in the proceeds. He had promised her that night, the time had come. He would take her away. The Duke di Malaspiga would find that his wife had run off with the Canadian artist he had befriended and there was nothing anyone could do about it. She sighed and let the gun hang slackly in her hand. She knew how to aim and pull the trigger, but she had never used it. She had been ready to shoot Katharine Dexter, at point-blank range. There was nothing in the world she wouldn't do for John Driver. Helping to kill Firelli had been more difficult than leading Katharine to the turret stairs. Her husband loved Katharine. Her perverted jealousy, inflamed still more by the knowledge of what physical passion could be, had fastened upon the American girl, adding a personal motive to the one she shared with Driver. She thought of what would happen at the top of the stairs and allowed herself a thrill of satisfaction which was honestly sadistic. She wished she could have been there to hear the final scream— Driver wouldn't show mercy. There was no one in the world capable of arousing his emotions except her. They had come together in mutual need. He, because he was consumed with ambitions that couldn't be satisfied, incapable of giving anything of himself, and she with the guilt of her only physical relationship, convinced she was an outcast.

John had changed that for her. She had felt inferior to Alessandro, afraid of the scale of his emotions. John and she had groped toward their love. He had shown her patience and tenderness, without reproach for the past. She had given him passionate gratitude, utter submission. She loved him, and soon they would be alone together for the rest of their lives. Out of the shadow of the Malaspigas forever.

When Alessandro sprang on her she gave a shrill scream of fear; the gun was wrenched out of her hand, and she was back against the wall, her husband standing over her. She saw his face and cowered away from him.

"Where is she?" Alessandro said. "What have you done with her?" Francesca didn't answer. He put the gun in his pocket and began to strangle her. "I will kill you if you don't answer me," he said. "Has she gone up to the east turret with John? Has she?"

He pressed harder and she choked, tears coming down her cheeks. Hate blazed in her and she looked at him and saw the loathing and suspicion in his eyes. She knew what his anger meant. It meant the extent of his love for someone else.

"Yes," she whispered. "She wanted to go. She wanted to see it." She tried to claw at his hands.

"At the point of a gun—" Alessandro released her. "If anything has happened to Katharine I will kill both of you." He turned and she sprang after him toward the door leading to the spiral stairs.

"John! John! He's coming after you—"

Malaspiga threw her to one side. She sprawled on the ground, the breath knocked out of her. He started up the stairs.

Katharine regained consciousness before they reached the top. She moved and gave a slight groan; Driver shifted his grip on her, holding her tighter. He rounded the last curve and they were out onto a landing. He let her slide down to the ground, and leaned her against the wall. She pushed the hair back from her face and looked at him. He had switched on a light and it was harsh, coming from a bare bulb in the ceiling. Sweat glittered on his forehead; he looked very pale and he was breathing hard.

"You're heavier than you look," he said. For a moment she couldn't speak. Her head was aching from the blow against the stone wall, her body was trembling and her legs threatened to give way. But the terror was returning. It came in waves, shocking her nervous system, fighting to take control of her completely. It was only physical weakness and confusion after her fall that kept it at bay. "Come on," John Driver said. "I'm going to shut you in here for a while." He stepped close and took her arm. There was a door set in the wall. It was blackened with age, hinged with massive wrought iron, and held shut by a bolt of wood that fitted into a socket in the wall. On the wall to the right, there hung an iron ring.

"In here," John Driver said, and pulled her toward it. Panic overwhelmed her, a terror so intense that she found herself able to fight. Strength flooded into her, summoned by the rush of adrenalin. She kicked and struck out at him, flailing at his face with her nails. He grabbed her, cursing and struggling. She clung to him, crazy with fear, shrieking wildly as he manhandled her to the door, and managed to swing the wooden bolt upright out of its socket. The door opened; inside was blackness and a gush of fetid air. Katharine made a wild effort to break free of him, but by this time he was in command of her, her body was turned toward that awful gaping doorway, there was nothing she could grip because he had twisted her arms behind her.

"Okay." He grunted the word. "Okay—in you go! Give my regards to Firelli!"

He gave a violent heave forward and threw her through the opening. The sound of her own horrified scream echoed back at her as the door slammed shut. In the total darkness, her senses failing, the terror was no longer blind. Not panic, but memory overcame her then. The memory of a little girl, so frightened by what she had been told that she hid weeping and trembling under the bedclothes. A story so horrifying to a child that the child had gratefully forgotten it.

Malaspiga Castle. It had always sounded sinister—the signet ring with its wreath and its spike growing out of the corn . . . Cruelty and death, a death invented by a human monster. She lay in a heap on the floor and sobbed in an agony of comprehension. She knew now why she had fought against going up the spiral stair, why the sight of that door had made her fight like an animal. She was in Duke Paolo's special room.

"Don't touch that!" Alessandro shouted.

With his fingers reaching for the iron ring in the wall, John Driver jerked around to see Malaspiga standing at the head of the stairs. The gun was pointed at him. The Duke began to walk toward him. "Take your hand away from that," he said. "Move away, or I'll shoot!"

"You can't," Driver said. "You can't touch me." He hooked his hand through the iron ring. "Kill me and she goes too."

Alessandro stood still. He had heard Katharine's agonized screams of terror as he hurled himself up the last few steps and into the passage.

Driver stood there, his right hand grasping the ring, with a mocking smile on his face. "If I fall," he said, "my weight will pull it down. And then what'll happen to your girlfriend?"

"Get away from that door and take your hand out of that ring," the Duke spoke quietly. "Otherwise I won't kill you outright. I'll shoot you, one bullet at a time, in every part of your body."

"You don't understand," Driver told him. He shook his head. "She can destroy us all. Me, Francesca, and you. You can't afford to let her get away any more than we can. I tried to warn you tonight, but you wouldn't listen. She has to die, Sandro. Put down the gun, and let me get on with it."

"Don't move!" The Duke took a step toward him.

"It's not what you think, Sandro," Driver said. "She didn't come here to find out about that. She's a narcotics agent. Drugs! That's what it's all about—millions of dollars' worth of heroin, stashed away in my crummy sculptures!"

"I don't believe you," Alessandro said. "I don't believe you. Let go of that ring!"

"You don't believe me—" Driver almost spat the words at him. "You arrogant bastard—you think I spent my time here working for *you?* Wasting my time on your little racket? I'm a millionaire! You want proof? Go and look in the storeroom—one of those little busts has had an accident. That's what she found— We've been running a Mafia operation for the last four years. And you try telling anyone you didn't know about it."

"'We,'" Alessandro said slowly. "You and Francesca. Working together."

"That's right." Driver had regained his calm—he even managed to smile and shrug a little. "Be sensible," he said. "The operation's just about blown anyway. But we've made millions. I'll talk to New York and they'll cut you in. We'll wind up the business here and nobody will be able to prove anything. She has to die, Sandro. She won't feel anything—it's very quick."

The Duke didn't move. Under the crude light his face was gray. "If you touch that ring," he said, "I am going to kill you."

"She isn't worth it," Driver said. "Jail for life, think of that. Think what would happen to your mother. Poor Uncle Alfredo. You'll get over it, Sandro. Just turn around and go back down that stair."

"*You* can get away," Alessandro said. "Take Francesca with you. I won't stop either of you. You have so much money —you can go anywhere in the world. Just forget about Katharine. I promise you, she won't say anything."

"I never thought you could be so naïve," Driver said. "You don't walk out on the Mafia. And you don't think you can open that door and expect her not to say anything? She works for the narcotics bureau in New York. She's a trained operator. Like Firelli, that antique dealer who came down here. He got into my workroom. I had to get rid of him the same way. I'm going to pull this handle, Sandro. Like my old dad said, there's nothing like a *fait accompli* for settling an argument."

The blackness had lost its total density. Slowly Katharine raised her head and lifted herself up from the floor. There was a feeble glimmer of light, and it came from a narrow slit in the wall. She was shaking violently, but the first wild paroxysm of terror was spent.

Numb, exhausted, she dragged herself upright; her legs almost gave way. At any moment it would happen. Perhaps he was delaying this long out of sheer cruelty, leaving her to suffer the ultimate in terror and despair. She couldn't see the door or judge how far she had fallen into the room when he threw her inside. She could only find a wall by going to the window slit. The air was foul and thick. A wave of sickness threatened her. Her legs refused to move. Panic attacked her then, keeping her paralyzed, like a dreamer in a nightmare who cannot run away.

The crisis came and she heard someone crying out to God to help them—the voice was her own—and she began to stumble in the darkness toward that slit of light.

"Stop!" Alessandro di Malaspiga shouted. "Stop! If you touch it I'll shoot—"

"You won't," John Driver said. "You won't throw everything away for one woman. And I won't let Francesca go to jail. After all, it was a Malaspiga who invented it." His fingers gripped the ring, and with a sudden jerk he pulled the handle down. Through the thick walls and the door, Alessandro heard a single scream. He shot John Driver through the chest. The scream was echoing around the passage. He fired again, stepping close, shooting into the sagging body, still clinging to the iron ring which was now depressed by several feet, at the end of an iron lever. Driver tried to say something, but the shots cracked into him, slamming his body in jerks against the wall. He toppled over, and the hand gripping the ring loosened and slipped free. He lay dead at Alessandro's feet, and there were no more bullets left. It was a second or two before Alessandro heard the scream again, a further second while its significance sunk in. He cried out, throwing the gun aside, and with all his strength he rammed the ring slowly upward into its original position.

Katharine had found the wall. She felt the rough stone against her hands, and she flattened herself against it, her fingers scratching at the surface for a hold. The window slit was above her head, there was nothing but blackness ahead. She didn't think or anticipate. Instinct kept her upright, terror kept her still and closed her eyes although she couldn't see. The crash came without warning, a rush of foul air blew up around her and she began to scream and scream. The floor had fallen away—there was a bottomless void at her feet. Now she was living the nightmare which had haunted her childhood. She was going to fall into the pit that lay under the room where Paolo di Malaspiga had imprisoned his victims. It was said to be two hundred feet deep, and at the bottom was a black well with waters that went secretly away beneath the mountain. Her consciousness reeled; she didn't know how close she was balanced to the edge of the void, but if she fainted she would topple into it. There was a thud and everything shook; she gave a single cry of terror and despair before she lost consciousness.

He found her lying face downward on the floor; the light from the corridor picked her out in the darkness. He stumbled toward her, choking in the fetid atmosphere. When he killed Driver he had thought it was her death cry he heard. Even when he brought the floor back, with the second and third screams as evidence that somehow, by some miracle, the mechanism hadn't worked, he hadn't expected to find her. No one had ever escaped . . . He knew, because he had seen the floor fall in daylight; there was less than three feet of solid flooring around the perimeter of that awful drop into the castle bowels. He lifted her in his arms and carried her into the passage. He stepped over Driver's dead body. It was lying on its side, one arm bent under it, the eyes still open and the mouth ajar. The floor was patterned with blood.

He laid Katharine down a little distance away and knelt beside her, holding her against him. She was as pale as if she were dead, and her breathing was shallow. Alessandro bent over her.

"My darling." His voice called her back, persistent, growing nearer. "My darling, you're safe. I'm with you . . . It's all right . . ."

Slowly, unwilling to return to the horror of the conscious world which she had fled, Katharine opened her eyes. The proud face was gaunt with emotion. He drew her tightly into his arms and she felt his kiss on her forehead.

"My darling," he repeated. "My darling . . . thank God! I killed him!" he said. "I shot him at the very moment I thought he'd killed you . . . Again and again."

"Don't," Katharine whispered. "I don't want to hear . . ."

He eased her upright, stroking her hair. He leaned forward and kissed her very gently on her cold lips. "I love you," he said. "I want you to do exactly as I say. I'm going to leave you for a moment, and while I'm gone I want you to turn your head and not look after me."

"No." Katharine caught at him. "No, don't leave me here —don't go away—"

"Only a few yards. I have to do something and I don't want you to see it." She looked past him to the huddled figure lying by the open door. She shuddered.

He laid his hand against her cheek and gently turned her head away. She heard him walk away, and instinctively her eyes closed, her body tensing. There was a muffled crash. It seemed a long time till he bent over her again. He helped her to stand, supporting her with his arm round her waist. He stooped and put the gun in his pocket. The corridor was empty, the door to the little room closed and bolted, the iron ring in place and the bloodstains on the floor smeared by something heavy.

"Oh, God," she whispered.

"I sent him the way he chose for you," Alessandro said. "I thought it was appropriate. Now we are going downstairs. I have to find my wife."

Francesca had stayed where she fell; it was some moments before she got her breath. Slowly she picked herself up; she was trembling. She gasped out John Driver's name as though he could hear her and be warned. Then the shots cracked out, echoing down the well of the narrow stair through the open door. She screamed, both hands clenched against her mouth. It seemed loud and shrill to her, but it was a thin cry, like an animal upon whom a trap has suddenly closed. She knew, as if she had seen it happen, that her husband had shot the man she loved. The firing went on—she moaned and swayed on her feet. She gave a last cry of agony, and then began to stumble down the stairs the way they had brought Katharine. Out through the gun room, past the passage and into the main hall. It was silent, dimly lit by the light from the wall sconces, empty. For a second she panicked and ran to the main door, struggling with the massive bolts to open it and run out into the night. Weakness and despair defeated her. Driver was dead. She was alone and at the mercy of her husband. She leaned against the door that held her prisoner and wept with terror. For years she had been afraid of him, afraid of his passion when they married, of his anger, his contempt.

She had helped to kill the woman Malaspiga loved. Her punishment would be fitted to the crime. She turned away and began to run up the stairs, not thinking where she could hide; instinct brought her to Driver's bedroom. She slammed the door and locked it. The sight of the room where they had been together, of the bed, his coat across a chair, the objects she associated with him, induced an outburst of hysterical grief, which subsided as suddenly as it had begun. John was dead. Her husband would be looking for her. She was shivering, but she was calm. She wiped her wet face and the kohl she painted around her eyes was smeared. She had to get away. The main door was locked and she couldn't risk going back to it. But there were other doors. The kitchen quarters—and the car was outside, ready to undertake the trip to Florence and establish their alibi for Katharine's murder. She went to Driver's chest of drawers and began searching; she found a roll of money clipped together. If she could get to Rome, to her sister . . . She thought no further than immediate flight. If she could get downstairs, around to the servants' quarters and to the exits at the back . . . She hid the money in her blouse. Switzerland. She knew the number of their account in the bank at Lausanne. There were millions of dollars there . . . She could disappear where Alessandro would never find her. She opened the door and slipped outside. She crept along the wall toward the stairs, pausing to listen for any sound that indicated he was near. She was still shivering. Down the stairs, waiting again, holding her breath, and then through the dining room and out, down a long cold corridor leading to the kitchen. Once she thought she heard him and she sobbed with fear. But the sounds changed direction. The old castle kitchens had been modernized. She had only been inside it half a dozen times during her marriage. The old Duchess was jealous of her privileges. Ordering life at the castle was something she had never given up and which Francesca had never wanted to take from her. She had always hated the place. She had hated everything connected with the Malaspigas. She looked around the clinical white and green kitchen, with its gadgets and ranks of gleaming stainless steel units, a central stove in the middle of the floor. It looked like an operating theater. Moonlight flooded through the window. She crept to the back door and very carefully slid back the top and bottom bolts. Outside, it was cold and brilliantly light. She hesitated, not sure which way to go. The walls reached up above her like cliffs; she felt as if they were pierced with eyes that watched her, mocking her hope of escape. She moved along them, looking for the outline of the western tower. Beyond that, and reached through a small gate, was the main courtyard where they had parked the car. She ran her hand along the rough stone, scraping the skin. It was unnecessary in the bright moonlight, but she was being moved by instinct, finding her way by touch as well as by sight. The gate was locked from the inside; she turned the key and opened it very carefully. The car stood in the shadows, waiting.

The first place Alessandro went was to his mother's bedroom. The habit of his lifetime was to make sure she was unharmed. He had left Katharine in her own bedroom, wrapped up against shock, and locked the door after him. She had looked small and defenseless lying on the bed, a look of despair and anguish on her face that he couldn't understand. He knocked on the old Duchess' door and went inside. There was always a small light burning in case she needed to reach out and ring for Gia, her personal maid, and by the light of it he saw that she was awake. She pulled herself up on the pillows, her thick dark hair hanging loose around her shoulders. At a brief glance she could have been a girl.

"Sandro? What is the matter?"

"Nothing." He came to the bedside. "Did I wake you?"

"No," his mother said. "I heard a door close, I think that was what woke me up. You look strange—is something wrong?"

It never occurred to him to tell her. His function was not only to command but to protect. His mother couldn't be exposed to what had happened. He bent down to her with a smile and kissed her.

"I wanted to talk to Francesca. I thought she might have come in here. She isn't in her room."

Isabella di Malaspiga hesitated. The door which had shut so loudly was across the passage. She knew it was where John Driver slept. It wouldn't do if her son were to be presented with the evidence of that affair. She gave a sweet smile in return and shook her head. "No, I haven't seen her. Why don't you wait till morning? It must be very late."

"You go to sleep," he said gently.

"You're sure there's nothing wrong?" She asked the question against her will, not wanting her fear of the unpleasant confirmed. She had only seen her son with that look of taut determination on his face once, and that was when he came back from his honeymoon. And he had never told her what went wrong.

"Go to sleep," he said again. He took the key out of her door without her noticing and locked it from the outside. His mother and Katharine were safe. He started back down the corridor to look for his wife. Chance made him glance through one of the windows as he hurried, and in the courtyard clearly visible in the moonlight, he saw the car. He took the last flight of steps to the main hall at a run. He felt for Driver's gun in his pocket. Francesca came out from the shelter of the gateway. There was no one in the courtyard— the main door to the castle was closed. She drew in a deep breath, unwilling to leave the shadows even though the car and safety were only a few yards away. A cloud crossed the face of the bright moon. She made a short dash forward and dragged the door open.

"Francesca!" She cried out in terror as he stepped forward; the moon burst through the cloud and she could see him clearly, pointing the gun at her. "Don't move," he said. "Or I will kill you."

The impact of terror left her. At one moment she was paralyzed, her hand on the open door of the car, rooted by fear. The next she felt nothing. Her shivering had stopped.

"Come away from the car," Alessandro said.

"No," she said. "She's dead, and you're going to kill me!" He took a step toward her.

"Why did you do it?" he asked her. "Murder—drug smuggling—why, Francesca?"

"Because I loved Elise," she said. "I'm not ashamed to say it now. I loved her. You thought you separated us, but you didn't. We deceived you. We arranged everything, she and I. The blackmail was my idea. I knew how you felt about me. You thought you were being so clever, making use of John—and all the time it was you who were being used! Then *she* came, and you had to put us all in jeopardy because you wanted her! I'm glad she's dead! I don't care if you kill me—"

"Katharine is safe," Alessandro said. "This time it didn't work. Uncle Alfredo saw you taking a man to the East Tower. The American dealer who called himself Firelli. You murdered him, just as you tried to murder her. But you didn't succeed. It's John who is dead."

She didn't move. Tears crept down her face. "You shot him," she said. "I heard you. Now you think you'll save yourself by killing me. Then nobody will know— But she's a narcotics agent—a spy! So we've destroyed you, John and I. You'll go to jail for smuggling heroin, and she's the one who will convict you! How much do you love her now?"

She looked wild in the moonlight, her eyes wide and staring, the makeup smudged by crying. She crouched by the car like an animal.

"I hate you," she shouted. The sound reverberated back at them from the high walls. "I hate you! Everyone I loved you've taken from me. Elise—and now John!" She suddenly jerked forward and spat at him. "He showed me how to make love with a man!" she said. "When he touched me it was wonderful—with you I wanted to be sick! Now you've killed him. But you won't escape, Malaspiga. I've nothing to live for without him, I don't care what happens to me now. But you're going to jail for the rest of your life!" She wrenched the door back and sprang into the driver's seat. She put her head out of the window and called him a foul name.

Alessandro took aim at the nearside tire of the car and pulled the trigger. There was a useless click. He had fired the last bullet into Driver's body. There was a roar as Francesca accelerated. The car shot forward, heading for the dark mouth of the main gateway. There was a screech as it turned, scattering stones and for a second its red tail light glimmered. He stood looking after it, the useless gun hanging from his hand. She had gone, God knew where. Insane with grief and hate, she was capable of anything. He turned and went back inside the castle. One of the servants was coming into the main hall, struggling into his jacket over pajamas. The noise of the car had awakened some of the staff . . . If the Duke required anything . . .

Alessandro had slid his hand in his pocket. There was nothing he needed. He told the man to go to bed. Then slowly he began to walk up the main stairs toward Katharine's room. When he unlocked the door and went inside he saw that Katharine had got up. She was sitting in a chair with the light switched on behind her. Her face was in shadow. When he came close he could see that she had been crying.

"You should have kept warm," he said. "You are suffering from shock!"

She looked at him. "You made a mistake," she said slowly. "You shouldn't have interfered. You should have let them kill me."

He felt in his pocket, threw the empty gun on the bed and walked to the table beside it. There was a silver box with cigarettes. He took two and lit them.

"Because of the heroin?" He crossed to her and put the cigarette to her lips. She took it in her fingers.

"That's why I'm here," she said. "I enrolled in the narcotics bureau just to come out and get evidence against you."

"I know that," Alessandro said. "Driver told me before I shot him. My wife just taunted me with it. She called you a spy." He stood looking down at Katharine. "Is that why you were crying—because you believe I am guilty, and you'd have to give me up to the police?"

"I haven't any choice," Katharine said slowly. "Unless you decide not to let me go. There's nothing I can do to stop you."

"Are you suggesting," he said quietly, "that I would hurt you to save myself?"

"You killed Firelli," Katharine said. "He died in that dreadful room."

"I see," he said. He looked at the end of his cigarette, blew a little to make it glow red. "So I am a drug smuggler and a murderer. But I saved your life because I am in love with you. Isn't that a little silly?"

"It's what happened," she said.

"I don't think your American policemen would agree with you. The Italians might, because we're great sentimentalists. And I should be tried in an Italian court. Perhaps there's some hope for me." He played with the cigarette again. "Anyway, I don't think you'll have to do very much. I believe Francesca will be the star witness."

Katharine looked up quickly. "She's gone?"

"Yes. I didn't kill her either. I couldn't even shoot the tires out on the car because there weren't any bullets left. I'd forgotten that. I'm not a very efficient murderer." Katharine got up—she felt weak and uneasy. His mood had changed completely. He seemed to be mocking her.

"Where has she gone?"

"To the *carabinieri*. Probably at Massa. They might not listen to anything so sensational in Malaspiga itself. They think quite well of me, I understand."

"But she can't denounce you—she was in it too!"

"I don't think she cares what happens to her. I think she started by trying to escape and when she left she was determined to have vengeance. For John Driver. My good friend the sculptor. It seems they were lovers, too. Before she gets back with the police, I want to ask you something. A favor."

"What is it?" Katharine didn't want to look at him.

"I want to show you something. Will you come and look at it?" She hesitated. She had hated and feared and finally loved him. The sight of him standing there, already ruined, with that smile on his lips caused her unbearable pain.

"All right," she said.

"Thank you," he said gravely. "I don't want you to think any worse of me than is deserved." He opened the bedroom door and held it for her to pass. They crossed the hall and through the armory. He didn't touch her or speak. He walked ahead and Katharine followed, past the sinister suits of armor, shimmering in the moonlight, retracing the steps she had taken that night. In the banqueting hall he paused and looked back at her. "We're going down to the storeroom," he said. "Be careful of the steps, they're very steep."

"I know," Katharine answered. "I was down there when Driver caught me."

He came back and took her arm. "Don't think about it," he said quietly. With the light flaring above them, they descended into the big room below the banqueting hall. A little earlier she had run for her life from it. She would never forget that moment, so like a classic nightmare, when the door at the head of the stairs flung open and she found Francesca waiting for her.

"Now," Alessandro said. "You wanted to look at this this morning. I wouldn't let you. You will see why in a moment." They were standing in front of the picture, shrouded in its green cover.

"That's why I came back tonight," she said. "To mark it for identification."

"Well, you shall look at it now." He stepped up to the picture and pulled the cover off. Katharine stared at it in disbelief.

There, framed in a magnificent Florentine wood frame, was the Giorgione she had seen in the gallery upstairs. The same exquisite coloring, the same grace and tenderness, the distinctive use of form and design which marked the great artist's work from all imitators. She turned to Alessandro. "You're selling this? But you said—"

"I said I'd never sell my Giorgione," he answered. "This is not the picture upstairs. This is a forgery." He pulled the cover back over the painting. "That was John Driver's great talent. He was a poor sculptor, as you were quick enough to recognize. But he was one of the greatest forgers of Old Masters since Van Megeeren. That picture was sold for a million and a quarter dollars to a New York collector. Through the agency of an antique dealer called Taylor. It is fully authenticated."

"But how? How could you get away with it?"

"Two art experts from Florence came here last week and saw the real Giorgione. They naturally gave it a certificate. John had spent a year in copying it. The collector believes he is buying the Malaspiga picture. As nobody will ever see my Giorgione again, and as John's work is indetectable— he's deceived experts from all over the world, long before he painted this—I shall never be discovered."

She said slowly, not looking at him, "And this was what you were doing . . . selling fakes? Not heroin . . ."

"Never heroin," the Duke answered. He took her by the shoulders. "Look at me, Katharine. I never touched drugs. I never knew anything about it, and I wouldn't have trafficked whatever the money. I sold fakes to people who believed they'd been looted from churches in Italy and were prepared to gloat over stolen paintings in private. I sold to rich men who thought they were getting a bargain at the expense of a poor Italian Duke who was forced to sell his family treasures. I cheated, and if you like to think of it, I stole a great deal of money. But I give you my word of honor, that nothing—not even the blackmail which started all this—nothing would have made me smuggle drugs. I beg you to believe that."

She gave a deep sigh, and suddenly put both hands to her face. "I do believe you," she said.

"If I were mixed up in drugs," he said gently, "I wouldn't have to sell anything else. Since I'm not a murderer or a dealer in heroin—can you forgive me for being a forger?"

He held her close to him. Katharine didn't move; she rested against him for a moment with her eyes closed. She felt suddenly too drained to think or reason.

"Whatever Francesca does, whatever happens," Alessandro di Malaspiga said, "I can survive it, so long as you believe in me. Now we're going upstairs."

"To wait for the police?" Katharine asked him.

He nodded. "I will get something for us to drink," he

said. "And while we wait I will tell you how it started." He put his arm around her shoulder as they walked to the stairs.

"I can tell that you believe me," he said calmly. "You've lost that look of misery."

As Carpenter remembered the map, he had reckoned he had less than two kilometers to go. At a bend in the road he saw the massive outline of the castle, silhouetted against the clear night sky, lights pinpointed from some of the windows. The road wound upward at a steep angle, overhanging the slope of the hill, studded with dark pine forest and patches of live groves which had been cultivated. Below him the town of Malaspiga was in darkness, the people sleeping. He had driven as fast as the winding streets would allow, and seen no one and not a single light in any house. He drove fast but carefully, hugging the side of the road away from the precipice at the edge. He had no plan clear in his mind, nothing beyond the rescue of Katharine. If he were in time.

There was a sharp bend, even by the standards of mountain roads in Italy, and he had slowed, swinging slightly into the middle to negotiate it better. As he did so a double beam of dazzling light cut across the windshield from a blind corner. Carpenter shouted and wrenched the wheel to the right, slamming his foot on the brake. His lights were dipped but they must have dazzled the other driver, and from the speed with which the oncoming car rushed at him round the corner, the effect could be blinding. He felt the thud and scrape of his car as it hit the rock bank and he came to an emergency stop. And then there was a fearful shriek of tires and a shattering crash which went on and on, reverberating through the darkness. He leaped out of the car and ran to the side of the road. Down below him, three hundred feet down among the pine trees, a burst of yellow flame flickered and then roared up in a cone of orange and crimson into the air. Carpenter stood staring down, numbed by the horror of the accident. The other car, traveling top speed, must have gone out of control and careered over the edge. It was burning furiously —some of the surrounding trees had caught alight. There was nothing he could do for anyone who had been inside it. He wiped his sleeve across his forehead; it was sticky with sweat. Among the tumult of crashing glass and metal, he had imagined for a second that he heard a woman screaming . . . He got into the car and drove on, holding close to the rock side. A few minutes later he had rounded a curve and saw the offshoot road that led directly to the gateway of Malaspiga Castle.

"It started a year after I came back from the States," Alessandro said. "By that time I had established a small reputation as a dealer in Renaissance antiques and my business was growing. I had a select clientele. I was making money but not nearly enough. Drink your coffee."

They were alone in the small sitting room. He had awakened his mother's maid Gia and told her to go and see if the old Duchess was asleep. She had made them coffee and Alessandro was sipping a glass of brandy. He seemed cool and unconcerned; he had reached out and taken her hand as he talked. When the maid came into the room he resisted Katharine's attempt to draw it away.

"I was in Florence when this American Taylor came to see me. He sent his card and asked for an appointment. I was delighted, I hoped to establish an opening in the United States. He came in the morning. I shall never forget it. We spent some time talking about antiques, and he was very knowledgeable—a very precise little man, not quite a homosexual. Then he said he had a proposition to make to me. I was very interested to hear it. He had a shop in Beverly Hills, and I thought I might do a lot of business. But it wasn't that kind of proposition. Francesca was visiting her sister in

Rome during that week. He took a photograph out of his briefcase and passed it to me.

"It showed my wife with Elise Bohun. I won't disgust you with details. He informed me that it was taken at a Rome hotel only a few days earlier, and that Francesca had used her sister as an alibi to resume the relationship which had started in Hollywood. I was stunned. I remember looking at that photograph, and there were others, equally filthy. And then I knew that I was going to be blackmailed. He was very direct, very businesslike. Unless I agreed to his proposition, those photographs would be sent to the police and a formal complaint made. Equally there are several newspapers in Italy who would have welcomed a scandal about one of the old aristocratic families. There was no question of compromise, or paying him off. Money didn't interest him. He wanted me to front, as he put it. To pass through art forgeries and authenticate them as having come from my collection. Nothing very big to start with, some thousands of dollars for a moderate fifteenth-century artist. Not spectacular enough to cause inquiries. He made it clear that there would be profit in it for me and that I need never worry about my wife being exposed after the first deal. This was sensible, because by then I would be personally compromised."

"Couldn't you have gone to the police?" Katharine asked him. "Why didn't you fight back?"

"There are many reasons," Alessandro admitted. "The first was my determination to protect my family name. That has always mattered more to me than anything else. I didn't want anyone knowing what the Duchess di Malaspiga really was. No vulgar *carabiniere* in Rome or Florence was going to gloat over those photographs."

"How did John Driver come into this?" she asked him.

"He was sent out to work here. Taylor said we had proved the market and were due to make substantial sums of money. He was in charge of the American end; he had opened a smart shop on Park Avenue and he had a lot of very rich clients. It would be simpler if the copyist worked direct from Italy.

And so John came. He enrolled at the Academy of Arts here, and we played out the charade of his coming to repair some of the statues at the villa and my becoming his patron. He worked on the forgeries at Malaspiga and a year after he came, we sold a fake Domenico Ghirlandaio which was so good a collector in Canada paid half a million dollars for it. He believed it had been looted from a church in Sienna during the German occupation and recovered by an American deserter who hid it for twenty years. As it was the property of the church, he couldn't put it on public display, but this didn't diminish his enthusiasm. As far as I know it is the pride of his secret collection. We sold him a Fra Angelico fragment, which I thought was Driver's masterpiece, until I saw the Giorgione. I became a rich man, working with Driver and using Taylor as my outlet. But I had no idea there was any other trade in progress. I didn't think Francesca knew any more about John than what I told her. A talented sculptor working for an exhibition and selling a few commercial pieces. Francesca said they had made a fool of me for years. She and that woman planned it all. Blackmail to get me involved in something illegal, and then the introduction of the smuggler. I liked John, that's ironical, isn't it! I knew he didn't have the talent he really wanted, and that forging other artists' masterpieces was some kind of revenge. I was genuinely sorry for him. When he hid his sculptures and wouldn't let anyone see them until they were finished, I sympathized. I respected his wishes. In fact, thinking back, I did everything to make it easy for them." He leaned back, still holding her hand. "Do you think anyone will believe in my innocence? I can hardly believe in it myself."

"I'll tell them what happened," Katharine said. "They'll believe me."

He looked at her and smiled. "As a narcotics agent, your word will carry more weight than anything Francesca says. And I shall need your help," he said. "The only way I can account for John Driver is by admitting that we were forging pictures. And I can never do that. One is certain disgrace and ruin for my family—the other way gives me a good chance. I want you to promise me something, Katerina."

"What?" she said, although she knew what he was going to ask.

"Whatever happens, you won't mention the art forgery," he said. "Even if it looks black for me, you won't think you'll help me by revealing that."

"I can't promise anything," she said. "I can't stand by and see you go to jail for life for something like drug smuggling."

"The sentence would be nearly as heavy for selling fakes," he said. "We Italians are very sensitive about our reputation in the art market. I would be severely punished, believe me. I will take my chance on the drug charge. At least I can plead innocent to that and be telling the truth. You're disappointed in me, aren't you?"

"Yes," she admitted.

"Women are very illogical," he said gently. "When you thought I was a murderer and a drug smuggler, you still loved me. You could love the black villain, but you are upset because you find that in fact he is a little gray. I can see it in your eyes—they show all your feelings. I remember saying that to you soon after we met. I could have been a hypocrite and pretended I was forced to sell the pictures. But I love you, my darling, and I want to be honest. I want you to love me for what I am. I saw the chance of doing everything I wanted for my family and for Malaspiga. The sale of the Giorgione copy will completely restore our fortune to what it was before the war. Does that make you unhappy?"

"Yes," Katharine said.

"At least my mother and Uncle Alfredo will have everything they want. As I have no children, I have arranged for the castle to become the property of the state after my death, with all its treasures. So at least our heritage will be preserved."

Before she could answer, the door opened. It was the old Duchess' maid Gia. There was a car in the courtyard, she said. Somebody was ringing the bell at the entrance. Alessandro got up, drawing Katharine with him. "She has acted very quickly," he said quietly. "I didn't expect them so soon."

He went out into the hall, still holding Katharine by the hand. They found Frank Carpenter waiting for them.

"Very ingenious." Raphael looked around at his assistant. They were in John Driver's studio. The evidence collected in the storeroom was already sealed up and documented. Alessandro had been unable to find a duplicate key for the studio and the police had broken the door open. Inside they had found John's unfinished work. Several small pieces, two more busts of children, similar in style to the two in the storeroom, a classical torso, two feet high. This was unfinished and proved to be hollowed out in the middle. Raphael inspected it silently. Then he spoke to his assistant. "Very ingenious," he repeated. "I should think this space would hold about ten kilos of heroin. Which would make this piece of statuary very valuable indeed." He glanced over his shoulder at the Duke.

"Was this his idea or yours?"

"I told you," Alessandro said. "I knew nothing about it."

"I know what you've told me," Raphael said. He lit a cigarette. "And I don't believe you. You say you are running a legitimate antiques business, and the fact that your New York customer is a proven drug smuggler is pure coincidence. I find that difficult to accept. But I find your ignorance of how the heroin was brought here and smuggled out in sculptures worked by a man in your employ—I find that quite impossible!"

"It happens to be the truth," Malaspiga said. "I have hidden nothing from you. And you have Katharine Dexter's word for what happened."

"Yes," Raphael agreed. He nodded several times. "You shot this man Driver, and you saved her life. You say he and your wife confessed to murdering Firelli. It is perhaps a little convenient for you that both these witnesses are dead?"

"I don't regard my wife's death as convenient," the Duke said coldly. He had spent the early morning down the side of the hill, watching the police remove the charred remains of a body from the twisted ruin of the car. The rear license plate had been found intact some distance away. He had identified it as belonging to the car in which his wife had driven away from the castle. Frank Carpenter had stood beside him. Alessandro had felt nothing except nausea; the place smelt of burned flesh. He hadn't pretended to feel grief. He was surrounded by enemies, and he preserved a frozen calm. He hadn't been allowed to talk to Katharine alone. Raphael and a squad of special police had arrived in the early hours, and he had found himself under arrest in his own house.

Standing in the storeroom, watching Raphael and his men examining the pieces, seeing the frame on the forged Giorgione split open looking for heroin, Alessandro had said nothing. When they came to the *poudreuse* he had said quietly, "Before you damage that, I must warn you it is a rare and valuable work of art." Raphael had looked at him with contempt, and then turned to his men. "Take it to pieces," he said. "I want everything in this room examined."

They had found nothing, except in the bust of the little boy, which was full of heroin like its companion. Nobody mentioned the Giorgione. They weren't looking for art forgeries. Now as he looked around at the work in Driver's studio, the enormity of the case against him couldn't be denied. The aggressive little Florentine policeman was triumphant, Alessandro recognized the type. A policeman with political bias against people like himself. Raphael had enjoyed discovering the sculptures, just as he had enjoyed watching his men dismantling the exquisite little *poudreuse*. The fact that there was no trace of heroin in it didn't seem to bother him. He was confident that what he'd already found was enough. He hadn't seemed to be impressed by Katharine's insistence that the Duke was innocent. Alessandro denied him the satisfaction of protesting or demanding his lawyer be called. There was nothing he could do to stop Raphael tearing down the castle walls at that stage, and he sensed that the policeman would have enjoyed a trial of strength which he was sure to win. The Duke said nothing, but the contempt in his silence goaded Raphael.

When the search was over, and Driver's studio was locked and sealed, he demanded to see the old Duchess and Prince Alfredo. Alessandro recognized this as a piece of provocation. "My mother is over eighty years old and there is nothing she can tell you because she knows nothing. My uncle, Prince Alfredo, is senile. In the name of common sense if not humanity, I must ask you to leave them alone."

Raphael felt in his pocket for another cigarette. "When it comes to murder and drug smuggling, Duke Alessandro," he said, "nobody's sensibilities are sacred. I will ask your mother and your uncle to come down together. I am sending Katharine Dexter back to Florence. There is nothing more for her to do here."

He was watching the Duke very closely, while pretending to adjust his lighter. He had the satisfaction of seeing his expression of indifference change.

"I should like to see her before she goes," Alessandro said.

Raphael shook his head; he held the little flame to his cigarette end and inhaled the smoke. "That won't be possible," he said. "She is the state's principal witness. I will see your mother and your uncle in the little room across the entrance hall. You will wait here. My men have orders not to let you leave the room, so don't make things unpleasant for yourself." He went out, closing the door, and sent one of the worried servants upstairs to bring down the Duchess and Uncle Alfredo.

"Kate"—Frank Carpenter had his hand on her arm—"Kate, there's nothing you can do. He isn't going to hurt them. He'll just ask them a few questions and then let them go." Katharine didn't listen; she pulled away from him and went up to the Duchess. The old lady was walking across the hall toward the room where Raphael was waiting. Uncle Alfredo, guided by a policeman in civilian clothes, was following behind.

Isabella di Malaspiga paused. When Katharine took her hand it was cold and limp.

"Where is my son? Who are these people?"

"There's no need to be afraid," Katharine said gently. "They're just making inquiries."

The Duchess looked at her. "I'm not in the least afraid," she said. "Something has happened. There are policemen here, and that must mean there's been an accident. Where is Alessandro?" For a moment her mouth trembled.

"He's here, he's perfectly all right," Katharine said quickly. Carpenter had come beside her. She could feel his impatience. At any moment he would take her by the arm and try to hurry her away.

The Duchess turned and spoke to Uncle Alfredo. He was making slow progress, chafing against the policeman's guiding arm.

"There's no need to worry," she said. "Alessandro will be with us; he will look after you, Alfredo. So come along and we'll find him together." She held out her hand, and the old man suddenly hurried toward her. He was nodding his head up and down—a tiny streak of saliva had gathered by the corner of his mouth. He didn't seem to recognize Katharine.

"It's the murder," he said. "I told him they were going to kill her . . . that's why the police are here."

"Prince Alfredo," Katharine said. He looked at her and then stopped suddenly. The Duchess had taken him by the hand.

"They didn't kill you then?"

"No," she answered. "Alessandro saved me."

"It was her fault," the old man muttered. "She was the wicked one—trying to send me away."

"Come," Isabella di Malaspiga urged him, and he pattered beside her, still mumbling to himself. She saw the door open and a brief glimpse of Raphael as he stood up and came toward them. They looked so frail and helpless, the old lady holding her brother-in-law's hand, that Katharine's eyes filled with tears.

Carpenter put his arm around her. "You've had enough," he said. "I'm taking you out of here right now."

"I want to see my cousin," she said. "They're my family—I want to know what's going to happen to them!"

"Raphael's got a warrant for him," Carpenter explained. "The old couple will be all right. Don't worry about them. Come on now—it's all over for you."

He thought she slept during the drive back to Florence, until he saw her face as they stopped by a toll booth on the way; the lights showed that she was crying. He didn't say anything, because he felt sure a few hours' sleep would bring her down from the nervous peak which was expressing itself in tears. He held her hand on the journey and whispered to her to try and rest. She didn't answer; she was safe and with her own kind. He had kept telling her so, while Raphael sat in Alessandro's sitting room, smoking and listening to her account of what happened. Carpenter had been soothing and protective as if she were much more shocked than was the case. The Italian had said very little, except that her part was over and she should leave the castle.

She had wanted to protest, to insist on staying, but they had taken the initiative away. They had separated her from Alessandro. Carpenter hadn't left her alone, or listened when she asked to say good-bye.

He drove to her hotel and came up to her room. It was lunch time. The lobby had been empty, the clerk reading a newspaper behind his desk. She had seen the restaurant through the open door. It was full and there was a cheerful noise of people talking. She remembered the first day she arrived there, and her disquiet at being given a special table and the manager's personal attention because of the name of Malaspiga on her passport. She had felt alien, resentful of a deference she felt was unbecoming for an American. She had come to Italy to destroy the Malaspigas, and it was the worst irony that because she was one of them, she had succeeded. Alessandro was under arrest, the impregnable walls of the castle breached by the modern judicial process, using as its siege weapon a piece of paper giving total power. She opened her bedroom door and turned, blocking Frank Carpenter's way.

"I'll rest," she said. "I'm so tired I can't think."

"I want to talk to you," he said. "But I guess it can wait." She saw how worn and tired he looked. He deserved something better than her frantic concern for someone else. But she couldn't give it. She couldn't have stepped aside and let him come into her room and try to resume what had been interrupted the night she left New York. That belonged to the girl she had been. It would never be possible for the woman she had become.

"I'm sorry, Frank," she said. "I have to sleep. Whatever you said now wouldn't make any sense to me."

"I'll call this evening," he said. "Raphael is bringing Malaspiga down. He'll want to see you, but I'll head him off till the morning."

"No," she said quickly. "No, don't do that—I'll be all right—"

"You're out on your feet," Carpenter said. "I can see that. He wants to go over your evidence with you, to help frame the charges. You've got to get everything clear."

"I'll see him today," Katharine said. "Late this afternoon. If you won't fix it, Frank, I'll do it myself."

"Okay," he shrugged. "If that's how you want it. I was only thinking of you."

"I know"—she caught his arm for a moment—"I know you were, and I appreciate it. But I'm thinking of an innocent man being held in prison. I'll see Raphael as soon as he gets down here."

"I'll come and pick you up," Carpenter said. His tone was abrupt. He turned away without looking at her.

She didn't intend to sleep. She lay on the bed, with an

arm over her eyes and woke with the telephone shrilling beside her. It was Carpenter; he was downstairs in the foyer,
waiting to take her to Raphael's office.

"You realize," Raphael said, "that you are my only wit-
ness? The contact in New York is dead, the bureau man who
was spying for him had a heart attack. The Duchess and the
Canadian. . . . There is no one who can testify against
Malaspiga except you." He paused and looked at Carpenter.
They were sitting in his top floor office on the Via Vecchia.
Below them the city was preparing for the evening. The shops
were illuminated, and the cafés filling with people.

"You've had a rough time," Carpenter said. He had been
silent on the drive from her hotel. Now he seemed intent on
making an effort and establishing the contact with her which
had been lost. "Naturally you believe his story about being
innocent. He saved your life and you want to believe him.
But look at the facts."

"He's guilty," Raphael said. "He's the head of the drug
smuggling ring, and everything points to it. His connection
with Taylor—coincidence? Maybe." He shook his head. "I
don't accept that and I told him so. He employs a man who
hides heroin in sculptures and he knows nothing about it? A
smuggling ring dealing in millions of dollars' worth of drugs
is being run from his home by his wife and this Canadian,
and in four years he never suspects anything? Why did he decide to play the patron to this particular artist—Florence is
full of starving young students—but he picks a criminal in the
pay of the Mafia? There isn't a jury in the world who would
believe he wasn't head and tail of it all!"

Katharine didn't say anything. He had been cool and
abrupt when she came in. Now he was walking up and down,
gesticulating angrily as he argued. He stopped suddenly and
came over to her. "You know he's guilty," he said. "Whatever
has happened between you—I appeal to your conscience not
to try and protect him. You came here to break this ring and

avenge your brother's murder—have you forgotten what they did to him? How they pumped him full of heroin and killed him to safeguard their pushers? This man, this cousin of yours that you say is innocent—he was responsible for that!"

"No," Katharine said, looking up at him. "He wasn't. He had nothing to do with it. I know that."

"How can you know?" That was Carpenter, taking up the questioning.

"Because he told me and I believe him. He had no reason to risk everything by saving me. And Driver himself said he was innocent."

"What?" Raphael swung around on her. "What is this?"

She hadn't prepared the lie—it just came out. She felt very calm, and she folded her hands on her lap to steady them. No jury in the world would acquit Alessandro when Raphael had presented his case. There was too much circumstantial evidence. He had been over-optimistic. It wasn't enough to defend him, to maintain his innocence. She had to lie, or tell the truth and break her promise. Expose him, not as a racketeer in drugs, but as a dealer in forgeries, employing a master craftsman to fake works of art. He would never admit to it himself. He would take the chance of an acquittal, which she could see now was nonexistent.

"What did Driver say to you? What story is this?"

She didn't hesitate. "When he found me in the storeroom. He said, 'You thought it was Alessandro, didn't you? But he knows nothing about it. The arrogant bastard thinks he owns me—but I've fooled him. We've been making millions behind his back, and he never suspected anything.' Those are his exact words. He hadn't any reason to lie. He was boasting about how clever he'd been." It was a trick of memory that recalled every word Driver had spoken. It made the lie she inserted seem completely real.

"You never mentioned this before," Carpenter said. "When you told us what had happened at the castle, you never said anything about it . . ."

"Of course she didn't," Raphael snapped. "She's only just invented it! Don't you see she's lying? Now, listen to me—whatever your reasons, you're in love with him, you're trying to protect your family—I don't know and I don't care why you've made up this lie, but don't think you're deceiving either of us. Don't think you'll get away with it!"

"It's the truth," Katharine said.

Raphael stood over her; his face was ugly with rage and contempt. "It's a lie, a deliberate lie. Why didn't you tell us this before?"

"I thought I had," she said. "I was very shocked; I must have been confused, and forgotten. But that's what Driver said to me and that's what I shall say in my evidence." The Italian swung away from her; she heard him swear blasphemously.

"Kate," Carpenter pleaded. "Kate, don't do this. Malaspiga is guilty as hell. Okay, you have a reason for doing this. Maybe Raphael's right. You want to protect your family . . ." He hesitated and then went on. "Or you're in love with him. But he's a murderer. Okay, the old man said the others killed Firelli. *He* says Driver admitted it. But what about your brother—what about the addicts back home, dying of heroin? He's killed thousands of innocent people and got rich on it. For Christ's sake, you can't protect a man like that!"

"If he were guilty I wouldn't protect him," she said quietly. "But I know he isn't. He had nothing to do with the drugs. Driver said so." She had grasped tightly on to the lie, and she kept on repeating it.

Driver had said nothing to exonerate Alessandro. Until he showed her the fake Giorgione, she had believed him to be the head of the organization. It distressed her to lie to Carpenter and see him turn away from her, bewildered and disgusted. But the lie was only an extension of the fundamental truth. She held fast to that too, and kept her courage.

Raphael came back to her. He stuck both hands in his pockets and rocked slightly on his heels. "I wonder how long you'll maintain this fairy story in a court," he said. "I think a good prosecuting attorney would expose you very quickly."

"If I give evidence at the trial," Katharine said, "I shall say the same there as I've said now. I know you want my cousin convicted, I know you believe he's guilty, but I promise you, you're wrong."

"You are a Malaspiga!" he spat back at her. "You don't know the meaning of right or wrong! You're just the same as all your kind— This is useless," he spoke to Carpenter. "She has been completely corrupted. It is hopeless to bring a case against him while an agent of the narcotics bureau insists on telling this pack of lies. I have no hope of getting him convicted! He would come out of the trial a hero!"

There was silence for some moments. Katharine didn't move. Raphael went and sat behind his desk. He lit a cigarette.

"Take her away," he said. "Get her out of my office." Katharine stood up, and Carpenter nodded toward the door. They went down in the elevator and got into his car. He drove through the slow traffic, looking ahead, as if she wasn't there.

"Well," he said as they approached the hotel, "I wish I could say I understood what you've done, but I don't. You've got him off the hook— There's nothing Raphael can do to him now. And that's what you wanted."

"There is a reason," Katharine said, "but I can't tell you what it is. He *is* innocent. I promise you that."

"You lied," Carpenter said. He didn't appear to have heard what she said. "I wouldn't have believed it. He got out on bail this afternoon—there was a smart lawyer waiting. As Raphael said, if he'd been an ordinary Italian citizen, he'd have stuck in jail for months and nobody would have given a damn. But there was so much political muscle being flexed about that bastard, Raphael couldn't hold him. He's out, so you can go right to him if you feel like it. Tell him what you've done."

"I won't see him again," Katharine said. "It wouldn't work. I'm going home, I'll see if I can get a flight tomorrow."

The car stopped outside the hotel entrance.

"I was going to ask you to marry me," Carpenter said.

"That wouldn't have worked either," Katharine said. "But thank you, anyway."

"Don't thank me." He turned and looked at her. His eyes were cold. "I had a different picture of you. I'll send a full report to Ben back home. From the bureau's point of view, I suppose it's been a very successful operation. We've cleaned it up in New York, and it's finished over here. But I'm sorry, I don't feel like pinning any medals on you."

He leaned across and opened the door for her. She got out.

"Good-bye, Frank." He drove away without answering or looking back.

There was a flight from Pisa to Milan that connected with Paris. From Paris she could get a seat on a 747 to New York. It was a grueling journey, but as the clerk in the ticket agency explained, it was a very busy season and all the direct flights from Rome to the States were fully booked. If she liked to wait a few days, he could find something better for her. But she didn't want to wait. She had left the hotel early that morning after a night when she woke several times to find she had been crying in her sleep. Alessandro was safe. A thought, so truly Italian that it surprised her, suggested that she had paid a debt of love.

When she told Carpenter that she was going home, she knew it was the only thing to do. There was no future for her with Alessandro. He lived by a code where family pride transcended ordinary moral values. Having sacrificed her integrity to save him, she realized that this alone made it inevitable they should separate.

She left the ticket agency with the flight tickets in her bag and began to walk, without purpose except to waste time. It was a magnificent morning, promising considerable heat later on. The sky was brilliant and devoid of clouds. She found herself at the end of the Via Vecchia, and glanced up at the building where Raphael had his office. It all seemed to have taken place a long time ago. She looked at her hand, at the little gold signet ring on her finger, with the wreath and the spike, surmounted by the Ducal coronet, and remembered how her childhood fears had made her hate it. It was a part of her which she had been unable to deny. But it had no place in the world to which she was returning. The real world, where she had been born and spent her life. The last weeks had been part of a dream regressing into the past. She came out into the Piazzale del Duomo. The great twelfth-century Cathedral reared up over the buildings in the square, above the crowds that thronged around it; its multicolored marble and the rose tiled dome were brilliant in the sunshine. For six hundred years people had been sitting on its steps. There was a timeless quality to the scene that made her feel suspended.

This too was a dream, like the silver olive groves and the marble mountains at Carrara, the castle of her ancestors standing guard over the town of Malaspiga. He had cheated and robbed without a scruple, to restore and preserve what progress had tried to take from him. She knew herself well enough to recognize she could never live with that and keep her love for him or her respect for herself. She would love Malaspiga for the rest of her life, but she would never see him again.

A group of tourists, tall Scandinavians, shepherded by a woman, surged past her, festooned with cameras and hurrying toward the Cathedral. Katharine turned away and began to walk back. She didn't want to linger in the city. She had grown to love it, and the parting caused an extra pain.

She walked to her hotel, and as she came into the lobby there was a disquieting sense of *déjà vu*. The clerk looked up at her and smiled and it was like the morning she received the Duchess Isabella's letter.

He waited for her expectantly, and she reminded herself that it was only to present the bill. He leaned toward her, and the smile was the same as on that other morning. "This was delivered for you," he said. It was a long package wrapped in paper and sealed securely.

"Is there a message?"

"Nothing, Signorina."

"Is my bill ready?"

"I sent it upstairs to your room."

In the elevator she pulled at the tapes and began unwrapping the parcel. It was half undone when she reached her room and opened the door. Alessandro was sitting in the chair. He got up, but he didn't move toward her.

"They told me you were leaving today," he said.

"Yes," Katharine answered. "This afternoon. Please, Alessandro—I don't want to say good-bye."

"I thought you would do something silly like this," he said. "Don't be angry with the reception clerk, I bribed him to let me in. The charge against me was formally withdrawn this morning. I understand that you were responsible. Why are you running away from me?"

"I can't explain it," she said. "You wouldn't understand."

"I understand everything about you," he said quietly. "You're a part of myself. I knew what had happened at the castle when I told you the truth. One should always tell lies to women. Please finish opening your parcel."

The wrapping came away and the parcel unrolled itself and hung down, the end curling over on the ground. The Giorgione Madonna nursed the Christ-child at her breast, serene and majestic, guarded by a kneeling St. Anne.

There were two big slashes right across the canvas.

"I hope," he said, "that you will accept it as a wedding present. I have decided to sell the real one."